John Morrow was born in Belfast in
1930. He left school at the age of
fourteen to work in the shipyards, and
has since worked as a navvy, furniture
salesman and insurance agent. He
began contributing short stories to
literary magazines in the late 1960s
and has since written extensively for
radio. His first novel, *The Confessions
of Prionsias O'Toole* was published in
1977, and *The Essex Factor* was
published in 1982. He has also
published *Northern Myths*, a collection
of short stories.

John Morrow lives in Belfast with his
wife and two sons.

Author photograph by Geraldine Sweeney

Sects And Other Stories

John Morrow

BLACK SWAN

SECTS AND OTHER STORIES

A BLACK SWAN BOOK 0 552 99256 9

First publication in Great Britain

PRINTING HISTORY
Black Swan edition published 1987

Some of these stories have been broadcast
on BBC radio. Others have been published in
The Honest Ulsterman, Quarto, Bananas and
The Ulster Tatler.

'The Humours of Ballyturdeen' and 'O'Fuzz'
were included in an anthology of modern
Irish stories entitled 'Paddy No More'
(Longship Press, USA, 1977 and Wolfhound
Press, Ireland, 1978). They also formed part
of my first collection of short pieces:
'Northern Myths' (Blackstaff Press, 1979). I
include them here because they seem to fit
into a loose chronological sequence.

A translation of 'Final Solution' ('Endlosung')
was included in a German anthology of Irish
stories entitled 'Erkundungen' (Verlag Volk
and Welt, Berlin 1979).

Copyright © John Morrow 1987

This book is set in 11/12 pt Mallard
by Colset Private Limited, Singapore.

Black Swan Books are published by
Transworld Publishers Ltd., 61 – 63
Uxbridge Road, Ealing, London W5 5SA, in
Australia by Transworld Publishers
(Australia) Pty. Ltd., 15 – 23 Helles Avenue,
Moorebank, NSW 2170, and in New Zealand
by Transworld Publishers (N.Z.) Ltd., Cnr.
Moselle and Waipareira Avenues,
Henderson, Auckland.

Made and printed in Great Britain by
The Guernsey Press Co. Ltd., Guernsey, Channel Islands.

Contents

Tommy Carlisle   9

Oul Cruelty   13

No Sundays on the Somme   17

Lonely Heart   34

Jason   50

The Coalman   60

The Gulp   65

Final Solution   71

The Gummy Lion   79

The Adjusters   87

The Humours of Ballyturdeen   95

O'Fuzz   109

Cromwell's Day   118

Chinese Knackers   126

Sects   133

The Gandhi Gong   143

Dublin Indemnity   165

The Visitation   195

Sects And Other Stories

Tommy Carlisle

When I was young, we knew where the devil lived. He lurked beneath a manhole cover near the gasworks, where the Blackstaff river meets the Lagan. Ordinarily, if you put your ear to one of the two small vents in the cover all you heard was a sound like a whisper in a cave; but at other times, mostly in winter, the roars of him could be heard the length of the street and gusts of evil-smelling steam would issue from the vents as if from the nostrils of a Walt Disney dragon. To go near him then, to get one whiff of that noxious breath, we were told, would mean, at the very least, two months isolation in the typhoid block in Purdysburn Fever. To fall into that terrible maw, if such a thing were ever possible, would mean certain death.

Our whispering, roaring devil was, of course, the most polluted river in Ireland, the Blackstaff, making its subterranean way through the city. I was going to write 'stretch of water', but by the time it reached the Lagan the percentage water content of the Blackstaff had plummeted into single figures. If there is such a person as the Devil, and such a place as 'The Sink of Hell', then the image of that black, sluggish, stinking broth is as good as any.

The manhole with the vents was one of many along its covered way – today they'd be called 'Service Access Points' – and when the awful soup below became too rich and thick, causing blockages, back-ups and flooding, the cover was removed and brave workmen, suitably protected, went down into the pit . . . It was at such a time, in the winter of 1937, that poor wee Tommy Carlisle went headfirst down the Devil's throat – and came up it a Saint.

Standing on the lip of the hole, I saw Tommy plunge screaming into the black, sliding ooze. Luckily, a workman was already down there and he managed to grab Tommy just as he was going down for the third time. They hauled him up, unconscious, sheathed from head to toe in sewage and industrial effluent, and carried him home to die.

Had it happened to any other of the juvenile trespassers cavorting around the hole that day, they might have stood a chance. Or so everyone said. But wee Tommy was only eight years of age, a year or two younger than we others; and forby that he was well known to be 'delicate', one of those large-eyed children with almost luminous skin and harsh, chesty voices, the runt of a large litter who, one knew, would not grow many grey hairs in those pre-penicillin days. To compensate for their short stay these fragile ones were often spoilt and pampered by their relatives, which made them a bit of a trial when they came out amongst their robust contemporaries. Such a one was wee Tommy, but all was forgotten and forgiven as we followed the procession of workmen and wailing women bearing him to his deathbed.

That it would be his deathbed no one, including the local doctor, had any doubt. Everyone knew the story of the workman who had gone down the hole in a pair of leaky gumboots and come up without toenails; of the fox-terrier that took a drink on a hot day and then bit three people and killed an Alsatian before itself dropping dead; of submerged pennies that melted before your very eyes.

We tip-toed in to view the small white face, corpse-like above the bedclothes, imagining the pints he must have gulped down, and we knew there was no hope. Suits normally deposited in the pawn-shop between one Sunday and the next were held out in anticipation of the funeral. 'You'll have to take a lift,' said my father, and proceeded to demonstrate for me the intricate footwork involved in the art of coffin bearing.

But wee Tommy lingered a week . . . and then a second week. People became irritated, and then began to lose interest. The rails in the pawn-shop began to fill up again.

Presently Tommy was sitting up and taking nourishment. Everyone said it was a miracle. His mother, who had kept an unbroken vigil at his bedside, had had a vision of the Deity in the small hours. In delirium, it was said, Tommy had spoken in strange tongues.

When Tommy next appeared in public view he was so well-mended as to be almost unrecognisable. He seemed to have grown inches, he had put on weight and his skin glowed healthily. Before, he had been a fractious, complaining child – a 'girn'; now he was cheerful and long-suffering of abuse from the rest of us urchins, whom he had robbed of a funeral. (I didn't get the chance to apply father's coffin technique until I was well into my twenties.)

Exactly when, or by whom, it was discovered that Tommy Carlisle had the gift of charming warts I can't say; but I do remember that he was very much in demand during a ringworm epidemic when I was twelve, which would make him ten at the time. Cataracts on elderly eyes were another early speciality of his; and on Christmas Day 1942, it is rumoured, he restored the sight of an Uncle who had gone blind while drinking methylated spirits on Christmas Eve. At the time there were cynics who said that a good dose of salts would have had the same result; just as today there are those who sneer at the gullible tens of thousands that queue all night for a place at a Monster Healing Rally conducted by that smiling six-footer in the white silk suit, the same wee Tommy Carlisle.

You've got to hand it to him: he's come a long way since those early sessions in a wooden tabernacle at sixpence a wart. Next to Billy Graham he's the biggest thing on the Bible Belt circuit in America, a dollar

11

millionaire ten times over. Of course, nowadays it's all much more subtle, a sort of spiritual psychoanalysis – and anyway, there's not as many warts and ringworms about as there used to be.

The last time he was over here on one of his World Wide Tours I watched it on television in the Salvation Army Home, where I am residing temporarily. The silver Rolls Royce; the ex-film starlet wife (more like his daughter); the bodyguard of New York Italians with wary hands inside their jackets; the collection buckets overflowing with paper . . . and all, I thought, because of that header down the hole all those years ago. Did he ever think of it, I wondered; did he realise what he owed it all to?

And there and then I resolved that some day I would confront him and bare my breast, spill the beans. Of course, he could very well cut up nasty; but he's a Christian man and I think he'll be inclined to take the larger view and express his gratitude in a substantial manner. For you see, if wee Tommy Carlisle owes his success to that dive down the Devil's throat, then he owes as much, if not more, to the fellow that pushed him.

Oul Cruelty

I'll call him Stanley, but in the years he sat on The Bench he was known universally as 'RSPCA' – or 'oul cruelty' for short.

The Bench itself sat just under the hooves of King Billy's horse at the corner of Railway Street. It was slatted and curved like an old, roll-topped desk, its wrought-iron end-pieces shaped in the letters V.R., and it had been stolen from the Ormeau Park in the early spring of 1919 by the six survivors of Railway Street's contribution to the Kaiser's downfall – six out of fourteen being about par for the course in that quarter of the city.

But Stanley, unlike the others, was not a city man, nor had he been a Rifleman. His tribe had originated in Loughgall or thereabouts, and he was so bitter about religious matters that on the outbreak of war he had joined the Black Watch, saying that he wouldn't wear a harp in his cap, crowned or not, even for Carson. He went away a quiet, dour lad and came home on four days of embarkation leave, kilted and spatted, with a thick Glaswegian accent and a terrible thirst for whisky. On the first day he broke a cue over the head of a bouncer in the local billiard hall; on the second he sent his own father to hospital with a cracked jaw; but on the third day, alas, poor Stanley fought his last battle.

He was on his way home, well-oiled, after paying a call on a cousin who worked in Dunville's distillery, when he was attracted to a disturbance centring on a terrace house which backed onto the railway embankment.

Pushing his way through a throng of childer and shawlies round the front door he came up against two RIC men who stood guard with carbines at the high port.

'Wassa matter here?' demanded Stanley. The childer crowded in around him, cheering . . . 'Bully Jock lad!' . . . 'G'wan Jock – you show 'em!'

The senior RIC man looked down from his great height at the kilted runt swaying in front of him. 'Just a bit of dog trouble, Sir,' he said in the thick brogue of County Clare, 'gone a bit daft with the heat. We have him cornered in the yard.'

'A dog!' exclaimed Stanley incredulously. 'A wee daft dog 'an they call out the Pope's Militia, armed tae the bloody teeth!'

The crowd, growing by the minute, howled . . . 'Steady the Buffs! . . . Forward the Forty-Twa! . . . Up yer kilt!'

Stanley threw off his Glengarry and tunic, handing them to an urchin in the front rank to mind for him, but first taking a long swig from the medicine bottle of first-shot Dunville's which had been the cousin's going-away present. He then rolled up his sleeves and faced the RIC men again. 'Outa my way,' he snarled. 'The dog was niver pupped that cud put the wind up me.'

The crowd, every one of whom was acquainted with the true nature of the problem, went wild. Compared with the heady days of 1912 things had been rather quiet since the boys went off to war. Crushed against the door, the two 'Pope's Militiamen' looked at one another, winked, and drew to one side, leaving the way open. The crowd, berserk now, surged forward and projected Stanley through the door, sending him sprawling up the hallway. But berserk or not, not one crossed the threshold after him. The lad wearing Stanley's tunic and Glengarry slammed the door and the crowd froze in silence. Then a shawlie, perhaps recalling the spirit of 1912, began to sing 'Oh God our help in ages past' and all joined in.

In the hallway, Stanley rose unsteadily to his feet and heard the singing outside. For Stanley, as for all his

14

generation, that particular anthem had an ominous portent ... the band awash on the boat-deck ... Titanic little Ulster being sucked down in the Fenian bog. For a moment, alone there in the dark hallway, his spirits sank, then Dunville's reasserted itself in the bloodstream. Anyway, what was a dog compared with his Da!

Here's tae us.
Wha's like us?
Damn few –
An' they're all deid!

Stanley marched into the small kitchen and looked through the window into the backyard with its waist-high wall verging the railway embankment. He could see no dog; it must have escaped onto the railway. Opening the scullery door he stepped out into the yard. And then, turning, he saw the dog. It had just emerged from its hiding place in the coalhole and it was the biggest dog Stanley had ever laid eyes on, a pure white Alsatian whose nearness to the wolf was a mere zoologist's quibble. What the keening crowd and the policemen – including the half-dozen lying on the far embankment with carbines trained on the yard wall – what they all knew and Stanley didn't was that it had been terrorising the district for a week and was suspected of being rabid. A small isolation ward in the City Infirmary had been filling up with its victims. The previous day it had tried to snatch a fireman from the footplate of a moving locomotive.

Stanley knew none of this: but he knew a big mad dog when he saw one. The dog, crouching to spring, growled and bared a mouthful of dripping teeth. Stanley heard the distant crowd go into the third verse of 'Oh God Our Help' and he reached slowly down to his right stocking top. If he had wanted to he might still have made it back through the scullery door before the dog reached him. It crossed his mind, but as he slid the cut-throat razor from his stocking (another relic of his Glasgow experience) the conditioning of the blood-weltering centuries was

15

too much – not forgetting, of course, Dunville's first-shot. Stanley flicked open the razor and launched himself at the dog's throat, uttering the battle-cry heard by the Peelers on the railway and passed from mouth to mouth in the following weeks of his glory – 'Heel, ya mad fucker ye!'

The Peelers waited until the howls of man and dog had subsided before moving in. When they did, two Wood-bines later, they found most of the Alsatian at one end of the yard and its head, firmly clamped on Stanley's left forearm, at the other. Stanley, though unconscious, still grasped his trusty Hamburg Ring.

Subsequent medical investigation revealed that the damage to Stanley's tendons which necessitated ampu-tation at the elbow had been done by his own razor; and the dog, it turned out, had not been rabid after all. This never became generally known, and even if it had would have had no effect on the legend that grew as it sped from lip to lip, across land and water. Even before it cleared the district all mention of the razor had been dropped, and by the time it reached France a third character had been added to the drama, the girlchild who cowered at one end of the yard with nothing but Stanley's bare hands between her and the ravening wolf (escaped from the circus).

And so it was that although Stanley himself spent the duration in Hospital Blues his battle-cry was carried to the brink of Hun trenches on the Somme and the Marne by waves of kilted furies – 'Heel, yis mad fuckers yis!'

No Sundays on the Somme

The 191st Company of the Belfast Battalion Boys Brigade stood stiffly, or otherwise, to attention, fronted and flanked by their officers, hemmed in by tiers of adoring relatives, facing the flag-draped platform soon to be graced by the presence of the Distinguished Visitor to this their Annual Inspection and Display. Six buglers stood poised to blow the 'General Salute' at a downward beat from the bandmaster, Lieutenant Bourke, known to all as 'Daddy', whose fat red face was grading to purple as his raised arms grew more leaden.

The buglers were sized 'tallest to the right, shortest to the left', the right-hand marker – number one – being an exceptionally tall and thin fifteen-year-old who wore thick, horn-rimmed spectacles. Number two, though more robust, was much shorter, the top of his head barely level with number one's shoulder, but a brave lad for all that ... At that tense moment, under Daddy Bourke's choleric eye, he chanced a final plea out of the right-hand corner of his mouth:

'For God's sake, Ken, don't!'

Ken, number one, didn't reply; couldn't, for just then a figure in battledress bounded onto the platform and Captain Walker, at the head of his men, screamed 'General Salute' and presented his walking-stick with a flourish worthy of a Hussar.

It was then that Ken did what number two, Jack, had begged him not to. The drill was that the red-tasselled bugle should be lifted – smartly – from the 'rest' position on the right-hand side of the navel and thrust out the

17

full length of the arm ('One') then brought – smartly –
to the lips ('Two'). But Ken now did it the French way:
when his bugle was at position 'one' he made a brief
circular movement with his wrist, causing his tassle to
fly up and wind itself round the body of the instrument,
a piece of theatre he had picked up from a film about the
French Foreign Legion.

If instead he had lashed out and booted Daddy Bourke
in the privates, it couldn't have had a more shattering
effect. Not only did it inject a fatal flutter into the timing
(one-birl-two) but also there was the fact that Daddy had
served with the BEF in 1914–18 and had a hatred for the
French such as he had never been able to work up
against the Germans. (It had all to do, seemingly, with
bared flanks as the fleeing frogs left the 'Contemptible
Little Army' to face the advancing Hun. Post-war revela-
tions in the memoirs of those who had a wider view,
proving that the flanks bared had been French as the
British Commander-in-Chief of the same name hurried
to the Boulogne boat, had done nothing to dampen
Daddie's Francophobia. Indeed, in the past few days, as
the BEF again made a 'tactical withdrawal', this time to
a place called Dunkerque, Daddie's 'Frogitis', as Ken
called it, had flared anew and he went round muttering
things like 'I hear they're poisoning the wells again').
In any event, his downbeat faltered in mid-swing and
became a pair of clenched, trembling fists; the 'General
Salute' richocheted off the sweating walls of the church
hall like the unsynchronised laments of six mortally
wounded elephants; the Distinguished Visitor winced
visibly; the back of Captain Walker's blond neck turned
puce.

God intervened in the person of the Reverend Eric
Cameron, Chaplain, who flung a three-minute-long
indictment at their bowed heads before introducing the
Distinguished Visitor . . . 'A soldier of Christ in the best
tradition of Gordon and Earl Haig, Colonel Wilkington-
Pike of the Flintshire regiment.'

The previous morning Ken and Jack had watched the

Flintshire training battalion march from the boat to take up quarters in the old mill warehouse. Ken's lip had curled (lips did this frequently in the novels of Percy F. Westerman and Ken had, with practice, managed to co-opt it with a flaring movement of his left nostril, which in turn caused his glasses to tilt slightly – all in all an intimidating performance, Jack found). 'Look at them rifles. Pigging,' he said scornfully. 'My Da says the Flintshires ran nearly as fast as the Shitty Shirts on the Somme.'

The other way, of course, Ken's Da's version of events on the Western Front in July 1916 being that the Ulster Division had run one way and everyone else, excluding the Germans, had run the other. Jack didn't doubt it; that would have been unthinkable even without the threat of lip and nostril. Ken's Da, besides being the neighbourhood's champion drunk and wife-beater, was the neighbourhood hero – M.M. and promoted on the field 2nd of July, 1916. Only once had Jack attempted lese majeste by retailing his own Da's conviction that the entire Ulster Division had had to be driven over the top by Connaught Rangers wielding bull's pisils. After a speechless few moments of curling, flaring and tilting Ken had said: 'And what would a stoker on a banana boat know about it?'

Jack often wished that his Da had gone and died along with his three brothers that July morning, instead of joining the navy. Then, of course, he himself would not have existed, having been born in 1926; but it would have been worth it just to see Ken's face. Dying was better than the M.M. any day.

'. . . even now,' said Wilkington-Pike, doing a bit of Dynamic Tension with his bamboo swagger-stick, 'our lads are executing a classic withdrawal and outflanking movement guaranteed to lure the Hun into the Allied net.' (Cheers.) 'Mark my words, Mr Hitler and his gang will be on the run before the turn of the year.' (Cheers. And Daddy Bourke yelled an approximate rendering of the Irish Fusiliers' battle cry 'Faugh a Ballagh!' which caused the Chaplain's wife to sit up straight.) 'But,' said

19

Wilkington-Pike, pointing the bamboo menacingly, 'let us not be caught napping, as we were in 1914. Because of, er, local difficulties, as you know, there will be no conscription in Ireland.' (Cheers.) 'But the Irish Volunteer has always been the backbone of the British army. So what I say to the young men here tonight who are approaching military age . . .'

'Did you see Fatty Hamill's face when he said that!' giggled Ken as he and Jack walked home through the blacked-out streets after the show. Fatty Hamill was a seventeen-year-old sergeant. 'He looked like he'd caught a mouthful of boke just in time. God! can you imagine maybe being stuck for days in a dug-out with Fatty's stinking feet!'

'Or having to send Yah-Yah Nixon with a life-or-death message for reinforcements!' cried Jack, breaking into his famous imitation of the afflicted corporal: 'S-s-s-sur, we are s-s-s-s-ur . . .'

'I'm not looking forward to the next Bible class, I can tell you,' said Ken glumly. 'What do you bet it'll be Daddy Bourke on Clive of India, Springheel Jack on Rhodes of Africa, or Walker himself on Gordon . . . Here!'

Ken had stopped suddenly. Jack pulled up and squinted through the murk at the towering outline of his friend. He saw the vertical pointing finger and knew without seeing that it was accompanied by Ken's 'Eureka!' expression, always a prelude to disaster.

'What now?' he asked, stomach sinking.

'I was just wondering if there was ever a holy sodger called Walker. Can you think? Anyway, even if there was there'd always be room for another one – or two . . .'

'Now don't go starting anything like that, for God's sake!' pleaded Jack. 'That bit of tassle birling'll have you in –'

At this point both were distracted by a burst of wild yodelling near at hand.

'There's Gene Autry on his way home to the ranch,' groaned Ken; 'I'd best go and pull his boots off before he gets to bed. I'll see you.'

Switching on his flashlight, Ken ran off in the general direction of 'South of the Border'. Jack turned off into his own street, but when he came abreast of the entry that linked his and Ken's street he stopped and listened. And, as always, up the funnel of the entry came Ken's final bulletin of the day: 'The two Chinks were the only ones inside the army age limits there tonight.'

And so they were: Terence Walker (the Captain) was 29 and brother David ('Springheel Jack', 2nd in command) was 25. They were the '& Sons' of a thriving butchery business in the district. 'Walker' himself had passed on ten years ago, but mothers in the district still sent their childer 'round to the Chinaman's' for a pound of minced steak. This sobriquet had had nothing to do with the shape of Walker's eyes or his colouring, for he had been a caricature of a burly pork-butcher.

The legend was that in the early twenties – 'with hardly a boot to his fut' – Walker had gone to Chicago via the Salvation Army emigration scheme. There he got a job in a corned beef factory, overseeing one of the huge vats into which whole, boned carcasses were flung to be scythed to mush by a blur of giant knives. Across the open top of this vat ran a narrow cat-walk for the convenience of maintenance men, and it was from this that Walker saw the Chinaman fall, without a sound, down amongst the whirring blades in a vat full of cubed cow.

Walker was the only witness. He shut off the power as quickly as possible and rushed to tell his immediate superior, who summoned the manager, who informed the directors . . . A caucus in a quandary: fifty thousand dollars worth of beef to be flushed down the hole because of one Goddamn Chink! But within the hour a decision had been taken. And Walker, with five thousand dollars hush money and a boat ticket home in his pocket, was given the honour of pressing the button that set the knives whirring again. (This tale is told of a successful butcher in every townland in Ireland. Another, to be applied in the case of a nouveau riche grocer, publican, bookie etc., is that he had been the one lucky

enough to purchase the tin with the pigtail in it . . . People
like to think that success is due to something other than
hard work.)

Walker had been a hard worker, had had a near way
with the knife, had known just how far to go with the
sausages (everything bar horns and hooves) and had
two sets of weights (one for the Inspector); all of which
he had passed on to his sons. But his success had been
due largely to his wife, a 'good-living' countrywoman
with a shrewd business head and the tongue of a tinker
when it came to bad debt. She treated Walker himself as
if he were a hired hand and raised their two sons in a
God-fearing, Victorian rigidity, her attitude to them a
mixture of maternal cosseting and scathing contempt
(though they were the ultimate possessions dear to her
huckstering heart, they were also reminders of her two
lapses into carnality – both occurring after the Master
Butcher's Annual Dinner).

The sign over the shop still read 'Walker & Sons', and
no one had any doubt that the real Walker still ruled
there. She and her boys lived in the flat above the shop,
and no female under the age of sixty had ever been
known to cross the threshold. Choirgirls might ogle the
handsome blondness of the brothers across the pews on
Sunday, but let one linger in the porch in the hope of a
word and she'd find her way deftly blocked by Mammy.

Not that the boys showed any interest. David –
'Springheel Jack' – was the athletic one. He had the
lean face and domed forehead of a scholar (though as
thick as two planks). Dressed, he was nondescript:
stripped, Superman, a bounding mass of muscular
vitality, a virtuoso of the parallel bars, a lord of the
rings. His delight at the end of each Brigade P.T. session
was to have a bout of tag-wrestling with half-a-dozen of
the senior lads. His only other function was to give a
monthly lecture on clean-living and the horrors of self-
abuse – a treat for all those in the Company who were
pursuing their own sex studies in the back entrys of the
district.

Captain Terence was the scholar of the family, an acknowledged (by the Bible Union) authority on the more bloodthirsty bits of the Old Testament. Though physically well-set-up he was not at all athletic, and had never been known to shed his coat or tie even on the hottest day at summer camp. His delights were drill and the minuiae of uniform and martial decorum. He would spend hours going round with a ruler ascertaining that every boy's pillbox cap was tilted exactly one inch above the right ear, as per Rifle Brigade regulations, or with a pacing-stick measuring the intricacies of the 'left incline', or demonstrating the old squaddy trick of burning brass buckles over a candle for better burnishing. The highlight of his year was when he led the company in the Battalion's annual march-past at the City Hall.

Captain Terence's delight can only be presumed: he never showed any. It was said of him that he looked as if he had suffered a stroke at birth ('the Chinaman's curse') or that he went in continual mortal terror of messing his trousers. Even at Bible class, detailing the mass slaughter of anti-semitic ancients, his delivery was usually of the dead-pan, throwaway sort such as a young company commander might employ when giving an enforced lecture on Proust to a squad of Glasgow keelies. The Sunday after the Display and Inspection it was, as Ken had predicted, Captain Terence on Gordon of Khartoum . . .

'Please sir – why did they call him "China" Gordon?'

The question, from Ken, burst like a grenade in the silence following the Captain's time-worn exposé of the Mad Mullah's beastliness.

The Bible class was held in a small room adjoining the church hall. The Captain stood at a lectern, flanked by Daddy Bourke and Springheel Jack. On the wall behind him hung an oil painting of Queen Victoria apparently battering a kneeling blackamoor on the head with an oversized Bible. The company sat on rows of backless forms facing the lectern. The place smelt of wax, dust and tired wood. Ken and Jack sat side-by-side on the back form.

Ken had called for Jack that morning, agog from research into the Life of Gordon . . . ' "China"! Would you believe it!'

'You're making it up', had been Jack's reaction, which he had call to regret.

'Alright – who better to ask than the expert himself –'

'Ah no!. . . Not the day. Look, I believe you. Are you satisfied now?'

Ken wasn't.

All heads in the Bible class swivelled to where he towered, hands and six inches of skinny wrists dangling like skinned rabbits from the sleeves of his older and smaller brother's cast-off navy serge. Fatty Hamill snorted. Somebody tittered. Jack closed his eyes and murmured 'Oh God!' 'Silence! Face yer front!' roared Daddy Bourke.

Springheel Jack tried to kill Ken with a hard look, cracking his knuckles ominously. But Captain Terence, when he finally raised his face from the lectern, was seen to be smiling – or as near it as atrophied facial muscles would allow.

'Because, Chambers,' he said with a stress on the surname that caused further muffled hilarity (Ken's nickname was 'Po'), 'General Gordon served with great distinction in that country during the Boxer rebellion. Alright?'

'Yes Sir.' Ken began to sit down, but the Captain then said: 'I'm glad you reminded me of your presence, Chambers. Mr Bourke has been telling me about your conduct prior to the General Salute last week. You are to return your bugle to Mr Bourke before the next drill session. Alright?'

'But Sir . . .'

'No "buts", Chambers; that's an order. Forby your gross behaviour with the tassle, there is also the problem of your increasing height. It would be different if it was accompanied by a proportionate increase in girth.

As it is,' – and here Captain Terence paused, glancing to left and right to assure himself that the line still held – 'you are getting to look more like a scruffy pull-through for a rifle.'

Everyone howled obsequiously, bar Jack and Ken himself. He kept standing throughout, grinning faintly, until the outbreak subsided. Then, in the process of folding himself to sit, he turned his head towards Jack and muttered something. Now Jack's laugh rang out and Captain Terence came craning over the lectern, not smiling now, pointing a trembling finger . . . 'Chambers! What did you say just now? . . . Come along, boy, what's that you whispered to –'

'I just said that it wouldn't be any rifle of yours, Sir,' replied Ken, standing up again, in a quiet, surprised tone of voice.

'And just what do you mean by that?' This from Springheel Jack, who had risen to stand beside his brother, flushed up and flexing the hidden muscles beneath his clerical grey.

'Only that being an officer, the Captain will have a sword or a revolver instead. Isn't that right, Sir?'

If the Walkers had had a sword between them at that moment they'd have hacked him to ribbons. Springheel Jack looked as though about to burst out of his chrysalis, like Batman, and launch himself across the room at Ken's throat. The Captain's unconditioned features writhed impotently, one half seeming to smirk and the other to glower alternately, like in a distorted mirror, shopping around the range of expressive moulds and finding none to suit.

What they would eventually have said or done no one will ever know. Daddy Bourke, who had been simmering away, chose that moment to boil over. He came to his feet, blood mottled and spitting, the squaddy of yester-year booting his way through the facade of select vestry-man, to scream at Ken: 'It's none of your bloody business anyway, you impudent ghett ye!'

'You're for it now, right enough,' said Jack ten minutes

later. They were standing with the others outside the church hall, watching Daddy Bourke being assisted into a car by the Walkers. 'He's bust a blood vessel for sure.'

'Notatall,' said Ken, with full lip and curl. 'Sure he had to do something after coming off with a mouthful like that in the church hall. He's faked many a wee turn before this, the same oul bugger.'

The car pulled away with the Walkers and Daddy in it and Willy Harper, Corporal, message boy for Walker & Co., wrestling companion of Springheel Jack and general toady, broke away from the crowd and made for Ken, brandishing his Bible. 'You're one rotten fucker, Chambers!' he cried, in his passion making the mistake of coming within the orbit of Ken's reach. The enormous fist, knuckles sharp and white, caught Willy judiciously in the throat (though he'd feel it all day, long after he got his breath back, there would be no marks to show the Walkers in the morning). But he would tell all.

'At the very least you'll be drummed out,' said Jack mournfully as they walked home.

But he wasn't, due either to the darkening days after Dunkirk, when everything tended to pale against the threat of invasion, or to the fact (equally traumatic) of the impending mission to the parish by the great temperance preacher, the Reverend Porter-Green.

'We should all be very proud,' said Captain Walker at Bible class, 'that this great man should make our parish his first stop on returning from his Grand Tour of the Antipodes. I personally look forward to hearing his own story of that great triumph when, like Gordon against the Dervish, he stood firm against the cut-throat brewers and whisky Barons of that gin-soaked country, Australia. You will all be given a copy of this pre-mission tract in which he describes how these ruthless men hired American gangsters to end his life, such was the effect his great mission was having on their ill-gotten gains. So when he calls for the pledge to be taken next Sunday I know that every man and boy in the 191st . . .'

Just to make certain that every man and boy would move in formation they had a rehearsal in the empty church that afternoon. The full company took up three rows of pews in the body of the congregation. Springheel Jack acted Porter-Green for the occasion . . . 'And now I call on everyone to come forward and pledge themselves to abstain from alcoholic lickers as beverages . . .' On this cue Daddy Bourke snapped his fingers ('one') and the company rose as one; he snapped again ('two') and all did a smart right turn; on 'three' the markers led off up the church in twos, each boy with pen in hand, ready to sign the illuminated pledges already blessed and witnessed by Porter-Green.

'My Da says he's a fruit,' growled Ken after the rehearsal.

'Springheel Jack?' asked Jack intuitively.

'No. Him,' said Ken, curling the lip at the photograph of Porter-Green on the cover of the tract: the long white locks and stern aquiline features that had caused aborigines to raise idols in his name. 'He used to wear perfume when he had the big Gospel tent in the bog meadows years ago, my Da says.'

Since they had repossessed his bugle everyone bar his immediate family circle and Jack was either a 'fruit' or a 'bastard'. Jack had never known him to take anything so hard. He had a talent for the bugle; he had 'the Lip', as they say (perhaps because of all the exercise he gave it); the only one in the squad able to play 'Danny Boy' on the mouthpiece alone. Two years ago he had blown the Last Post at the Battalion remembrance service at the cenotaph. Now, he knew, the Walkers would make sure he never blew again, anywhere.

'I'll fix them,' he said, while un-fixing Porter-Green into two, four and then eight pieces. His tone of voice filled Jack with an awful foreboding.

'Ah God no, Ken! Don't do anything more. They'll put the black on you for sure.' (The Walkers were also big wheels in the Masonic, and Ken had hopes of an apprenticeship in the shipyard.)

If he had known beforehand what Ken was going to do, would he have had the guts to join him? The question was to haunt Jack far into his middle years. Only when the memory of the church parade that mission Sunday grew dim was he able to persuade himself, sometimes, that he just might have.

The church was packed to overflowing; so much so that the verger expressed fears for the structure of the normally little-used balcony. The Lord Mayor, several Aldermen, the local MP and other office-bearers occupied the front pew in the nave, beneath a vast rampart of flowers banking up to the pulpit. Behind them sat the elders of the Select Vestry and their families, and in the centre pews the Boys Brigade, the Life Boys, the Girl Guides and the Brownies. From the stained-glass windows dust-laden shafts of sunlight bathed the congregation, bringing a touch of colour to pale, pinched faces, a new lustre to bald heads and homemade millinery, a faint luminosity to the starched crossbelts of the Brigade and the high, hard collars of the vestrymen. The organist, possessor of the most expressive backview in Christendom, excelled himself, causing some of the more worldly in the gathering to smile knowingly, remembering when he used to rise twice nightly out of the floor in the Ritz, a local cinema – and occasionally fall off the stool in mid-passage. He was the local organiser for Alcoholics Anonymous.

Porter-Green himself came as an anti-climax. The photograph on the tract had been taken thirty years before. The flowing locks were there in abundance still, but the matinee-idol features had shrunk to the appearance of a much battered champion chestnut, the piercing eyes that had put the fear of God and the straitjacket into many a confirmed drouth now mild and watery. The verger had to help him up the six steps to the pulpit.

His voice matched the rest of him, an old man's chesty whine, and most of his message was inaudible even, apparently, to those in the front pew. Within minutes the MP's chin was on his chest, snoring gently, and the Lord

Mayor was seen to be carrying on a heated argument in *sotto voce* with an adjacent Alderman. Near the end Porter-Green did manage to capture his audience momentarily with the information that he had in his possession – in a glass jar, in the vestry – the pickled liver of an alcoholic aboriginal, and the promise that anyone signing the pledge that day would be vouchsafed a peek at the abomination. But generally it was with a rustle of relief that the congregation heard him appeal to everyone to come forward and 'pledge themselves to abstain from alcoholic lickers as beverages'.

Daddy Bourke snapped thrice and the company, led by the Walkers and himself, moved in twos towards the altar – or so everyone in the company thought, including Jack, who was so intent on 'facing his front' that he was halfway there before he realised that he was unpaired. The congregation in the balcony were the first to notice, causing the structure to creak alarmingly as they surged forward to gape at the figure sitting alone in the centre of three deserted pews. Captain Walker noticed when, after pledging himself to total abstinence for the thirty-first time, he turned to lead the company back to the pews. At that moment, some said, he looked as if the long-dreaded had come to pass and he had indeed shit his pinstripes . . .

'Private Chambers standfast – the rest of the company – Dismiss!'

On the roadway outside the church hall Jack did a smart right turn, saluted, and wandered onto the pavement with the dismissed rest, leaving Ken alone for the second time that day. The Captain and Springheel Jack, both wearing thunderous expressions, had gone on ahead when the company paraded from the church and were now in the Bible classroom preparing for the court-martial. Daddy Bourke now fell in behind Ken and, perhaps feeling a bit ridiculous because of some civilian onlookers, whispered 'By the left, quick march.'

As Ken and Daddy disappeared into the hall, Fatty Hamill said: 'They'll ate him.'

'Serves him right,' said Willy Harper; 'thinks he is somebody.'

The company dispersed homewards – more quickly than was usual after a parade, Porter-Green's long ramblings having brought the proceedings to the edge of darkness. Before long Jack was alone on the steps of the church hall, shivering in the bitter east wind that had started to sneer at his light, Sunday-best suit. He could hear a rumble of voices from within, the Bible classroom being at the front of the building, its one blacked-out window just a few yards beyond the railings that lined the steps. Once the coast was clear Jack vaulted the railings and pressed his ear to the window.

Captain Walker was saying: '. . . and what you thought or did not think has nothing to do with it, Chambers. An order was given and you disobeyed. You out of all the company chose –'

Ken: '– But I just didn't want to take any pledge, Sir.'

Captain: 'Oh, you didn't! And what makes you so different from the others? They were willing to obey orders.'

Ken: 'I thought it was my own choice, Sir. Colonel Wilkington-Pike told us the war might go on for years, like the last one, and they'll need every man-jack they –'

Captain (shouting): 'Don't ramble, boy! What's all this got to do with today's disgraceful behaviour?'

Ken: 'Well, Sir, I want to join up as soon as I'm the age . . . So I can't very well take the pledge, can I, Sir?'

Long silence, broken only by what sounded like a giggle from Springheel Jack.

Captain (nonplussed): 'Well . . . I never heard . . . What you're saying, Chambers, is that because you're joining the army you have to be free to drink all you like . . . Is that it?'

Ken: 'I didn't mean –'

Captain: 'Never mind what you meant – what you're

saying is that your idea of being a soldier is one long whisky binge! Well, we can guess where you got that from, can't we –'

Ken: 'My father drinks rum, Sir. And he got his first tot from the army when he wasn't much older than me. The 2nd of July, 1916. You never know when you'd need something like that. Y'know, Sir – like Gordon at Khartoum? The book I'm reading says he got through two bottles of brandy and soda a day.'

Jack groaned.

Captain (roaring): 'What! You ... you guttersnipe! I will not have you maligning the memory of a great Christian man. Do you hear me?'

Ken: 'But, Sir, it's true –'

Springheel Jack (threateningly): 'Just you be careful what you're saying, Chambers. Not only about Gordon; listening to you you'd think the whole Ulster Division went into action in a drunken stupor.'

Captain (breathlessly): 'Some needed to be, I suppose. But there were plenty of decent, sober, Christian men there too, you know. Lieutenant Bourke was there, a man who took the pledge today for the fifteenth time, he told me. But I suppose you'll say he was full of rum too. Eh? What do you say to that, Mr Bourke?'

Daddy Bourke made no reply – at least none that Jack could hear. There was a long pause. Then he heard Captain Walker ask, in a puzzled sort of way: 'Mr Bourke, are you all right?' Another pause – then the unmistakable sound of Daddy's iron-shod clock-killers crossing the room, a door opening . . .

Jesus! thought Jack; he's twigged me!

He hurdled the railings, spracleing heavily on the steps before taking off across the road and into the maw of an entry, from which position he could watch the door of the church hall.

But when that door opened some minutes later it was

Ken who came out, not Daddy. Jack ran back across the road and met him on the steps, 'What happened? ... What happened? ... I was listening at the –'

'I know. I heard you doing the bunk,' said Ken. He then put a finger to his lips and beckoned, 'Listen.' From the Bible classroom came the sound of raised voices, but now the one predominating was that of Daddy Bourke.

'What happened?' Jack asked again. For answer Ken took him by the arm and started to run. They covered a good few hundred yards of main road at full gallop and were deep in the tangle of small streets near home before Ken stopped, panting, and said: 'Now, I'll show you what happened.' From under his coat he produced his bugle, presented it, flourished the tassle in the French way, and blew the chorus of 'Marching Through Georgia'.

'Where the hell did you get that?' gasped Jack, having visions of a sudden snatch and run job.

'Daddy Bourke,' replied Ken, prior to spitting another wild blast.

'I don't believe you!'

'I'm telling you. Without a word he marches over to the cupboard, takes out the bugle, hands me it and says: "Away on home and get in a bit of practice".'

'And what did the Walkers say to that?'

'Bugger all. Just stood and gaped the whole time. God! I bet they're giving it to poor old Daddy now.'

'But why did he do it?'

'Search me. Sure you wouldn't know with these oul fellas, either shite or sugar. I've seen my Da crying like a ba over nothing at all.'

'Crying? Why, was Daddy Bourke crying?'

'Well, I think he was when he gave me back the bugle. But mind, don't you come over that to anybody or I'll break your bloody neck!'

'But . . .'

Jack's further inquiries into Daddy Bourke's curious behaviour were forestalled by a high, nasal rendering of 'Mexicali Rose' breaking out close at hand.

'Oh God!' groaned Ken. 'You'd think he'd at least sing hymns. I'd better go and collect him.'

'Where the hell does he get it on Sundays – in this place!' cried Jack, angry at being deprived of a long post-mortem. But Ken was already half-way down the street.

A bomber's moon had come up and Jack watched until his friend's gangling figure had turned a corner and out of sight before continuing his own way homeward. But when he came to the entry mouth and looked up, the pair of them were silouetted at the far end, tall Ken supporting his short Da in a semi-fireman's-lift. And above the last verse of 'Mexicali Rose' he heard Ken's last bulletin of the day echoing up the entry:

'There was no Sundays on the Somme.'

Lonely Heart

One blacked-out evening in January 1944 a jeep-load of
drunk Yanks mounted the pavement alongside the one-
and-ninepenny queue at the Ritz cinema and squashed
him dead against a blind lamp-post. At the moment it
happened the one-and-ninepennies began to move in, so
when a joint patrol of Yank MPs and British red-caps
came on the scene minutes later there were no witnesses bar the jeep's cargo, and they were paralytic.
When the British red-caps saw, by flashlight, that the
broken heap lying at the base of the bent lamp wore a
khaki greatcoat with a British lance-jack's stripe on the
sleeve, they wanted to kill the cargo, or at least the
driver, there and then. The Yank MPs, naturally,
wouldn't hear tell of it. Angry words were exchanged,
lead-loaded flashlights brandished, gun butts fondled in
dark confusion. Only the arrival of a civilian policeman saved the incident from developing into something
really nasty. Turning the heap over with his toe, he said:
'Och sure, it's only oul Lonely Heart. He's a busker, a
shell-shock case.' And they saw then that the greatcoat
was faded and threadbare, and that the right hand still
clutched a battered mouth-organ. One of the red-caps, a
long service man, noted that the few remaining buttons
on the greatcoat bore the insignia of the Horse Artillery
and remarked to himself the incongruity between this
and the crossed rifles of a marksman on one sleeve:
damn few of those in the horse-guns.

The legally necessary post-mortem on the remains of
Thomas Woods, known as Lonely Heart to generations

of cinemagoers, was held the next day. One thing brought to light was a fragment of a German dum-dum bullet which had been wandering around in his puddings for twenty-eight years. Giving evidence at the coroner's inquest, the city pathologist said that the deceased must have lived in almost continual torment. The coroner declared that it showed again just how beastly the Boche were, recorded a verdict of accidental death, and the one hungover newsman present came away with the impression that Lonely Heart, writhing in agony, had fallen in front of the jeep. Those responsible for inter-allied harmony in the city heaved a sigh of relief.

People read about his death, and about the dum-dum nagging away all those years, like a grain of sand in a barren oyster, and their sadness was tinged with remorse. Lonely Heart had been a case, a character on a par with 'Andy Gump', 'Oily Boke', 'Skin-the-goat'; all tattered derelicts who prowled the city, minds turned by war, drink, love or, in the case of one who lectured pigeons on the Customs House steps, 'The Books'. They'd called him Lonely Heart because he had never been known to play anything other than the mournful dirge 'I Wandered Today to the Hills, Maggie', his appearance at the head of a cinema queue the signal for a chorus of cheerful abuse and a barrage of small missiles. And through it all he had played his dirge, the mouth-organ in one hand and his extended cap, clinking, in the other.

His funeral column was the longest in living memory in his home district. At the cemetery the laid-out wreaths covered a dozen graves on either side of the waiting pit, most of them from people who had never known his proper name ... 'For Lonely Heart – from the girls in Murray's snuff room'.

But there was one other, a small spray placed far back and almost hidden behind a neighbouring headstone, which puzzled those few of the mourners who noticed it when, after the service, they made the traditional tour of the tributes to make sure their florist hadn't welshed.

'For Shooter,' the card on the spray said. 'Quis Separabit'.

Tommy Woods had been a gunner in the Horse Artillery. Unlike most of his Belfast contemporaries in the Ulster Volunteers (Carson's Army) – Hostilities Only men – he was a regular and had been one of the first on French soil in 1914, retreating from Mons almost as fast as the contemptible Field Marshal French himself. When the armies were bogged down in trench warfare in 1915 Tommy was unhorsed and given a rifle, and it was as an infantryman near Ypres in early 1916 that he stopped the German dum-dum with his guts. They managed to extract most of the fragments in the field hospital, after which Tommy was sent to a rest camp near Abbeville to convalesce.

He had been courting a girl called Aggie Gamble on and off since they had been half-timers at the mill school together, and they had corresponded regularly since his enlistment. They had talked of marriage, but always as a post-war happening – until the wound. Aggie's letters suddenly became very torrid and peremptory: all her friends were getting married; she was nearly twenty – she'd be left on the shelf; she'd heard of 'Blighty wounds' – surely Tommy's was one; an Easter wedding would be nice . . . Tommy applied for leave in February, it was granted on the first week in March and Aggie set in train arrangements for them to be married on the Thursday of Easter week.

And so, in the early morning of Tuesday the 25th of April, 1916, Tommy Woods stood in a crowd of other happy 'Blighty Ones' at the rail of the Holyhead-Kingstown ferry as the gangplank thumped onto Irish cobbles. He could see the Belfast train lying just up the wharf, steaming on the leash, welcoming doors gaping. He also noticed a hobnailed scurry of military activity on and around the wharf – but being wartime, that was only to be expected. One of the returning warriors made a joke about 'Fireside Fusiliers' and Tommy, full of beery euphoria, was still laughing as he clattered down the gangplank . . . his last laugh ever. He had one foot on the cobbles when a hand fell on his shoulder. Its owner was a middleaged Sergeant of the Dublin Fusiliers, very white-faced and nervous. 'Thanks be to Christ, an artilleryman!' he cried, thumping Tommy's shoulder. 'Tell us, do you know anything about eighteen-pounders?'

'Aye, but what . . .' Tommy stuttered.

'Never mind,' said the Sergeant. 'Come with me.'

He started to drag Tommy by the arm across the wharf in the direction of some army lorries. The Belfast train made shunting noises, its doors banging impatiently. Tommy found his tongue. 'Here . . . hi . . . that's my train,' he fairly yelled, wrenching free from the Sergeant and hoking in his tunic pocket for paybook and leave pass. 'I'm getting married the day after –'

The Sergeant took hold of Tommy by the webbing with one hand and half-drew a revolver from its holster on his belt with the other. 'She'll have to wait,' he said through his teeth, close to Tommy's face. 'Everything'll have to wait. If Christ himself walked up that harbour this minute and knew one end of an eighteen-pounder from the other he'd be up on that wagon double quick or I'd blow his fuckin' head off. Jump!'

Tommy jumped. He had seen men like the Sergeant at that stage of hysteria before and he knew it was either jump or be crippled. The authority of such men rested on sincere presentation of stark choices.

For part of the way along the Dublin road the lorry ran abreast of the Belfast train. Then road and line parted company and Tommy felt as though his stomach was about to fall out. 'Cheer up,' said the Sergeant, shoving a lit Woodbine between Tommy's lips. 'The day after tomorrow, is it? Sure you could be on the evening train. They brought up four eighteen-pounders from Athlone this morning. They'll soon winkle the bastards out.'

He took it for granted that Tommy had heard of the Sinn Fein rising, which he hadn't. It wasn't until long after the event that its true nature dawned on him, and then only as part of the long dream sequence his past life had become, a brief illumination in the fog behind him, quickly snuffed.

As the lorry clattered through deserted suburban streets and the familiar boom of eighteen-pounders and the fitful sparkle of small arms grew louder, Tommy barely noticed. He was thinking of Aggie. She'd be leaving work today. The girls in the mill would truss her up with hanks of flax, daub her face with loom grease and wheel her around the streets in a trolley, chanting:

Here comes the bride
Forty inches wide
See how she wobbles
Her big backside . . .

The lorry stopped close to the roar of guns. The Sergeant screamed: 'Out!' and they dropped off the tail-board and ran crouching behind a wall beside a river. Two eighteen-pounders at either flank of a wide bridge . . . black-faced gunners training and laying. As Tommy and the Sergeant reached the nearest gun it fired. Tommy swivelled to look and saw a wide street of tall buildings with, in the centre, tallest of all, a thin pillar, masonry crumbling. 'Close, fuck yis,' howled a Bombardier. 'Mind what the General said, knock the one-eyed matelot down an' yis are all on a fizzer!'

The Sergeant thrust Tommy forward and shouted into the Bombardier's ear. The Bombardier glared at Tommy's cap badge and growled: 'Christ! The galloping peashooters, that's all I needed. Come on, King Billy – at least you'll be no worse than that huer on the breech. I've been waitin' for his sporran an' bollocks to go scatterin' up Sackville Street.' A private of the Black Watch staggered to the rear and Tommy took his place. 'Prime . . . load . . . brush . . . fire!' And so began the waking nightmare of Tommy's life.

For two days he stoked the gun, with brief respites for

bully and char and, once, champagne and cold chicken from the kitchen of a wrecked hotel. The air was still and the smoke and fumes hung around them, growing thicker by the hour, turning day into night and night into a small room containing the gun and themselves, lit spasmodically by muzzle flame.

Once, during a lull whilst ammunition was brought up, Tommy wandered out of the stour and over to the parapet of the river bank. It was night time. Across the stretch of flame-tinted water the big street burned. A four-storied shell glowed like a Hallowe'en turnip and then, as he watched, collapsed like an old gas-mantle. But the one-eyed matelot still posed on his pillar, and that was all the Bombardier cared about. 'Come away ar' that, King Billy, and lave that river alone.'

The rest spells became more frequent throughout Wednesday, and at dusk the word came to stand down – they'd run out of ammo. Most of the crews dropped where they stood, asleep before they hit the ground. The Bombardier came across Tommy sitting on a shell box, curled up in a knot, heaving silently, holding what had been a khaki handkerchief over his mouth; it was now sopping red. 'Jasus! Is it the lung rot ye have?' asked the Bombardier, slapping his back. 'You should have spoke up. That cordite's a bastard.'

Tommy managed to explain that the blood was from his stomach, not his lungs; they'd told him this might happen, and not to worry. The Bombardier went away and came back with two thick horse blankets. He wrapped Tommy from head to toe like a cigar and, lifting him bodily, carried him to one of the waiting lorries. Stretched in the back, blanket-cowled head on his pack, Tommy didn't hear the engine start up or feel one jolt of the cobbled journey.

He awoke in familiar surroundings. He lay on a low camp-cot between two high hospital beds, all around him the muted hubbub of an early morning ward: a steady base of groaning and coughing overlaid by the clanking of utensils, the scurry and squeak of orderlies' feet, the raised voices of nurses. An RAMC stretcher party picked its way through rows of cots down the centre of the ward. For a dazed moment Tommy thought he was back in Abbeville; then everything came back to him . . . Aggie.

'How are ye now, Rip Van Winkle?'

A Belfast voice, issuing from a hairy face with Woodbine attached, framed in bandages, glaring over the edge of the bed to his right.

'What time is it?' asked Tommy.

'Eight o'clock or thereabouts. The way you've been snorin' you should be askin' the day, not the time.'

Tommy thought back frantically, heart in mouth. 'It's Thursday,' he said.

The man wheezed joyfully. 'There y'are! . . . Rip Van Winkle. They gave you a quare doze of somethin' when they carted you in. You've slep the clock roun' an' then some. It's bloody Friday mornin', an' if you don't believe me, just take a whiff . . . bloody fish! They start boilin' it at the scrake of dawn so's all the good'll be out of it by dinner hour. Fenian bastards! Here, where are you off to?'

Tommy was pulling on his trousers. Luckily they had piled his clothes and pack, army fashion, beside the cot. 'Home,' he replied, 'as soon as I can get a train.'

'They'll niver let ye.'

'They'll never notice, if I know anything about these places.'

Neither they did, all their attention being taken up at that moment with an intake of wounded from the field stations. Tommy pushed his way through a jam of bearers and stretchers and cadged a lift in an ambulance that left him off not far from Amiens Street station.

The city lay under a haze of smoke from the fires of Sackville Street. From there still arose an incessant rattle of machine-gun and rifle fire. But the vicinity of Amiens Street was quiet enough as Tommy hurried towards the station. In the almost deserted entrance hall he asked a railwayman about trains for Belfast. 'No

40

civvies or leave men,' was the reply, 'only goods and troops-in-transit.'

Nevertheless, Tommy ran towards the platforms – and into the Dubliner Sergeant, who now wore the red armband of an RTO . . . 'King Billy! I heard you were in hospital. When's that weddin' of yours?'

'Yesterday,' said Tommy. 'And I want home as soon as I can get. They say it's all troops-in-transit.'

The Sergeant, suddenly grim-faced, again laid hold of Tommy by the webbing and started running him towards a train that was making its first jerky shunts out of platform one. He shouted in Tommy's ear: 'Say you're attached to the Sherwoods. Give my name . . . McKenna.'

Sergeant McKenna wrenched open the door of the last carriage and heaved Tommy in and across the legs of twelve tired Sherwood Foresters. They cursed, but none queried him and he settled on the floor for the long journey home. He tried to think. Aggie, the whole thing a bloody shambles. What'll her people say? But no matter how hard he tried he couldn't grasp the fragments, and the harder he tried the worse his guts ached; like ducking for apples in a bucket; wits gun-scrambled. He'd seen it too often in others.

It was late afternoon when Tommy marched up Railway Street to his own house. The train had crawled all the way because of the danger of derailment by the rebels. In the hallway of the house he met two of Aggie's six brothers coming out, one a sailor on leave, the other a shipyardman. Without speaking they launched themselves at Tommy, knocking him back through the front door. The neighbours, who had been watching from behind curtains, swarmed into the street and managed to drag the berserk brothers off him, but not before the sailor had cracked the toe of his boot on Tommy's ear and the shipyardman had planted his clog, several times, in his gut.

His father and brother carried Tommy into the house while the neighbours saw off the still belligerent

41

Gambles. Tommy's guts were on fire and the blood started coming again. The doctor was sent for, and being ex-army himself and knowing something of the ways of wandering foreign bodies he prescribed coagulant and a sleeping draught. In the meantime Tommy had been told that Aggie, ashamed to face her mates at the mill, had left on the Liverpool boat the previous night. Mercifully, the draught combined with the residue of that given to him in Dublin knocked him out almost immediately.

On Saturday Tommy awoke as the person he was to be for the the rest of his days. The family were puzzled. He talked to them quite cogently, about France, about his wound – but never a mention of Aggie, or of the happenings in Dublin. Still, he seemed to be well enough physically considering, and very placid in himself, so they thought it a 'wee kink' that would pass.

Tommy stayed in bed, sleeping most of the time, until Tuesday morning. Then he got up, washed, shaved and polished his boots. His ten-day pass included travelling time, so his return warrant was made out for the five-thirty train to Dublin that day (though there would be no connecting boat from Kingstown until Wednesday morning). At two o'clock his father and brother accompanied him to the Crown bar opposite the station, and between then and train time all three made fair inroads on Tommy's wedding money – so much so that when train time came the Da, footless and maudlin, was unable to cross the road to see Tommy off, and the brother wasn't far behind him. Tommy had matched them drink for drink, but he marched to the train stone sober. Throughout the drunken garrulity of the afternoon no mention had been made of Aggie or the wedding. Afterwards, the brother said that Tommy had been so strangely calm he had been afraid to say or do anything that might draw blood.

Before the train drew to a halt in Amiens Street Tommy saw Sergeant McKenna on the platform. He appeared to be on the look-out for someone, scanning faces at the window of each carriage as it passed. He spotted Tommy. 'How's me oul son? Come on down an' have a cuppa char. You've plenty of time, there's no boat the night.'

Tommy followed the sergeant to an RTO hut at the end of the platform. They had the place to themselves. The sergeant put a kettle on a coke stove and said: 'I've been wondering how you got on. What about the weddin'?'

At this point he had his back to Tommy, poking the stove to get a flame. When no reply came he turned and faced him. At first Tommy looked puzzled, then his eyes closed tightly and he moved his head slowly from side to side. He held his big square hands clasped to front, the thumbs circling one another frantically, clockwise then counter clockwise. They reminded the sergeant of mice on a treadmill.

The tea when it came was twenty-five per cent Power's whiskey, causing Tommy's guts to burn pleasurably. 'Rest easy, lad,' said the sergeant. 'I've a billet for you the night and we'll get you down to Kingstown in good time for the morning boat.'

After the tea they went to a nearby pub and the sergeant ordered hot whiskies. The place was packed with troops, a rag-tag-and-bobtail of all the units in Ireland plus a few press-gang jobs like Tommy. Tommy sat at the bar while the sergeant circulated, quartering the company with an appraising eye. When he rejoined Tommy there were two men with him, one an elderly corporal of the South Staffords and the other a youthful private in the Irish Rifles who hailed from Cullybackey, a raw looking ganch.

More hot whiskies, which the Cullybackey man threw into the flat remains of his pint. The sergeant went off on another tour, and after they'd been talking for a while Tommy noticed that both men wore crossed rifles on the sleeves of their tunics, the insignia of a marksman. When he commented on this, the Stafford corporal said: 'That's why we're drinking whiskey instead of beer, mate.'

'Aye mon, we're the boys for the job!' cried the ganch, spitting on his hands and slapping them together.

'What's the job?' asked Tommy.

The ganch started to reply, but the corporal caught him by the arm and said authoritatively: 'If the sergeant wants him to know he'll tell him soon enough.' The ganch winked conspiratorially.

When the sergeant returned again he had another man in tow, a Cameronian. Tommy looked at his sleeve . . . crossed rifles. He waited until the three marksmen were engaged in a separate conversation and then broached the subject.

'What's the job?'

McKenna hesitated for a moment, pondering. Then he said: 'I was going to tell you. That's why I kept a look-out at the train. But then . . .'

Tommy sensed what he meant, though even now Amiens Street and the RTO hut seemed years behind him. Now was a clear circle in the fog that closed rapidly at his back and swirled impenetrably a yard in front of his face.

'I'm all right now,' he said.

'You're not, not near it,' growled the sergeant. 'But then who in the name of Christ is. I'll tell you, but under your hat, mind.'

He told Tommy, briefly, the nature of the job.

'How many?' asked Tommy.

'Thirty . . . three tens . . . one apiece,' sighed McKenna. 'And hard enough to scrape up when the huer-in-charge wants them all crossed rifle wallahs.'

'How many do you need still?'

'Three.'

'What about me? I'll do it for you.'

The sergeant doffed his cap and took something from the inside band. He laid it on the bar between them, a khaki patch embroidered with crossed rifles. 'There's not many of them in the Horse Guns, but the bastard'll never notice. Are you sure now?'

'I'm your man,' said Tommy, and pocketed the patch.

They visited two other pubs that night and Sergeant McKenna got rid of the last two patches from his cap band. He also had a needle and thread in the cap band, and in the packed lorry on the way to the billet he affixed the patches to the appropriate sleeves by the light of a carbide lamp. Tommy stood and looked out over the cab of the lorry as they ran in under a lighted archway to the billet. He saw a name carved in the stone above the archway but couldn't make it out in the dark.

Almost the next thing he remembered was a hand on his shoulder and McKenna's voice saying: 'Stand to. Up you gct, oul son.'

It was still dark. In the dim gaslight, only two small mantles at either end of the long barrack hut, hungover men struggled into cold-stiff uniforms. On the bed next to Tommy's the Cullybackey ganch spewed noisily into an enamel bucket. Sergeant McKenna and two corporals roved around like sheep-dogs, snapping at the heels of each man until he was ready and on his way to the square outside. At the door each was handed a rifle from a rack of thirty.

In the square they formed up and dressed off in a single line. After being inspected by the 'huer-in-charge', a young captain, they formed twos and then wheeled into six lines of fives. The paired lines were designated squads one, two and three; Tommy was in number two, rear rank. By this time one side of the sky was beginning to lighten.

'Number one squad, stand fast! Number two and three squads, dismiss!'

The corporals shepherded the dismissed men to a hut in the corner of the square in which there was a tea urn and a tray of wads. Tommy drew himself a mug of tea, but didn't feel hungry. He noticed that very few touched the wads. From the hut window he watched number one squad being inspected again by the captain; a rifle was found wanting and another fetched; the bamboo cane flicked a piece of maladjusted webbing and Sergeant McKenna adjusted it; the encroaching light erased the last weak stars from the patch of sky bounded by the high roofs of the prison blocks. The sergeant's commands to move out were subdued. The squad marched off and disappeared around the corner of the main block.

'Any minute now. They don't keep you waiting,' whispered a man beside Tommy. It was so quiet inside and out that Tommy could hear the first chirruping of sparrows. The two corporals stood on either side of the hut door, facing inwards, scanning the company and drawing nervously on cupped fags. It was full daylight now.

The crash of the volley cannoned wildly in the square, sending hordes of sparrows hurling skywards from the high eaves. Tommy saw the fag drop from a corporal's hand as he crossed himself. From down the hut came the thud and rattle of a body, rifle and tea-mug hitting the earthen floor: the ganch had fainted.

There was a lot of noise after that. The corporals pounced on the postrate ganch and hauled him onto a bench. Everyone crowded around and everyone seemed to be shouting. The Catholic corporal kept slapping the ganch's face and screaming, 'Wake up, you thick bastard!' Then Sergeant McKenna was amongst them, pushing, using his fists, bellowing. The men fell back and shut up – all except the corporal, who still screeched and lashed at the horizontal ganch. McKenna signalled to the other corporal and they took an arm apiece and ran him out of the hut. Some of the men managed to get the ganch sitting upright and poured tea down his throat. He awoke choking and immediately went into a bout of violent sobbing. When McKenna and the corporal returned, McKenna lifted the ganch's rifle off the floor, handed it to the corporal and shouted: 'Number two squad – fall in.'

'Just my bloody luck,' growled the corporal, opening the breech to check the barrel for dust.

The sergeant stood at the door of the hut and patted each man on the shoulder as he passed. Tommy looked at him as the hand fell, but it was as if the sergeant didn't see him, his lips forming the word 'seven'.

The captain was tall, thin and droop-moustached; a

young Kitchener. He was the first officer Tommy had seen wearing a sword. Everything was to his liking until he came to the corporal, who had taken the ganch's place beside Tommy in the rear rank. He tapped the corporal's right sleeve with his cane and said: 'This man is not a marksman, sergeant.'

'Sah. We had a bit –'

'Report to me at stand down, sergeant. Carry on.'

'Squad . . . left turn. By the left, quick march.'

They rounded the corner of the main block and entered a narrow tunnel, the crash of hobnails deafening. Emerging into daylight, they were halted almost at once, the front two men close to a high wall.

'Left turn. Order arms.'

Tommy could see that they were drawn up at one end of a narrow yard, cramped between high walls, but not much else because of the tall fellow in front.

'Front rank – one pace forward. Front rank – kneel.'

He saw, at twenty paces, a sand-bagged wall and a black-painted post. Just then the captain emerged from a door on the left of the yard, followed by two sergeant-majors with silver-knobbed canes clamped under their oxters, marching on either side of a small man in dark trousers and a white shirt.

'Rear rank – port arms.'

When the little procession reached the black post, one of the S-Ms pulled the man's arms around the back of it and the other knelt in front. Tommy saw that there were straps on the post, one to circle his body, the other his legs. As they were doing this the captain stood facing the man and appeared to be reading something to him from a piece of paper. Their job done, the S-Ms marched back through the door. The captain finished his reading and fell back to take up position beside the squad.

Tommy could see the man clearly now. He had long grey hair that fell down over his ears. His eyes were closed and his lips were moving. Tommy could hear the drone of his voice in the drum of the killing alley, but indistinctly, as though very far away . . .

The captain's sword slid from its scabbard. He gave the orders now.

'Squad – load.'

Working the rifle bolt, Tommy kept his eyes on the man. His lips were still moving and his eyes were open now.

'Squad – present.'

It was the heaviest weapon he had ever hefted. His left arm started to tremble and he had difficulty centring on the white shirt . . . steady the Buffs . . . what the hell was keeping him? Tommy raised his eye from the sighting line to the man's face. He was still talking.

'Fire!'

Most of the white shirt vanished; the head slumped, grey hair spilling forward. The corporal beside Tommy dropped his rifle and clasped his ears, face twisted in agony. Tommy didn't hear it fall because he was stone deaf: the noise in the enclosed space had been shattering. McKenna moved to the front of the squad and made gestures as he shouted the commands to retire. The return march through the tunnel was a shambles. As he left the yard, out of the corner of his eye Tommy saw the captain remove plugs from his ears before moving towards the post, unholstering his pistol as he went. And he wondered if the talking man had known that the captain's ears were plugged.

For the twenty minutes or so it took number three squad to do its work, Tommy sat in the back of a lorry with the nine members of number two squad. Number one squad was sealed in a lorry alongside, another awaited number three. Their kits had already been loaded; all were for the boat, whether they wanted to or not. Curiously, no one talked or even smoked until the muffled crash of the third volley; then matches flared and voices were raised in obscene complaint about being shipped out without as much as a by-your-leave, and without as much as a decent breakfast. Presently number three squad marched out and the convoy set off for Kingstown, Sergeant McKenna riding with number two squad.

At Kingstown the sergeant stood at the bottom of the gangplank and counted-off the men as they embarked. When his hand fell on Tommy's shoulder, Tommy paused and turned to face him.

'What was that fella talking about, sergeant?' he asked.

'Damn all of interest to the likes of you or me,' McKenna replied testily. 'An' for Christ's sake remember to take that patch off your sleeve before you report to depot. Damn few of them in the Horse Guns.'

But Tommy never did remember; and nobody noticed until one blacked-out evening twenty-eight years later, when a jeep-load of drunk Yanks mounted the pavement alongside the one-and-ninepennies at the Ritz.

Jason

If his Da had put an idle shoulder to the corner and spat the day away like any other decent man in the idle 30s, instead of taking a WEA course in the Greek Classics, he'd never have saddled his only son with a name like Jason. Indeed, if he had waited six months, he would certainly have been dipped 'Joe' after the great Bambrick, for by then the Da had come out of his literary coma, was working again, and leading the bass section of the Spion Kop choir at Windsor Park every Saturday. As time went on the old fellow, perhaps realising that someone called Jason would never be allowed to play centre-forward for the Blues, became increasingly embittered towards the lad and in his early dotage took to calling him 'Billy' – if he addressed him at all, which was seldom.

Nowadays, shout 'Jason' in any classroom and a dozen small heads will swivel. But in the late 30s, to be a schoolboy called Jason in a world of Willy Johns was character-building, especially if you were always a head taller than your bull-runty classmates, and slight with it. But he was a cut above the rut in other ways, our Jason – not academically, mind you, for to be called Jason and to be in the A stream would have been too much for any lad to support and stay sane. He coasted down the placid C stream and eventually emerged into the torrent at fourteen as unlettered as the rest, but with a reputation for being 'brilliant' in ways that earned him more respect from his fellow prospective bin-men than if he'd carried off the scholarship.

Jason had, as they say, hands for anything – and eyes. This flair first showed in the senior infants drawing class, where his precocious grasp of perspective was remarked by the teacher. If such a thing happened now, of course, the prodigy would be plucked out and nurtured to the door of the Art College; but in those days art, having no place on the examination papers, was for infants and idiots. In the backwater of the senior Cs we were allowed to draw, read comic-cuts, play cards, do anything as long as we did it quietly and without too much bloodshed, allowing the As and Bs to get on with their competitive subjects in peace.

In this atmosphere Jason's talents flowered. He drew, studied aeroplane books (it was wartime now), became an expert modelmaker, bicycle-mechanic, airgun-fixer and morse-tapper. He didn't participate in any sport (because of weak eyesight) but he read about all of them, fast becoming our acknowledged arbiter in disputes over, say, who played left-half for whom when they won the cup in 1905, or the span of Jess Willard's right paw. (He also became our oracle on sex, dispeller of many fond myths on the subject and retailer of a string of horrifying statistics about VD cribbed from *The Red Light*).

But principally the young Jason was a maker and decorator of things; of enormous, many-flanged box-kites in the Japanese tradition; of canoes on the River Lagan; of those vehicles known in America as 'soap-boxes', elsewhere as 'guiders', and in the Holy Land district of Belfast, inscrutably, as 'cherryactors' (possibly from the misreading of 'charioteer' by some long-dead semi-literate). We all made cherryactors, and we all began with the same template in our heads; but only Jason could give an old knotty plank its second childhood or transform a pair of butter-boxes into a plush wagon, gaudily 'hippy' at a time when the word still meant a lady with a big arse. Hands for anything.

At age twelve he stood out from his C stream contemporaries like a clean finger. He was an only child, as I've mentioned, and his Ma was a small Lurgan woman with energy enough for an orphanage matron. Grubby children who called at the house for Jason were liable to be dragged into her scullery and scrubbed with red carbolic while they waited. Jason himself sparkled continually from head to toe and had the great gift of being able to emerge from Belvoir Park after a morning's birdnesting as spotless as a juvenile dummy in Spackman's window. This antiseptic aura was particularly remarkable when springtime brought the 'nit' man – a doctor with a fine comb – to the school; often he was the only one in C stream not dipped and shorn by order the following day, sitting among the donkey fringes like the woolly Judas ram kept to lure the sheep to the scissors (a comparative hirsuteness which his Ma encouraged all the year round for mildly snobbish reasons, and which, along with heavy-rimmed spectacles, gave him that arty appearance he has affected into middle-age).

I've always held that it was this, his appearance, that got Jason the nice job in the sample room of the mill warehouse when we left school. It certainly wasn't anything else, for besides having no qualifications he carried the headmaster's curse for having defaced the Leaving Certificate examination paper with a very creative doodle. I and another degenerate from the C stream attended the same interview; he was sent to help stoke the boilers and I went to the packing-room.

I didn't see much of Jason in the following years, even though we worked for the same linen lord. A matter of temperament, I suppose: he never was the booze, jiggin' and hussies type. But I heard of him from time to time and it seemed that his talents were being recognised above, for he was attending day-release courses in the Tech. with a view to taking up damask designing. I met him occasionally in the street, and we had a quick word about grand old days in school. He had developed into a very natty dresser in a muffler, gloves and overshoes fashion way beyond his years. To see him dandering down Linenhall Street, with the long hair, the horn rims, and with that faraway look as though he were always working out a fifteen-cross-double in his head, you'd have sworn it was some BBC producer from around the corner taking his ulcer for a walk.

I, in the meantime, had been made foreman of the packing-room, and our other schoolmate was in charge of the boilers. So all us old C streamers were doing very nicely (considering that the A stream scholarship winner of our year, an accountant by trade, was in his second of five years in Crumlin Road gaol). Then the boom came down.

The old Lord died. His son and heir – and ex-model daughter-in-law – decided to sell up and build hotels in Spain. The purchaser was an insurance company that wanted the site for redevelopment, so we were all on the street within the week.

Unfortunately this coincided with the general slump from which linen has never fully recovered. Our mate in the boiler house got himself fixed up quickly enough – boilers being much the same everywhere. But I had a few months on the dole before deciding to make a clean break from the trade. I became an insurance agent (dirty dexter, bicycle-clips and all). Nearly three years were to pass before I heard anything of Jason.

In that time I grew to realise that some talent of my own had been wasting in that warehouse. I got on very well with people and, consequently, very well in the job. I liked the fresh air, the flexible hours, and the fact that the wife could never be sure where I was, or who I was at, added a stimulating tension to our relationship that had never been there before. Of course the job had its drawbacks, one of them being the amount of corpses I had to view in the course of my duties. In fact it was while attending the funeral of a client that I next ran into Jason. Outside the house of mourning I turned, and there he was, waiting with his four minions to receive the coffin from the relatives, in top-hat, tails, buttonhole and traditional umbrella – an undertaker's Major-Domo!

I must say he did look the part: benign, other-worldly,

with just a touch of the sinister. I spoke to him at the graveside and he seemed truly delighted to see me. When he'd been sacked from the warehouse, he told me, he'd taken up driving and tinkering with motor cars. He'd been a driving instructor for a time, until his ulcer started; then he'd driven a hearse; then promotion . . .

'Do you fancy it?' I asked.

'Not much,' he replied, shivering; 'too many grave-yards are on hills. You can get your death hanging about in this gear. But I'm studying –' I never found out what he was studying, for at that moment the principal bereaved came over with the driver's perks and I didn't get the chance to speak to Jason again.

After that I kept an eye out for him when attending funerals catered for by his firm, but in vain. Not long after our meeting I asked one of his fellow Major-Domos about him. 'Oh, Jason's inside now – lucky bastard!' was the teeth-chattering reply.

So that's what Jason meant, I thought: studying for management; the morning-suit with the water-proofed shoulderpad . . . 'Come this way, Modom. It's a grief we all come to bear in time.' Bully Jason lad, thinks I. Face up C stream! You can't keep a good lad down!

But I was mistaken.

Two years later the last of my grannies, the paternal one, dropped off at the age of 82. The other, a saintly silver-haired lady in the Spring Byington tradition, had gone on fifteen years before, a judgement of the Almighty's for which my Mother has never quite for-given Him. It is beyond her comprehension that one so immaculate in her person and habits should have been taken three days short of drawing her first pension and the other left to squander hers on snuff, red biddy (hot) and untipped Woodbines.

The last time I'd seen the old girl alive her face, or what I could see of it behind a veil of smoked hair, had resem-bled the bed of the Connswater in a dry spell. But when I accompanied my aunt into the parlour and looked down into the coffin I couldn't restrain an exclamation. 'Jasus!'

Cheeks like peaches; hair of spun gold; ruby lips; a sleeping cliche in well-preserved middleage awaited her iron-stomached Prince! (I noticed that they'd even polyfilled the attenuated slits in her ear-lobes from which a pair of brass curtain-rings had dangled for 60 years.)

'Jason,' corrected the aunt. 'Isn't he marvellous!'

An undertaker's plasterer!

Granny was buried ten years ago; and but for a chance remark overheard recently that would have been the end of the Jason story so far as I'm concerned.

I left the insurance game some years ago and so had lost sight of Jason – and his handiwork, thank God. In the course of my new job (whisky salesman – a progression not uncommon in the rat-race) I was standing in the public bar of a client when a voice from a snug attracted my attention.

'I'm really worried about Harry.'

I thought for a moment that someone had switched on the television; it was that kind of voice, so I wasn't surprised when I turned and found that it belonged to an actress. I haven't been inside a theatre in twenty years, but I'd seen this one on the box often enough. (The pub was within staggering distance of the local television centre and much used by all classes of arty itinerants.) The man she had spoken to, and who sat beside her on the narrow plank seat of the snug, was a mature, short-back-and-sides person – one of those solicitors or doctors, I surmised, who prefer to keep their sponsorship on a personal basis.

'Really worried,' she boomed again, and my attention was drawn to the fact that they both seemed to be staring into space, or at something on that side of the half-enclosed snug hidden from me. Curious, I sidled along the bar and followed their gaze. 'If that's Harry, love,' I wanted to assure her, 'you've very good grounds for being worried.'

At first I thought it might be a woman; perhaps one of

55

those chain-smoking oddities who lurk on the fringes of Grub Street. It was wearing a sort of Kaftan thing, powder-blue, and wisps of shoulder-length black hair straggled across its face, having an effect like cracks in a delft doll. Then it stirred, belched a cloud of fag smoke and groaned something unprintable in an unmistakable basso. A Henry, I decided, not only very far gone in drink, but also one of those poor men with little resistance; a messy, sweaty, farty drunk on whose physique every bottle leaves an indelible mark. He gulped a mouthful of smoke into his windpipe and went into a spectacular coughing fit, at each cough his face changing colour, from grey to green, to red, to puce, to purple, as though each rictus rang the changes on a battery of strobe lights inside his skull. He subsided to greenish-grey again and the actress, wiping particles of flung spittle from her sun-glasses, said again: 'I'm very worried.'

Just then the door of the bar burst open to admit a wild-looking, shirt-sleeved young man with a clipboard and pink glasses, closely followed by two large fellows in the uniform of the television centre's security force. The young man ran over to the snug, looked down at Harry and screamed, 'Oh, my Christ!' The two large men, without a word, pushed past him into the snug, from which they extracted the boneless lump of Harry with an effortless ease that spoke of long usage. The young man danced behind as they went out through the door with Harry's toes trailing between. 'Twenty minutes to go! Oh my God!' he shrilled. 'Take him straight in. I'll get Jason.'

The name didn't register just then, for as I've said there's thousands about nowadays; and anyway, at that moment the landlord came along, just in time to see the exit of posse and captive.

'Harry's cutting it a bit fine the night,' he grinned, glancing up at the clock.

'Who is he?' I asked.

Aghast, he cried: 'Where've you been! Harry Boal, the

newsreader.' (I didn't try to explain that I hadn't heard a news bulletin since September 1969.)

'Newsreader!' I exclaimed. 'I always knew they could get away with murder on radio, but that –'

'Radio! yer arse!' he said scornfully. 'Bar bomb or powercut Harry Boal'll be on that box up there, in full colour, fifteen minutes time.'

'You're joking!' I challenged.

'All right, wait and see,' said the landlord, pouring me a large Powers (one of this job's drawbacks). 'Get that inside you while I take a look at the stock.'

On his way out he switched on the telly and we waited through the last ten minutes of Children's Hour. Actress and man-friend had shifted their position to get a better view. 'Oh God!' I heard her moan, 'I hope they managed Jason in time.'

Jason, I decided, must be the standby newsreader. It was beyond belief that the puking shambles I'd seen dragged through the door would be able to sit upright within the next 24 hours, let alone read the news. Anyway, landlords are inclined to affect an exaggerated pride in the resilience of their hardcase clientele – a way of mitigating their own profitable collusion, perhaps.

The opening clangour of the news brought the landlord scurrying from his stocklist to watch. The actress strained forward, savaging her fingernails, until the captions cleared away to reveal the smiling features and upper person of a neatly trimmed young man who bobbed his head engagingly and said: 'Hello, good evening. Our first item is, of course, the power crisis. Our industrial correspondent –'

'Oh thank God!' howled the actress, slumping dramatically. 'Isn't Jason bloody marvellous!' Manfriend said he was, patted her knee, and poured her a half-pint of red filth from a black bottle.

The landlord tapped my shoulder. 'Well, what did I tell you?' he said, thumbing at the screen.

It crossed my mind that he was going the way taken by

so many of my vintner clients. I thought for a moment of humouring him for the sake of business, but decided against it.

'You said that Harry Boal would read the news come hell or high water,' I pointed out ... And suddenly I knew there was a catch; he was grinning craftily. 'And that's Harry Boal!' he cried triumphantly, jabbing at the screen. I looked again at the young man mouthing away and confirmed that my client was indeed draining the heels. 'You don't believe me?' he said; 'right ... Miriam.'

The actress turned and smiled dazzlingly. 'Yes darling!'

'Is that or is that not Harry Boal reading the news?'

Her laugh tinkled. 'Now Bob darling. Dearly as I love you I don't wish to become embroiled in one of your awful –'

'It's not me,' the landlord protested, 'It's this fella here. He won't believe that that's Harry Boal.'

She gave me her standard 'A Handbag!' look and said coldly; 'Of course it's Harry Boal. Who on earth do you think it is?'

With the growing feeling of being involved in some sort of three-handed confidence trick I replied truthfully: 'Somebody called Jason. I overheard –'

Actress, manfriend and landlord whinnied with mirth. 'Jason!' gasped the actress. 'You can't know Jason or you'd realise how gloriously funny ... a true genius in his way but hardly a performer!'

'Now, doubting Thomas,' said the landlord, swinging me round to face the screen again, 'Take you a good hard look at that fella up there.'

I did. The young newsreader just then turned his head slightly and I caught a glimpse of what could have been a shadow behind his left ear – or a bun of clubbed hair? But no, it was ridiculous to even speculate. Then suddenly, the camera zoomed in. I'm told it isn't a normal manoeuvre at news time. The close-up of the newsreader's face was brief, so I presume it was an aberration – or the action of a vindictive cameraman – but it was enough to convince me that it was, without doubt, Harry Boal. The eyes did it; like black stones – expressionless; the eyes of a blind man, or a ventriloquist's dummy; as though peering through holes in a cardboard cut-out.

'Merciful God!' I exclaimed, much to the landlord's delight. 'How do they do that in twenty minutes! It's impossible.'

'Nothing's impossible for Jason,' he said sternly, 'the hands of a saint. I once heard an old actor say that he must have been indentured to God for seven years. Sure the Equity Senior Citizens gave him their 'Lazarus' award three years running . . . Hands for anything.'

Face up C stream!

You can't keep a good lad down!

The Coalman

He smiled his plump, self-satisfied smile to the last.
Unlike most of his fellows he had always faced the street
rather than the enemy, giving the impression that he
was employing his out-thrust sword more as a pointer
than as a weapon, perhaps indicating to a gathering of
17th century war correspondents on the North bank of
the Boyne the rout of Sarsfield taking place on the South
bank. Or at least it had seemed so until some vandal had
drawn a cartoon bubble from the Royal lips and decided
that his message to the world at that moment of victory
had been 'Elvis Lives!'

Sadly, in the autumn of last year one of the Housing
Executive's big balls swung and struck approximately
at the point where the right hoof of his white steed had
been threatening the head of a floundering Jamesite for
fifty years, and 'The Coalman' collapsed in an explosion
of brick dust, a martyr to redevelopment.

That he had a name at all was extraordinary, though
not unprecedented. In another part of the city a gable-
end artist called Ferguson, a perfectionist, had been
somewhat over-realistic with regard to the gender and
anatomy of the horse, a touch which led to the speculation that all James' cavalry, just as realistically depicted
on the far bank, had been mounted on mares – and to
the naming of his creation 'Ferguson's Bull'. Another, in
a small mill town in the Lagan valley, was known as
'Powderpuff Billy' because of a curiously angled sword-
arm and a limpid gaze that seemed to beckon to fates
other than glorious death in battle. Even the horse had a

hypersensitive look about him. Their creator, a Sunday School superintendent, fled the parish the day after the unveiling ceremony.

'The Coalman' was named so because the artist had also been the local dispenser of fuel, a well-doing bellman called Bulmer who had had some early training as a signwriter. But this alone would not have caused his creation to be named thus, any more than the nearby dozens painted by navvies, red-leaders and caulkers. And anyway, in their case the unspeakable hubris which led to Bulmer the coalman being commemorated in this way would never have been allowed to happen, most gable-end projects being carried out over a period of days in full view of the populace, which was never slow to provide a running barrage of advice and criticism: 'Wud ya look at them legs! If yon horse was a table yi'd hafta ate yer dinner aff the floor!' ... 'God help us ... aren't you learnin' ivery day – I niver knew King Billy was tully-eyed' ... 'Here, take a look at the galloping consumptive. There'd better be an iron lung at the far side of that water or that poor cratur'll niver see the day out!' – and so on.

'Boss' Bulmer was not the sort to appreciate criticism or to accept raillery at his own expense. With three coal-carts on the road, owner of half-a-street of houses, employer of six men – including two sons, who also called him 'Boss' –, select vestryman, Mason, Pastmaster in the Order, Chairman of the Buffs club, Bulmer was a citizen of substance and some style.

Physically, he was 'a fine figure of a man' in the Edwardian sense, meaning overweight and ponderous, with a face the colour of raw beef. On full dress occasions, when he paraded the family to Kirk on Sunday morning, at Lodge meetings or on the Big Walk, he wore a curly-brimmed bowler-hat in the old style, tipped forward over the eyes, and a suit of good navy-blue serge, the coat almost three-quarter-length and split at the back in the horsey fashion, the trousers tapering to a pair of well-buffed brown boots. And across the full bay-window of his waistcoat, strung in two glittering loops from pocket to pocket, was Bulmer's pride, his 'Gold Guard', the chain of his giant gold Hunter watch adorned with gold sovereigns and the precious insignia of three secret societies. It clinked richly at his every step, and no matter how inclement the weather no closed coat was ever allowed to obscure its glory, the symbol of his worth and standing.

So, when it came to gable decoration, not for a man like Bulmer the ignominy of exposure on a rickety ladder and the coarse jeering of the hoi polloi. The preparations for the Sistine Chapel job could not have been more elaborate. Before a chalk-mark was made or a brush laid, Bulmer's two sons and four hirelings erected a scaffold the width of the pavement and the height of the gable. They then draped it from top to bottom in tarpaulins, front and both sides, leaving the top open to let in light.

Bulmer too had been making his preparations. Unlike other hit-and-miss gable daubers, he, the skilled man, had already measured-up and conceived an overall plan of which he had made small-scale drawings. So when he arrived on the scene early one morning and was asked when he expected to be finished, he could confidently reply that one full day working and a day's drying would do it. The anxious inquirer was not only the owner of the gable but also the current Worshipful Master of the local Lodge, which meant that this year the traditional banner-lifting ceremony before the Big March would take place from his house. The reason he asked was because it had been decided that the banner-lifting and the unveiling of Bulmer's epic should be a joint ceremony, to be performed by Lady Blackstaff, wife of the County Grand Master. As it was now the sixth of July, with less than a week to go to the Big Day, he thought Bulmer was cutting it a bit fine. But he needn't have worried – at least not about that.

Bulmer mounted the platform armed with his paints and brushes, a cork-screw and a case of bottled stout;

the sons stood by for fetching and carrying; the hirelings patrolled the foot of the scaffold to ward off inquisitive childer. Except for two breaks while the platform of planks was lowered, Bulmer worked solidly from eight in the morning till one the next morning. He was already working on the ground when the light went at ten o'clock or thereabouts and the sons set up a couple of carbide lamps and carried in a second case of stout. And at one o'clock all was finished, including the stout.

The next day, luckily a fine one, was for drying-out and touching-up; and the next, a Saturday, was the day of the unveiling ceremony, scheduled for the afternoon. Early on Saturday morning the sons and hirelings affixed a wooden baton high up on the gable, to which they lightly nailed a long tarpaulin to cover the entire scene. The scaffolding was then taken down, a barrier erected on the pavement to keep off childer and incontinent dogs, and all was ready.

At three o'clock the district assembled in front of the gable to watch the Lodge parade in, headed by a flute band; to applaud Lady Blackstaff as she descended from her open Rolls; and, not least, to see the artist himself, in full fig, being presented. Then came the big moment when Lady Blackstaff, flanked by Bulmer and the Worshipful Master, said that it gave her great pleasah, the sons and hirelings swung on the tarpaulin, ripping it from its moorings on the baton above, and Bulmer's 'Battle of the Boyne' was revealed to the multitude.

At this point the flute band was supposed to render a verse of the National Anthem – but it died halfway through the first drumroll, as did the initial burst of applause from the crowd. The stunned silence that followed was broken by the inevitable wag, ever ready with the apt phrase . . . 'Hey, Billy, throw us in a bag of slack!' The great howl of laughter unleashed by this observation was nothing compared with the pandemonium caused by the next. 'Look at the waistcoat!' For not only was King William the Third's full-frontal image that of a younger, more refined Boss Bulmer, but across the Royal midriff was a loop of gold that the artist later swore was a bit of ornamental frogging, but which looked suspiciously like a gold watch chain.

Bulmer himself stood frozen to the spot throughout the ensuing hubbub, transfixed in the eye of his own image. He saw clearly what had happened. Immersed in detail, restricted by the scaffold that his pride had erected around him, he had lost sight of the whole. The enormity of his gaff bore in on him as gales of derision mounted on all sides.

'God in Heaven,' groaned Bulmer.

'Oh, is that your next commission, Mr Bulmah?' drawled Lady Blackstaff.

The Gulp

The young American got off the bus from Belfast at 10.30 am on June 17th 1962. Mrs Teresa Cullen, manageress of the Northern Lights ice-cream parlour, remembers him vividly. She describes him as having blonde hair, crew-cut, and wearing rimless glasses and one of those 'mad' sports jackets that Americans go in for. His only luggage was a khaki-coloured hold-all, a portable typewriter and a camera bag.

The reason why Mrs Cullen could give such a detailed description to subsequent inquirers was that on descending from the bus he made straight for the Northern Lights – at a jog-trot. Mrs Cullen was in the pavement kiosk at the time, dispensing cones and sliders to a charabanc of school children from Belfast. The young American didn't enter the Northern Lights, she says; he stopped dead, panting slightly, just outside the doorway, dropped the hold-all and typewriter to the ground and, gazing up at the huge sign above the door, shouted: 'Eureka! Oh my Gad! Eureka!'

When this scene occurred he was so close to Mrs Cullen that she could later describe his spectacles as being like the bottoms of two jam-jars.

That was the first sighting; and in 1962 the seaside hamlet of Porglass was not so accustomed to exotic visitors for it to be the last. Yet in Victorian times even an excitable young colonial would have gone unnoticed in the throng of well-to-do eccentrics drawn annually to the plushness of the nearby Grand Royal Hotel – now the Agricultural College – and the picturesque fishing village nestling in the sheltered bay, flanked by miles of flawless strand. At that time people came down to the sea to look at it, to smell it, sometimes to paddle in it, but seldom to immerse themselves in it. When it became fashionable to do so, Porglass stopped growing. It is today almost exactly as it was on that fateful day in 1909, when Mr Bartholomew Forsythe, an overweight dentist, disappeared into the flawless strand, the first of many. During a mindless upsurge of the sea-and-sand cult in the thirties, the Porglass 'Gulp', as the locals call the most carnivorous stretch, achieved a fatality record equal to that of the Bondi Beach sharks in Australia. And nothing can be done about it – a complex matter of subterranean soil erosion and variable currents far beyond human remedy: one minute a stretch of near-white, hard-packed strand, the next a voracious quicksand, undermined by the incoming tide. Local people say that they can tell when and where it is about to happen by such esoteric signs as the schooling of seagulls and the smell of seaweed. But when, in 1946, an incipient post-war boom was nipped in the bud by the widely syndicated photograph of a bread-cart being swallowed in full view of the main promenade, it was pointed out that the bread-server had taken the same short-cut across the strand for twenty-five years. Since then Porglass has been a mere half-hour stopover for coach trips, time enough to suck an ice-cream while counting the 'Danger!' posts, and a haven for dedicated drouths, its one hotel, The Nome House, famed far and wide for its ever-open back door.

It was there, in The Nome House, that the next significant sighting of the young American took place. The bar manager, Mr Mick Cooley, says that he came in just after lunch on June 17th, still carrying the hold-all and typewriter. The main bar of The Nome House is dominated by a life-size portrait in oils of the Klondike poet Robert Service, topped with the head of a gigantic moose and flanked by a pair of genuine Yukon snowshoes. It was in front of this montage that the American staged a repeat of his emotional display at the Northern Lights that morning, this time declaiming a full verse of *Dangerous Dan McGrew* at the top of his voice. Luckily there was no one else in the bar at the time, says Mr Cooley, or there might have been trouble, the regular daytime clientele being of a very morose nature, punters and the like. He admits that he himself was a bit alarmed, so much so that he approached the customer with a bung mallet held ready under the bar top. But the young American soon put him at his ease, first by standing him a large vodka, then by asking about the connection between Robert Service and The Nome House.

It was a tale Mr Cooley could recite in his sleep, and often did: the saga of young Peter Connolly, a boot boy in the old Grand Royal Hotel, who ran away to America in the 1880s to make his fortune; of how he had trekked to the Klondike in the first wave of gold fever, climbing the Chilkoot Pass in the dead of winter – 'In them very snowshoes,' declared Mr Cooley –, and of how, after much backbreaking toil and disappointment, he had struck it rich beyond the dreams of avarice. Years of the good life followed for Connolly, old Sourdough buddy of Robert Service, owner of yachts and racehorses, escort of the lovely 'Diamond Lily' Langtry, friend and confidant of Presidents. Then, in the midst of it all, the great yearning for his home place, Porglass.

At this point, Mr Cooley says, he had to break off his narrative due to the extraordinary behaviour of his listener. He was howling with laughter, thumping the bar top with agony of it. And when Mr Cooley, naturally huffed, asked him what the hell he thought was so funny, the American wiped his thick glasses and apologized fulsomely for his bad manners. He was, he explained, doing a Ph.D. in modern history at Wisconsin University, and for the past two years he had been gathering material for a definitive book on the Klondike gold rush. That's what had brought him to Porglass, the home town of 'Cathouse' Connolly.

'Who did you say?' asked Mr Cooley, wondering if he'd heard aright.

'The great 'Cathouse' Connolly, that's who,' said the Yank gleefully. 'What slayed me just then was your wunnerful visualisation of Connolly packin' up the Chilkoot in them snowshoes. 'Cathouse' Connolly! – he was packed up in a sedan chair by relays of Chinese coolies! And as for striking gold! Hell, that guy didn't need it. He already owned a string of saloons and cathouses in every state in the Union – the Klondike operation was only a branch of the business. In the gold camps the real money was in booze and broads. Of course, it's something people don't talk about afterwards, at least the people who write about it don't. But, boy, am I gonna put that right! I hit this place by accident, he sure did a good job covering his tracks. So I thought I'd have a helluva lot of digging to do when I got here. Then I steps off the bus and – wham! – he hits up the kisser from all sides. The Northern Lights, Proprietor P. Connolly, The Nome House, P. Connolly, licensed to sell ... The Whitehorse Amusement Arcade ... Man, for me this is pay-dirt!'

Mick Cooley could have told him that Connolly had also purchased most of the village and 200 acres of farmland fringing the strand just north of it. But Mick was momentarily speechless – with anger, not shock. The credibility or otherwise of what the American had said never crossed his mind. It was as if he had alleged that Pope John had once run numbers for Capone; a blasphemy.

Mick found his tongue and the handle of the bung mallet at the same time. 'Take yerself outa here this minute,' he said, advancing round the end of the bar, the darkly-stained mallet held at the ready, 'or ah'll open ye.'

The American took no chances. Grabbing holdall and typewriter, he walked backwards to the door, protesting as he went: 'Now look, buddy, no offence meant, just doing my job. And it can't hurt the old guy now. A few more details, a shot or two of the grave, and I'll be gone.'

He was half-way through the door at this point. Mick,

closing rapidly, shouted: 'What grave? Sure he's alive an' kickin', y'eejit ye!'

The expression on the American's face as the door closed on it told Mick that he had made a terrible mistake. Looking out over the half-glazing he saw him running down the main street towards the post office. They'll tell him, thought Mick, and then he'll be out to the farm like a liltie, badgering. Not that he'd get anywhere near the old fellow – the Three Graces would see to that. But the thought of him slabbering all that stuff about 'Cathouse' Connolly sent Mick running to his car, shouting for the bar-boy to take charge.

He went out the coast road like a rocket and was pulling into the yard of the Connolly farmhouse five minutes later. Connolly's daughters, the Three Graces as they were known locally, came out to meet him. As always, they were dressed exactly alike, in the long billowy smocks sometimes called 'Mother Hubbards', so that at a distance they looked like three little girls. The old man had married three times, fathering one daughter on each wife, but never a son. Theresa, or 'Teesy' for short, the eldest at 62, had been born in America. She was the dominant one, a stern, swarthy person with the shoulders and upper arms of a navvy. Mary, 55, was very stout and had the chalky pallor of a chronic asthmatic. Kate, the baby at 47, was still as pretty as a doll, her fair hair tonged and crimped in the fashion of the Hollywood '40s. She now smiled at Mick in the shy, secretive way that had turned many a male head in days gone by, earning her a reputation expressed in the less reverend name the townland had for The Three Graces: Teesy, Wheezy and Easy.

Mick delivered his warning about the impending visit of the loony Yank. He hadn't meant to mention the 'Cathouse' allegations, but Teesy's dark gaze probed his bluster.

'Did he call Da-Da names?' she asked.

Mick stammered that well, yes, now that he came to think it, he had said some daft things about cats. At this,

Wheezy went into one of her frequent coughing kinks. Teesy, slapping her on the back vigorously, said: 'The next bus out is in half-an-hour. Time to sniff the seaweed. It'll do you good, dear.' She led Wheezy, still coughing, across the yard and into the short boreen that ran from the main road to the strand.

Mick turned to go, but Easy, fingering her curls, moved closer to him and asked: 'Would you like to take a wee peep at Da-Da, Mr Cooley?'

Nowadays it was a privilege seldom vouchsafed anyone outside the family. Mick followed Easy round to the back of the luxury bungalow which stood on the site of the old farmhouse. And there, through a massive, double-glazed picture window overlooking the Gulp, he viewed the 95-year-old, blind and almost stone-deaf remnant of the old Sourdough, cushioned in a deep club chair and muffled to the mouth in the skin of his first grizzly bear. The coat, and a peaked sealskin cap, left nothing actually in view bar nostrils for breathing and mouth for periodic injections of 'Ole Grandad' Bourbon whiskey, a half-bottle of which stood on a nearby table. The room was ringed with dwarf palm trees; caged singing birds hung from the ceiling.

'Isn't he lovely, Mr Cooley?' breathed Easy, very close to Mick's ear. And Mick, knowing her of old, took to his heels.

The driver of the bus on which the young American took his last journey recalls seeing the Three Graces coming down the boreen as he alighted, still carrying hold-all and typewriter. The Three Graces say that he had tea with Da-Da and then set off to walk back to Porglass across the strand. That was the final sighting. A month later the Gulp regurgitated a hold-all and a pair of spectacles like jam-jar ends. The Three Graces laid them to rest in a shallow grave dug high up in the dunes amid thick marram grass. Already interred therein were the bits of two tape-recorders, a light meter, the bloated remains of a passport and a notebook, and a baseball cap embroidered with the words 'Utah Hi!'

Final Solution ('68)

The experienced eye of the Sergeant Commissionaire picked out each man from the stream of sleepy-eyed clerks pouring through the revolving door into the main hallway, and as each paused and looked around he barked across the echoing distance: 'Upstairs; second floor; first on left', with a peremptory lift to the last syllable he had not dared use to anyone in years. It pleased him that each wheeled and obeyed without question.

The letter each man had received the previous morning had stated tersely: 'Initial briefing – 10.00 hours prompt', the familiar phrasing causing a comforting glow in many a tattooed breast.

In the windowless room there were two dozen chairs in six ranks of four facing a dais. Each man entered by a door to the left of the dais, thus having to run a gauntlet of massed scrutiny by the earlier birds. Some brassed out this ordeal with a swagger; others, spotting a familiar face from Cyprus, Malaya or Aden, smiled or waved a greeting only to be cut dead in accordance with the service tradition which lays down that wheresoever two are gathered together a third is not only outnumbered but is a rookie and beneath contempt; one unfortunate measured his length on the polished parquet.

No one lit up – though there was no forbidding notice; no one spoke – though all took turns at coughing to break the awesome silence. By ten o'clock most were familiar with the number and pattern of boil craters in the neck of the fellow in front.

At ten o'clock precisely two men entered by a door on

the right of the dais. One was a tall, burly person of unmistakable stamp despite his clerical grey ensemble; the other a shortish, iron grey, droop-moustachioed man who walked to the dais with the affected, horse-spavined strut of a tank commander. The latter sat down behind the green baize table on the dais and began to arrange the wads of paper which his colleague unloaded from a brief-case. When all was to his satis-faction he gave a signal and the large man faced and quartered the assembly with a glare that stilled any incipient murmur.

'My name is McTavish,' he threatened in a thick Glaswegian accent, razor seams glaring raw on the blue skin of his cheeks; 'ex Sarnt'Major, 1st Cameronians. This gentleman is Major Wilkington-Pike, late C.O. of the 191st lancers. I will be your direct superior, responsible to the Major for general discipline and administration. The Major will now give a short talk on the motivation of our operations.'

In the time it took the Major to rise and arrange his varicose cells there was a general stir of relaxed tension as legs were crossed, coats unbuttoned, noses blown and fags got ready in anticipation of what they knew would be his first sentence. This was the cosy order of things as they'd always known it: an Englishman in the saddle, a Scotsman hanging on his stirrup and they eat-ing dust and dung behind.

'You may smoke,' he said, and a dozen match heads exploded on the period. 'My first duty,' he went on in a high-pitched lisp which would have made his life impos-sible in the lower ranks, 'is to welcome you on behalf of the Ulster Government, of which you are now servants. At the outset I would remind you that you have signed the Official Secrets Act document, and that anything you hear in this room is – ah – secret.'

He paused to take a swig of gin disguised as water and let his words sink in. McTavish's scowl promised an obscene end for anyone caught tattling. 'The Govern-ment has been persuaded that the only approach to the problem in hand is a military one, so everyone here has been chosen because of his Army background. All of you were long-service front-line infantrymen and, I may say, the backbone of any army.' (He did not say that all had been long-service Privates and were what had been left after the Prison Service and the Parking Meter Department had taken their pick of the NCOs). 'Furthermore, you are men who have had actual physical contact with various species of trouble-making wog over this past decade. I well remember,' digressed the Major, raising his eyes from the text and then lowering them again to find out just what he did remember well, 'I well remember standing in my scout car at a road-block in Aden, watching the gallant lads of the Argylls rummaging for arms in the filthy nighties of those murderous swine, and thinking what self-discipline and devotion to duty . . .' As he rambled on in this vein for a moment, the thoughts of some old Aden hands in his audience turned to balmy nights spent rummaging expensively up the none too clean nighties of female swine. And in the minds of at least one there occurred the speculation whether the Major might himself have preferred to rummage up the kilt of an Argyll.

'And now to Operation MALTHUS,' said the Major portentously. 'Everyone here is of the 'Reformed Faith', as they say, and your backgrounds as regards political loyalty have been gone into thoroughly. I need not hesitate, therefore, to call a spade a spade and tell you that this operation is to do with population control; specifically, the control of the R.C. birthrate in certain well-defined areas.'

'I need not tell you men of the problems this birthrate has caused your Government over the years.' Their collective expression assured him he need not. In each the little pod of gall which had been his only birthright, now began to swell and disseminate its bitter vapours throughout the bloodstream. The Major, pleased with the effect, wondered briefly if there might be something for him in this Irish political lark.

'Hitherto,' he continued, 'the effects of this annual explosion in marginal areas has been offset by judicious realignment of constituency boundaries – gerrymandering, as the Shinners choose to call it. This has become increasingly difficult since the Mainland went Bolshie and some of the leading Bolshies took to poking their long noses into our affairs, aided and abetted by the Shinners. Furthermore, the problem recently has been rendered more acute by the almost gluttonous appetite for the Pill amongst people of the loyal persuasion.

'The crux of the problem is, of course, that the Shinner's mumbo-jumbo forbids any form of birth control – especially of the slot-machine variety.' Sniggers all round. 'But since the Pill, the R.C.s of other countries – and, I may say, they're a different proposition from this lot – have shown signs of coming round to the civilised way of thinking. The word is that there will be changes in the mumbo-jumbo in the near future. But again, the 'near future' as regards religious yapping matches, the Government realised, could very well mean fifty years elsewhere, and perhaps another fifty before it filtered through to these bog Bishops! In view of this they took the unprecedented step of sounding-out clerical opinion on the entire matter.'

Pause for gin. From previous experience during lectures on regimental history, the Major had expected to lose his audience at about this stage and he was not disappointed. It didn't worry him: all part of the White Man's Burden; any manifestation of intellect amongst the troops always meant trouble anyway. A man in the back row, a product of one of the more primitive tin tabernacles, expertly smothered a yawn and hoped that they at least would situate the gas chambers on a bus route. McTavish marked the table savagely with a ruler, causing the film to fall temporarily from four dozen eye-balls. The Major went on:

'The result of this recce with the Bishops was indeed surprising. They also, it appeared, were concerned about the problem, and their concern was based on two factors: one, the increasing strain on facilities in their parish schools, which get little or no subsidy from the Government; two, the increasing part being played by a bolshevik element in the Shinner's party, agitating in the ghettos about housing conditions, religious discrimination, and so on. Any dramatic increase in population, causing further over-crowding and unemployment, they realised, would play into the hands of these rabble-rousers.

'The Bishops, of course, could do nothing officially until they get clearance from the Eyeties – which, as I've said, could be fifty years hence. But, after protracted negotiation during which they extracted promises regarding increased subsidies for their schools, an unofficial approach to the problem was agreed upon. The kernel of this approach is what we term "Passive Enforcement".

'The Dogma of the church, y'see,' explained the Major, encouraged only by McTavish's understanding nod, soporific in its regularity, 'much like Common Law, can be bent by precedent. And the precedent in this case, the Bishops concluded, was that of those nuns in the Congo who were raped by the niggers and had children. If their purity was considered to be unsullied by an act of violence, there can be no question of mortal sin in the case of a woman to whom the Pill is administered forcibly.

'Now, how to do this? There was the suggestion that it should be introduced into the water supply disguised as fluoride; but this was discarded by us as being too random, and by the Bishops as being too sneaky and much too widespread. It was they who first pointed out that the problem was most acute in certain defined areas, and indeed offered to supply details of certain tribes and individuals whose fertility makes them prime targets for the approach finally agreed upon. Mr McTavish . . .'

McTavish had been creaking about adjusting a screen on the wall behind the table and setting up a slide-projector at the back of the room. He now flicked off the lights and settled the first slide on the screen. It was a coloured map of the city with certain areas circled in red. 'These,' said the Major, indicating the circles, 'are your target areas. As you see, twelve in all, each to be worked by a unit of two men. Next slide.'

Also coloured, this was of a large, jolly-looking lady with a head of curlers and a butt smouldering on her lower lip. 'This person is, unbelievably, only twenty-eight. She has ten children and a potential of at least the same again. She is also a good example of what you'll have to deal with, which brings me to the matter of enforcement.

'To enforce anything on this person against her will would be extremely unpleasant, if not highly dangerous. Three months ago she bit the ear clean off a bailiff who tried to repossess her television set. But here, in your case, is where the power of the Bishops comes in. They will give out, unofficially of course, an edict of non-resistance and a blanket absolution which will guarantee your safety at all times.'

The next slide featured a pretty, blond young woman whose languid gaze left no doubt about where she would like to have the photographer. 'This one,' said the Major severely, 'represents a different kind of danger. At twenty-six she has produced eight times – indeed, goes on producing throughout her husband's lengthy jail terms. The hazard here is that traditionally associated with milk-roundsmen and I must warn you men that default of this nature will not be tolerated!'

The light came on again and McTavish returned to his place on the dais.

'And now,' said the Major, 'to the actual operation. The problem, then, was how to forcibly administer a contraceptive pill at the prescribed, regular intervals to pin-pointed targets, and to administer it in a manner which would not compromise the recipient's passivity in any way. The method I shall now outline meets these requirements in full. Mr McTavish, with the assistance of two volunteers, will demonstrate as I speak.'

76

McTavish snapped his fingers at two in the front row. These sprang to the front and took up positions in accordance with McTavish's muttered instructions, the three forming a tableau with McTavish and volunteer A side by side facing Volunteer B.

'Now this triangle,' explained the Major, 'represents the working unit. Mr McTavish and Volunteer A on his left are administrators and, behind an imaginary door, Volunteer B is the prospective recipient. The first movement of the action is made by the lead-man on the right, McTavish here, who knocks on the door . . .' McTavish got a laugh by rapping sharply on Volunteer B's forehead '. . . and I draw your attention to the important fact that he used his *left* hand.'

The Major went on: 'Movement number two is the emergence of the recipient.' Here he had to pause while McTavish helped Volunteer B overcome his stage fright with dire threats in *sotto-voce*, eventually getting him to mime the door opening and take one step closer. 'This is the most crucial stage of the entire action. The recipient is there facing you; she knows what you're there to do, but she cannot assist you in any way. Movement number three, therefore, must be to get her mouth to open involuntarily. It proceeds thus: the second man in the unit, here Volunteer A, reaches out and firmly grasps the recipient's nostrils between finger and thumb.' Volunteer A, a bright lad, did as bidden. And sure enough Volunteer B's mouth fell open, causing a round of admiring applause. 'The second man in all units, of course,' added the Major, 'will be issued with rubber gloves.'

'Movement number four is the actual administration of the Pill. And here again we come up against the passivity question. The lead man, you say, could now place it on the recipient's tongue and that's that. But the Bishops contend that the recipient would then have to swallow the Pill and this could be looked upon as an *act* of acceptance. A system to overcome this had to be devised.

77

'I now draw your attention to the instrument in Mr McTavish's *right* hand; a hard plastic tube, twelve inches long, half-inch diameter, standard size as used by veterinary surgeons. So, with second man still in the nasal position, lead man now inserts the Pill into the tube's mouthpiece, places the muzzle smartly between the recipient's lips and blows sharply. Thus the Pill is propelled so far down the recipient's gullet that any muscular reaction on her part could not be construed as voluntary by even the most hostile theologian!'

At the Major's request McTavish and the volunteers went through the motions again and again, each time gaining noticeably in speed and efficiency. 'Knock – nose – blow – recover. Knock – nose – blow – recover,' chanted the Major in time with each movement. 'This is the basic action. This afternoon Mr McTavish will organise you into similar units and begin your practical training. In the meantime, I will finish this introductory talk by mentioning one or two occupational hazards. First, the Pill itself: avoid oral contact at all times as this could have nasty side effects over a period; watch out for blow-backs – our pilot teams found that some of these people have a very curious sense of humour; and make absolutely certain that you find the right target – we don't want a deluge of complaints from home-helps and visiting relatives!'

'My last word,' promised the Major, glancing at his watch, 'is on appearance. We wish to avoid looking like Mormons or insurance men; the keynote should be informality, even gaiety, in dress and general comportment. Longish hair will be encouraged and certain men will be told to grow beards.'

'And now,' said the Major, a trifle sheepishly, 'in accordance with Government regulations concerning official gatherings of more than three people, we will finish by singing the first verse of *God Save the Queen*. Mr McTavish will accompany on the bag-pipes.'

The Gummy Lion
(Ulster – a Protestant Myth)

'– Stand hat hease! Lance Corporal Webb – Sah!'

Captain Wilkington-Pike allowed the Sergeant Major to complete his time-honoured solo passage for heel and floor-board before bidding Webb to stand easy. Then followed a pause while the Captain busily made marks on a roster sheet and Webb, eyes fixed on the regimental crest on the wall behind the Captain's chair, wondered what the hell it was all about. The Vandals v Hooligans soccer match organised by the 'Hearts and Minds' committee had not gone at all well – but that had nothing to do with him. Indeed, but for his presence of mind and a handy C.S. pistol the Captain would most likely have gone on record as the first referee in the game's history to be throttled by the chain of his own whistle.

His eyes still protruded slightly, Webb noticed when the Captain at last flung the rosters in his out-tray and looked up.

'Well now, how's the leg today, Lance-Corporal?'

'Not so bad, Sir. They dug the last bit out yesterday.'

'Yes, so I see; I have the quack's report here somewhere. Ah yes, "full set upper dentures, female, in nine fragments." A not very appetising jig-saw, what! Still, let's hope the dental chappies will be able to reconstruct the thing to Mrs What's-her-name's satisfaction.'

'Mrs Concepta Flaherty, Sir,' supplied Webb, scarcely believing his ears. 'Do you mean she'll be getting them back, Sir?'

'I'm afraid she must, Lance Corporal,' replied the Captain, avoiding his eye; 'they are her property, after all. There's a list somewhere – yes, here it is . . . "Articles allegedly looted from the premises of . . ."!'

'But that old bag tried to bite me on the . . .!'

'Hold yer tongue!' screamed the Sergeant Major.

'I understand how you must feel, Webb,' said the Captain evenly. 'But you too must appreciate the difficult position we're in here. A question in the House about how Mrs Flaherty lost her dentures is the last thing we want at this moment in time. It's the sort of incident which could be very effectively used by extremist propaganda. The next thing would be an article in the *Sunday Mirror* about British soldiers selling old ladies' gold fillings on the black market – accompanied by a full-page zoom picture of Mrs Flaherty's naked gums, no doubt! No, we cannot have anything like that just now, so the word from above is that Mrs Flaherty and teeth are to be forgotten, forthwith. All right?'

'What about the dump, Sir?' Webb persisted boldly, again causing the Sergeant Major to grunt and snuffle indignantly.

'All right, Sergeant Major,' soothed Wilkington-Pike, doodling frantically on the margin of a fresh roster sheet. (The regimental head-shrinker, after that bit of man-management bother in Aden, had had no difficulty connecting those chains of small triangles with the man-sized iron one – still darkly stained – which had been supporting roses on the Wilkington-Pike Stately Home for over a century. In the great days of the Raj, mounted on a bullock cart, it had taken pride of place in the train of General Redfers Wilkington-Pike, the Captain's Great-Grandfather. On it, with no more provocation than a cloudy button, the General had flogged entire battalions in every outpost of the Empire.)

'Come now, Webb,' he said, ' "dump" is taking it a bit far, don't you think? You might call seven semi-automatic pistols and related ammo. "a good haul", but hardly a "dump"! Also, that would tend to suggest Mrs Flaherty's prior knowledge of the articles found behind the fish fingers in her fridge, and she states – I quote:

"They must have been there when the man brought it."
Intelligence thinks it could well be the work of *agents provocateurs*, so let's not be hasty in our judgments, Lance Corporal. All right? Good. Now perhaps we can proceed to the primary object of this interview. I have your particulars here somewhere . . . where the . . . ah yes . . . "Rodney Webb, Religion: Non-Conformist".'

The Captain sat back and frowned deeply.

'Pretty vague, wouldn't you say, Webb?'

'What, Sir?'

' "Non-Conformist". To what do you not conform so religiously?' Though somewhat surprised at his own turn of phrase and wondering where on earth he'd cribbed it (*Soldier* or *Reader's Digest*?) Wilkington-Pike glanced slyly at the Sergeant Major and elicited the regulation guffaw.

'My parents are Baptists, Sir,' explained Webb, convinced now that the whistle chain incident had sent his Captain over the wall. 'I'm agnostic, but the Recruiting Officer said I must put down something.'

'Quite right,' said the Captain sternly; 'there are no agnostics in the British Army – officially. Unofficially, having stated that you are one, I'm sure you'll not mind if I amend this section to read Church of England, will you, Webb?'

'Why, Sir?'

'All right, all right, Sarnt Major . . . Because, Webb, of strategy. Your lack of conformity at church parades has been noted and reported by the local Peace Vigilantes. You have been . . . What the . . .!'

A petrol bomb flared up the heavily grilled window of the company office, followed by a patter of stones. The hysterical shrilling of a guard whistle, and, above all, the old Celtic battle cry – favoured on both sides of the religious divide – 'Gerratyafugginbasters!', completed a familiar pattern. The Captain glanced at his watch. '*Tempus fugit* – the Primary school is going to lunch. Look lively, Sarnt Major, and get in those pickets before anything nasty occurs.'

'Now, Lance Corporal, where were we . . . ah yes, the Peace Vigilantes. You see, Webb, anything smacking of serious fundamentalism tends to raise their hackles. C of E is as far out as they'll tolerate, so I've arranged with the Padre for a special combined Baptism and Confirmation service for all those in the company not already C of E. The Peace Vigilantes will attend, as observers, of course, as will representatives from each of the forty-six republican factions, the Maoists, the P.D., the Glasgow Celtic Supporters . . . Yes, Sarnt Major?'

'Sah! They've got Private Briggs' rifle. Sah!'

'Christ! – was it the Primaries?'

'No, Sir, the Backward Boys, Sir. They dragged him through the window of their mini-bus. Most of his uniform's gone too. He's in a bad state of shock – Sah!'

'Damn bad show! But when you think of it, impartially, I mean,' mused Wilkington-Pike, 'they do have this terrific community feeling, no one is allowed to feel out of it. That incident down in C Division last week, for instance – where else in the world would a full Colonel of Life Guards be badly mauled by a Darby and Joan club on their evening out? Still, a rifle's a rifle and battalion inventory comes round shortly. Get a couple of our fellows down to that road-block below the chapel, Sarnt Major; the Coldstream will be poncing around all limp and elegant and they'll have no difficulty swiping a replacement for Briggs. By-the-by, Briggs is in your litter, isn't he, Webb?'

'Yes, Sir.'

'I thought so. Cut along with the Sarnt Major and see how he's doing, will you. Report back here immediately.'

When they'd gone the Captain looked down at the roster on his blotter and said, 'Damn!' The little triangles had spilled out of the margin and across the page, rendering it useless for anything save further evidence for the head-shrinker. Crumpling and throwing it into the waste basket, he sat back, lit his pipe, and began to ruminate on the life and times of his Great Grandmother, Sybil. (A morbid deviation which puzzled the Captain – normally his idle mental moments were taken up with erotica of a highly technical nature. The regimental head-shrinker, of course, had never divulged the significance of the triangles to his patient.)

Sybil Wilkington-Pike, even more so than her flagellant husband Redfers, was indeed a strange subject for quiet reverie. A keen horticulturist, she had accompanied Redfers on his blood-spattered tours abroad, building up the collection of exotic flora which now resides in the British Museum. But not included in that collection are the odd trophies which fell to her busy secateurs during the long retreat to Peshawar in 1840. Contemporary gossip suggests that the death of her lover, a Havildar Major in the Poona Foot, had first prompted her to join the native women on the battlefield after dark. Whatever the reason, the products of her nocturnal snipping, strung on a length of piano wire and worn as a necklace, had caused ripples of envy at many a hunt ball on her return to England. When Sybil died in the late '80s the necklace disappeared or was destroyed – it was thought, by a daughter far gone in the fashionable puritanism of the times; but by the turn of the century it had begun to turn up again, or rather remnants of it had, now unstrung, in all sorts of odd corners in the family mansion. The Captain himself remembered a hushed furore when his parents discovered just what a housemaid had been using to buff a high shine on the family brogues. And quite recently his elder brother, heir to the Stately Home and death duties – 'Private Zoo, Dodgem Cars, Sauna Baths, Restaurant' – had spun him a garbled tale concerning a short-sighted cook, a batch of mushroom soup and a coachload of affluent Pakistani bagmen.

The Captain's grisly daydream was broken by the return of Webb.

'Sir. Private Briggs is under heavy sedation, so I couldn't get much out of him. The medics say he'll be all right in time.'

'Jolly good. What else . . . Where . . . ?' The Captain found his pencil and began defiling a virgin roster, his train of thought quickly falling in behind the small triangles. 'Ah yes, Webb, your theological problem. I don't wish to labour the point – as I say, *tempus fugit* and the Grammar School will soon be upon us. I know that you, as a good soldier, appreciate our difficulties in this situation. If it's not one thing with these people it's another. This time last month, you'll remember, it was the Racial Purity League about Corporal Mashimba. We thought we'd got over that one by creating an entirely new liaison post for him in the University, thinking he'd blend well with the colour scheme up there. Now, more trouble – this is in strict confidence, you understand – two nights ago Mashimba was caught in a police raid on a pot party. Carried off to the loony hatch wearing love beads and screaming about Black Power! Another good NCO down the hole! And on top of that there's Lieutenant Levy. He has, quite naturally, refused plastic surgery on his nose, so we now have to get him on the boat before Good Friday or else. So you see, Webb, any sacrifice. My Christ! What is that racket?'

From the outer office came the sound of splintering furniture and a loud voice, curiously guttural, rising in anger. At that moment the Sergeant Major, ashen-faced, came backing through the door, slamming and holding it tightly closed.

'What on earth is it, Sarnt Major?' the Captain demanded.

'The Right Honourable O'Lig, Sir.'

'Ah Christ! – the one who spits?'

'Yes, Sir,' confirmed the Sergeant Major, wiping his face, 'the juicy joker.'

The voice outside rose to crescendo pitch and the door shuddered under the impact of the Right Honourable's industrial toecap. 'For God's sake hold that door shut until I'm ready, Sarnt Major!' cried the Captain, grabbing his flak-jacket and helmet. 'I'll go out to him – don't want everything in here saturated. What's he on about anyway?'

'Sergeant Greeves' tattoo, Sir.'

'Who? Oh, I recall now. The one whose jacket they set alight. When he stripped off they spotted the thing on his forearm – "For Queen and Country" wasn't it? What the hell does O'Lig want us to do? They flayed it off Greeves there and then as I remember!'

'Yes, Sir, they did. He's waving it about out there now, Sir, stretched on a frame as evidence. It seems he wants the whole company inspected for provocative decoration of this sort and appropriate action taken, Sir.'

The R.T. in the corner of the room began to bleep madly.

'Oh God! Everything at once!' groaned the Captain, striding over and snatching up the hand-set. 'Hold that door for your life, Sarnt Major . . . B company base, B company base. Over.'

A voice crackled over the speaker: 'Hello B company base. This is C platoon on patrol, Lieutenant Parkes reporting. Over.'

'Hello Parkes. Company Commander here. What's the trouble? Over.'

'There's a mob gathering outside a pub down here, Sir – looks a bit dodgy. They're singing party songs and doing a lot of flag-waving. Over.'

'Tread carefully, Parkes,' barked the Captain sternly. 'No precipitate action. Diplomacy is the watch-word at all times. Understood? By the way, state your exact position. Over.'

'Understood, Sir. Position is . . . junction of the Shankill Road and-ah-Snugville Street, Sir. Over.'

'What!' The Captain's demeanour changed abruptly. He pointed down the mouthpiece like a gun-dog. His voice quivered. 'Parkes. Listen and answer carefully. What flags are they waving? Over.'

'Ours, Sir – Union Jacks. Oh and some other white and orange thing. Over.'

For Webb, watching, the transformation wrought on his Captain by this intelligence was remarkable. Gone was the old 'Wafflington-Puke' of barrack-room derision; the back straightened, liverish cheeks flooded with colour, a free hand smoothed suddenly turbulent, though nonexistent, moustachios. Had there been a jaw at all it would have jutted. When he spoke again his voice seemed deeper, his manner clipped and urgent.

'Parkes. Listen carefully. We must nip this in the bud at once. I order you to open fire – repeat – OPEN FIRE! Written confirmation will follow. Understood? Over.'

'Understood Sir. Over and out.'

Replacing the hand-set, Wilkington-Pike stood for a moment in silence, breathing deeply, savouring the orgasm of decision. Then a great splashing howl from outside signalled a renewed assault by the O'Lig.

'Sir!' appealed the Sergeant Major, bracing himself against the door.

'All right, all right, Sarnt Major,' snapped the Captain irritably, shoulders slumping back into the mould of the flak-jacket. Lowering the perspex riot-visor on his helmet he moved over to the door and faced it manfully. 'When I give the word let go and stand well back, Sarnt Major. Oh, and I shall want the company paraded, stripped to the waist, in five minutes. Understood? All right, Sarnt Major, open the box.'

The Adjusters

He awoke with the echo of the telephone's first assault in his ears. During the second the luminous dial on the bedside table told him it was 2.30 and the blown rain spattering on the window told that the weather, as forecast, had turned foul. He quenched the third summons in mid flow and lifted the receiver to his ear, the butterflies which would later become bats stirring in his stomach. He didn't speak, nor was he meant to. The familiar voice at the other end said: 'Number 24 in fifteen minutes. Scramble.'

'Z.2 – Roger,' he said and replaced the receiver gently.

Beside him Margie stirred and murmured, 'Bob?'

It never ceased to amaze him. She could sleep through telephone, force 9 gale, thunder, and once when a carbomb had gone off two streets away she had snored obliviously; yet one syllable from him and she was awake. He had pleaded with the Major to let him drop the 'Z-2 Roger' business, but the Major had been adamant: regulations were regulations. 'After all, Margie could have a fancy-man for all we know,' he had growled, his one little red eye leering obscenely.

Margie sat up in bed and switched on the light. 'Oh Bob, not again!'

He heard the sob in her voice and inwardly cursed the Major and his regulations.

' 'fraid so,' he said with forced nonchalance, pulling on trousers and choker over his pyjamas. 'A dirty night for it too.'

'But why always you. This is twice in ten days!' she cried, angrily tearing open a fresh box of tissues which he knew would be depleted by morning.

'Well, there's only Connors and me since Frank –'

He smothered the sentence, but the damage was done. She turned on her side abruptly and buried her face in the pillow.

Fully dressed now, gathering his bits and pieces, Bob thought of the cemetery that dark November afternoon, shouldering Frank's coffin beside the Major, trying to keep time with the idiosyncrasies of the Major's wooden leg. He remembered thinking that if big laughing Frank were looking down he'd be splitting his sides at the sight. Thinking of it now, he found himself laughing uncontrollably. Margie turned towards him again, eyes wide, aghast, 'You're mad!' she cried suddenly. 'You're all mad!'

Sobering, he moved to comfort her, but she had turned her face to the pillow again. As he closed the bedroom door he heard the floodgates of grief burst open behind it.

The short drive through the blacked-out streets was uneventful. Bob kept his headlights dimmed for fear of illuminating a prowling foot patrol. Edgy soldiers could get very stroppy over a thing like that.

Irish Street was a row of derelict terraces in a deserted ghetto area. The windows and doorway of number 24 were bricked-up. Bob parked in the alley behind the row and entered via a hole in the backyard wall. Two other cars were parked in the alley.

In what had been the living-room the Major sat at a folding card-table. The only light came from a hand torch propped on the ruined mantelpiece. Young Connors stood in the shadows to the left of the table.

'You're late,' barked the Major, fixing Bob with his little red left eye and flicking the black patch over his right socket, a glimpse of empty horror that did nothing for jaded nerves. He always did it, deliberately, just as he always barked 'You're late!' no matter when you arrived.

Having long since ceased to be affected by the Major's

little ways, Bob said briskly, 'All the more reason to get on with it. What's the job?'

The Major had placed a dark cheroot between his teeth. Before replying he lit it, slowly, rolling the end in the match flame. Without looking, Bob could feel the tension radiating from young Connors.

'Mappins in Tomb Street,' said the Major, 'four-story warehouse: expensive electronic equipment.'

'How much?' asked Connors, his voice vibrating with suppressed excitement.

'Two million quid, give or take a thousand. It's a big one.'

The Major unrolled a plan on the table and they gathered round, going into the well-drilled routine of deposition, method, vulnerability, and so on. Making a point, young Connors laid his right hand, the two-fingered one, on the table. Bob thought of the effect that hand would have on the promotion board in three weeks time and he marvelled again at his own charmed life. Frank dead, the Major half-blind and crippled, Connors, with only six months service, maimed in the best place possible, and he still unscathed after five years of front line work. How long? Perhaps tonight . . .

'Right,' said the Major, 'time to get going.'

Connors produced the battered black suitcase, laid it on the table and opened the lid. Bob, the expert in these matters, pulled on rubber gloves and began checking the contents. The grey sticks were bone dry, he noted with relief, any trace of sweat at this stage would be disastrous. He bound four together with wire, incorporating in the bundle a timing mechanism consisting of a rigged wristwatch and detonator. From the suitcase he also took a dozen or so wired detonators which, along with the deadly bundle, he placed carefully in a soft leather briefcase.

'Ready,' he said. Connors' two-fingered hand, trembling slightly, darted out to rest on the briefcase. 'My turn, I think,' he said quietly, causing Bob's stomach to tighten with sudden rage. Enthusiasm was one thing, but the insatiable ambition of Connors was beginning to wear on him; especially since he'd lost the fingers. 'As good as five years service,' he'd been heard to boast to an awestruck junior, flaunting the stumps. For a moment Bob hesitated, his own hand still on the briefcase. The Major saw the tension on the faces of the two men and smirked contentedly. 'Fair's fair, Bob,' he said, and Bob relinquished hold on the briefcase, knowing it was an order. Still seething, he turned on his heel and made his way out to the cars.

Tomb Street was ten minutes drive by the shortest route through the city centre. They went in Bob's car, Bob driving and Connors with the briefcase on his lap, humming tunelessly to himself. It was always a tense time; all it needed was a nosey foot patrol and the contents of that briefcase could mean five years apiece. A red halo in the sky marked their destination.

They parked the car on the main road and approached Tomb Street on foot. Turning the corner was like opening the door of a giant oven. Mappin's four storeys glowed, illuminating a seeming chaos of fire tenders, tangled hoses, police cars, soldiers and the ubiquitous television crews. Extension ladders soared above the blazing building, but Bob could see that any effort from now on would be control-of-spread to other premises. Mappins itself was a write-off.

Suddenly a black-faced rifleman confronted them, demanding identification. Bob said 'Acme Insurance' and proffered the card which he had held ready in his hand – reaching for a wallet at the point of a gun could be very dicey. For one heart-stopping moment, as the soldier squinted at the card and eyed the briefcase under Connors' arm, he thought they'd had it. Then came a shout from the direction of some landrovers and a young policeman came running to assure the soldier of their credentials.

The man who had shouted was crouching in the lee of a landrover, sheltering from the wind-blown heat. He greeted them, grinning sardonically, 'Well, if it isn't the men from Acme. I'd a notion this was one of yours.'

'It is indeed, and a big one,' said Bob.

'How does it look, sergeant?' asked Connors.

Sergeant Mahaffy indicated with a toss of his head. 'Just as you see it, a write-off. Oh and by the way, let me introduce Cadet Thompson, my new apprentice.'

The young man who had rescued them from the inquisitive soldier touched his cap. There was a red flash on the epaulettes of his tunic, indicating officer material . . . also danger, thought Bob. Probably already at University, on his way to a law degree . . . have to be careful . . . Cadet Thompson's accent confirmed his forebodings.

'Is it usual for insurance officials to attend fires at this time of night?' he asked.

The sergeant answered: 'If you've a boss like the mad Major it is . . . And how is the oul brute?'

'Bearing up,' said Bob. 'Oh, and he sends you his best regards, sergeant.'

'I'm sure he does,' said Mahaffy dryly. He and the Major were old enemies, veterans of many a verbal battle at numberless conflagrations in the small hours. 'The Major is the Acme Insurance Claims manager,' he explained to Cadet Thompson, 'and a holy terror if ever there was one. I've seen me having to put a hammerlock on him, actually lay him on the ground and sit on him, to stop him charging into a fire after the evidence. You'd have sworn every penny was coming out of his own pocket.'

'Evidence of what?' asked Cadet Thompson.

'Of malicious intent involving sabotage by three or more persons,' intoned the sergeant. 'Did you never read the small print at the bottom of your policies? There's a bit that says: "Exclusion clause – Northern Ireland: Acts of War or Civil Disturbance". That means that if they ever hijack your car and use it for planting a bomb, you can whistle for your money so far as your insurance company's concerned. And the same applies to this.'

As the sergeant indicated Mappins, an inner wall collapsed with a roar, sending a fountain of sparks shooting up to engulf the tops of the extension ladders. While the sergeant had been talking Bob had been watching the progress of the fire, noting how the wind was driving it to one end of the main block. To the windward end there was a smaller, two-storied section which housed the shipping and transport department. Though attached to the main building this section was of a different vintage, having been part of Mappins original warehouse. Bob recalled these details from the Major's briefing; what interested him now was that it seemed thus far to have escaped serious damage due to the wind direction. He managed to draw Connors' attention to it while the sergeant continued lecturing Cadet Thompson. 'Y'see, if the damage is the result of a firebomb, the government pays; if not, it's the insurance company's baby. That's what drove the Major mad, y'see, not being able to get the evidence before it was all destroyed. Of course there's no need if somebody hears the bomb going off – but that doesn't always happen.'

It was a cue for Bob to put the vital question. He tried to keep his voice steady. 'Well, sergeant, is it or isn't it?'

Mahaffy grinned and nudged Cadet Thompson. 'What did I tell ye!' he cried. 'The mad Major can't get about himself now so he gets his boys outa bed. Well, Bob, you can give my best regards to the Major and tell him that as no explosion was heard by the adjacent residents and no smell of inflammable materials reported by the firemen, he'd better start getting his wee purse open. And stand well back when he starts to foam at the mouth.'

The die is cast, thought Bob. At one end of the main building the holocaust had mounted to a roaring crescendo. They were bringing down the extension ladders, a sure sign of lost control. But at the other end the two-storied shipping section still stood, though flames were now discernible through the window gaps. It was now or never.

Bob yawned and said, 'Well, I suppose that's that. No

sense us hanging about. You'll send us your report, sergeant?'

'I will that,' the sergeant promised. As Bob and Connors moved away he called, 'Have the strait-jacket ready when you tell the Major!'

Bob saw with satisfaction that the television cameras were still trained on the blaze. No better evidence than the media. Neither man spoke until they were clear of Tomb Street and nearing the car. Connors broke the silence: 'The shipping end?'

Bob nodded. 'If we drive down the next street on the left it should bring us close enough. Let's hope there's not many about.'

There was a couple of fire tenders with hoses leading to the main building. As they drove past they saw that both crews were concentrated down there, leaving the shipping end pretty well deserted. They followed the narrow street along the wall that bounded the end of the building until they came to a gateway. They were now shielded from the fire tenders by the curve of the wall. The gate was a twenty-foot high affair of wrought-iron lattice-work through which they could see the gable-end of the shipping department. Smoke gushed from the windows, but there was no sign of flames as yet.

'From the top of the gate, I think,' said Bob, and Connors nodded.

Bob extracted the main bundle from the briefcase and set the timing for four minutes. Connors had taken the bundle of loose detonators and was standing ready at the foot of the gate when Bob finished. Then, with both bundles thrust in the capacious pockets of his duffle-coat, Connors began to climb the gate. The smoke issuing from the windows was very thick now. Bob heard Connors choking as he straddled the top of the gate, poised for the first throw. He held his breath . . . Connors threw . . . bullseye! straight through the main window. The second bundle, the detonators, he scattered inside the yard. He had just unstraddled the gate in preparation for descent when he went into a particularly violent bout of coughing; then he plummeted fifteen feet onto the concrete. When Bob helped him to his feet he screamed, clutching his right leg. Aware of the seconds ticking away, Bob lifted him bodily and flung him in the back seat of the car.

The boom came as Bob tooled the car into a maze of little streets near the city centre, well clear of Tomb Street. Another two million saved for Acme, he thought with satisfaction. Then Connors groaned in the back seat, reminding him of the promotion board in three weeks time, and his heart sank. Now he had a two-fingered hand *and* a limp to compete with. And knowing Connors, it would be a very bad limp. Ah well, thought Bob, between now and then I'll just have to be less careful and hope for the worst.

The Humours of Ballyturdeen

'We'll have less of that sectarian nonsense, Jeffers, if you don't mind,' said Mr Sanders, re-aligning the signed photograph of Mr Bob Cooper ('Alliance – Voice of the Silent Majority') in relation to his immaculate blotter. 'The fact is,' he went on, 'that there are units in Ballyturdeen crying out for repair and until we can arrange a replacement for Baxter –'

'– Who chose the Prison Service sooner than Ballyturdeen,' observed Jeffers firmly, causing Mr Sanders' hands to ball suddenly into small fists.

Jeffers was sure of his ground; the brawn drain of men to the Prison Service, the Police Reserve and Securicor was one of the Sanders' own hobby-horses at Rotary Club luncheons.

'You know as well as I do, Mr Sanders,' he said, 'that soldiers get DSOs just for having been in Ballyturdeen. On the television only last week, when the Queen Mum presented colours to the 2nd Flintshires, what do you think was the new battle honour on the battalion flag, below El Alamein and alongside Waterloo?'

'I know, Jeffers, I know,' cried Sanders, 'we all watch –'

'– Ballyturdeen,' stated Jeffers, making his point. 'So I'll have triple-time or my cards.'

'Triple!' yelled Sanders, causing his Girl Friday in the outer office to hunt out the yellow pills. 'My God, Jeffers, this is blackmail – industrial blackmail – and I will not have it. Do you hear me, Jeffers? I will not have it! I will not allow myself to be intimidated. People like you are worse than the bombers and gunmen, using the troubled times in our dear land to further your own selfish ends. Industrial bully-boyism! That's what it is. But remember, Jeffers, at the end of the day "We must love one another or die"; "No man is an island", Jeffers.'

Jeffers listened patiently. He knew there was no real harm in the man. And the decibel count was rather less nowadays than when he'd joined Spinduo as a boy ten years ago and Sanders had been a leading light in amateur dramatics (the memory of those daily, Bard-laden confrontations still gave him the shudders). Since then he had seen Sanders through Humanism, Moral Rearmament, the Jehovah's Witnesses, and he'd found that when the quotations began to fly the best attitude was the stonewall. Other men, skilled in WEA dialectics, had shouted Sanders down, confounded him, left him with his Faith (in whatever) tottering – and received their cards and holiday money in the next morning's post. As one long gone agitator had said of him, 'His heart's in the right place, but his head's full of mad dog's shite'.

Ten minutes later, after a performance by Sanders of all but the tail-end of Beethoven's Ninth on bumpaper and comb, Jeffers went through the outer office and said to Girl Friday, 'Triple-time now, love. That's official.' She, anticipating the frantic bleeping of her dictaphone and hurrying Sanders-wards with yellow pills and water, growled, 'Red-flagger!'

'Blue knickers,' replied Jeffers, administering a deep reverse goose with twist and sending Girl Friday, water and pills in three different directions. Sanders bleeped piteously.

But once on the motorway at the end of which, somewhere, lurked Ballyturdeen, Jeffers' spirits sank. Behind him lay the homely, smoking ruin of Belfast; there he knew where he was, or where he shouldn't be, at any given time, in his head a tracery of invisible battle-lines created by polarisation ('git out or be brunt [sic] out, ya taig/prod basters'); a city of vast pigeonholes – including a burgeoning ghetto of Chinese waiters around the municipal baths – in which he had become attuned to every nuance of change that spelt danger; the midday stillness that might herald a sudden swarming from side-streets, like maddened bees from a smoked hive, as some hunger-striker gasped his or her last; the abrupt acceleration of a police Land Rover for no apparent reason; the look on the face of a searching paratrooper that told him not to remark pleasantly on the state of the weather or England's position in the World Cup.

But Ballyturdeen? What did he know of it beyond the three names familiar to every Dervish and Bushman with a transistor tuned to the BBC World Service: 'Kilbraddock's Braes' and 'Turberry's Meadows', its two Housing Trust kraals, and the notorious 'Cut', a blood-spattered no-man's-land which separated them and which for three years had vied with Sinai and Penang Province for the attention of the world's camera crews. There, only six months ago, an entire CBS unit had been wiped out in crossfire after failing to come to a suitable financial arrangement with either side. And there too had occurred the terrible massacre of a delegation of C of E liberal vicars. (Though, in mitigation, a case of mistaken identity due to poor visibility and misted gunsights – for one side the profusion of fuming briar pipes had been enough, for the other a brief glimpse of flared houndstooth and one flowered kaftan.)

Yet when Jeffers pulled off the motorway an hour later and made a tentative probe into the Ballyturdeen outskirts, all seemed very quiet. He left the van at the barrier which closed off the main street to all traffic (including, hopefully, car-bombers), intending to present his list of calls to the nearest shopkeeper and ask directions. Shutters everywhere – it was whole-day closing. Cursing his luck, Jeffers walked the street both sides, but the only living thing he encountered, a hunch-backed septuagenarian dressed up as a traffic warden, scuttled away up an entry as he approached. The alternative,

Jeffers decided reluctantly, was that last resort for anyone wanting to get anywhere in the shortest time possible: the police.

He had passed the barracks on the way in; a fortress, with all but the front wicker gate sandbagged and the entire building caged to the roof in an anti-bomb screen. When he rang the bell on the gate a voice crackled over an intercom from within. 'Who are ye? What d'ye want here?' After he had stated his business there was a hiatus while they conferred and took a long-lens photo, he supposed. Then the voice said, menacingly, 'Stay where ye are. I'm coming out.'

What came out first was the muzzle of a Sterling machine pistol, and behind it a grizzled, brick-faced retired farmer in the uniform of the Reserve force. Jeffers first presented his identification for scrutiny and then his list of calls. The Reservist squinted at the list, whistled, pushed his cap up from his forehead, muttered something rural like 'Boys-a-dear!', and fixed Jeffers with a look of fatherly concern. 'The man that give ye this lot, son, didn't much like ye,' he commented ominously.

'Why's that?'

'I'll tell ye why; two of them's in Kilbraddock's and three's in Turberry's. That's why.'

'Oh ... Well, what's it like in there now? Quiet?' asked Jeffers, wondering if he should turn around, go home, and bugger the triple-time. But if only he could get in and do one job in each area ('Not-at-homing' all the others) Sanders would then have no excuse for welshing on the triple-time – as he knew Sanders would try to do in any case.

'Quiet? I dunno,' growled the Reservist. 'Nobody knows. They could be atein' each other for all anybody knows.'

'Do you – I mean the police – do youse patrol up there?'

'Patrol! Yer jokin!' the Reservist guffawed at the idea of it. 'The only patrollin' done up there is from an Army helicopter on very dark nights. An' I hear tell all it does is hover a fut or two off the groun' long enough for one fella to jump out, shout "Goal!" and jump in again!'

An exaggeration, Jeffers knew: that was another branch of his antennae developed over the troubled years; the wilder the tale, he's always found, the milder the basis of it. 'Well, I think I'll go out and take a look anyway,' he said, folding the list. 'What road do I take?'

'On yer own head be it, son,' sighed the Reservist, turning and pointing the Sterling. 'Keep on the way yer facin'; over the ramps; through the barriers at the Army sangers there an' you'll come to the internment camp on yer left; follow the wire to the end, take the first on yer right an' about a hunnerd yards up yer into the Cut. I wouldn't chance the van in it, if I was you – you could wreck the sump in them mine craters. But you can take side lanes into the estates – Kilbraddock's is on yer right, Turberry's is on yer left . . . Oh aye, an' if ye run across any TV men up there that wants an interview, it's ten quid a time, mind. We don't want youse city fellas .comin' up an' spoilin' the rate. OK?'

'OK,' said Jeffers, and was turning away when he remembered . . . 'Oh, Constable, you said three in Turberry's and two in Kilbraddock's, but what about these other two here?'

He began to unfold the list again, but the Reservist forestalled him. 'Oh aye. Yer alright at that end. It's a private estate – shally bungalows. I live out that way myself,' he said proudly.

Five minutes later Jeffers, heart in mouth, bumped along the Cut and turned off in the direction of Turberry's Meadows. The entrance to the estate was marked by the burnt-out husk of an Army scout-car, the insignia of the Life Guards still visible on the turret. It swarmed with squealing youngsters and barking dogs, reminding Jeffers, ironically, of those recruiting exhibitions that tour country towns on market days. He eased the van past without attracting so much as a look, let alone a stone.

Encouraged, he drew up alongside two ladies gossiping

over a gate and asked the way to his first call (all the
street nameplates and door numbers had been removed).
They directed him volubly. One, noting the firm's name
on the pocket on his overalls (he had decided to use an
unmarked van) said, 'Ma Gilmore'll be glad to see you.
Thon oul hurdy-gurdy of hers has been stone dead for
months.'

No wonder, the motor housing crammed with old,
boiled cabbage secreted there by Ma Gilmore's five
greens-hating urchins. But before getting round to that
diagnosis, having been greeted like the Prodigal by Ma
Gilmore, Jeffers had three cups of tea, half-a-dozen
Paris buns and a lot of reassurance.

'Niver heed a word them shits of Peelers tell you, son,'
said Ma Gilmore, a cheerful, chain-smoking goitre victim. 'There's nobody'll lay a hand on you this side of the
Cut. An' there's no need to tell you to steer well clear of
them savages on the other side.' (He'd thought it better
not to mention his calls in Kilbraddock's.) 'I'm still sure
an' certain that's where my Tommy is,' Ma Gilmore
went on bitterly, the saucer eyes that go with her ail-
ment beginning to overflow, 'lyin' stiff as a board with a
bullet in him under somebody's garden in Kilbraddock's.
My own brother swears he seen him fallin'-down-drunk
outside a pub in Scunthorpe, but nothin'll ever convince
me he wasn't waylaid by them animals. Ethel thinks the
same about her Frank. Isn't that right, Ethel?'

Ethel, seated on a low settee, smiled and nodded and
tried to stretch the hem of her skirt another inch
towards her crossed knees (only another six to go).
Ethel – Mrs Lavery, twenty-four-year-old mother of
two – lived next door and her Frank had flown the coop
four months ago. Jeffers observed that she had not
allowed grief to affect either the bond or the elaborate
dressing of her false eyelashes. He also noticed some
other outstanding things about Ethel and was wondering if she had a Spinduo machine when Ma Gilmore, as
though reading his mind, said, 'Why don't you get Mr
Jeffers to have a look at your fridge, Ethel? It hasn't been

defrosting properly since Frank went. Isn't that right, Ethel?' Ethel smiled and nodded. 'There's such a lot goes wanting where there's no man in the house. Isn't that right, Ethel?' Ethel giggled and Ma Gilmore, the neighbourly soul, gave Jeffers a meaningful look.

It was a form of social work in which Jeffers had had a wealth of experience – the only sort for which a degree is not required, only talent. So after digging a bucket or two of putrid cabbage out of Ma Gilmore's hurdy-gurdy he accompanied Ethel to her house, leaving her two children happily unravelling Ma Gilmore's surgical stockings – a favourite treat.

Knowing nothing about fridges anyway, he got down to the task in hand without delay (pure habit, for the time factor wasn't as crucial as when working a tight call schedule in the city). Ethel's reaction from start to finish was in keeping with her social repartee – 'Oh . . . Oh? . . . Ah!!!' – after which he had a job keeping her awake long enough to get her from the kitchen floor to the sofa.

He left her snoring and returned to Ma Gilmore's who, thoughtful soul, had a cup of tea waiting. 'Well, you can't say we're not full of hospitality in Turberry's Meadows – you dirty brute ye!' she cried, punching him playfully. The sudden thought that Ma Gilmore might be contemplating an agent's fee in kind caused Jeffers to gulp his tea and bolt for the van.

So far so good, he thought, tooling gingerly around the craters in the Cut: one call in Kilbraddock's and we're home free. (Of his other two calls in Turberry's, one tribe had flitted in the night a week before, Ma Gilmore had told him, taking with it the bath, the upstairs toilet, every inch of copper piping in the house and the roof-tiles, and the other lot, friends of hers, were using the complaint ploy to stretch their HP terms to infinity. Against the first Jeffers wrote 'Derelict house' and against the second 'Con-artist'.)

In every respect save wall graffiti Kilbraddock's Braes was a mirror of Turberry's Meadows. True, there were no war relics quite so dramatic as Turberry's scout-car, but a seemingly haphazard pile of builder's rubble near the entrance to the estate, Jeffers noted, had no missile in it more than handsized. On the Green a mixed group of teenagers played a game – a not very nice game – with the rubber baton rounds the army used for mob control. Some spectators who lounged beside a stand of Japanese motorbikes wore the remains of policeman's caps, mutilated to resemble Brando's headgear in The Wild One, recently revived on television. But Jeffers reached his call unmolested.

His first sentiment on meeting the lady of the house, a Mrs McKenna, was heartfelt pity. All the fear and insecurity of the times seemed personified in that little beak of a face peering at him round the door-jamb. 'Spinduo service, Missus,' he announced – and immediately regretted it. The face went all open-mouth-and-staring-eyeballs before disappearing inside.

Jeffers heard her running up the hallway crying, 'Spinduo, Teddy, . . . Oh dear God, Teddy, Spinduo . . .' and, following, he thought to himself that here was the end product of it all: the bombs, the bullets, the night searches, the whole gruesome business of near-civil war.

At the kitchen door he was confronted by Teddy, the man of the house – large, toothless, badly in need of a truss, but still brutal looking about the tattooed forearms. He held a quivering finger under Jeffers' nose and shouted, 'And about time too! Either you fix that bloody thing in there or take it to hell outa here or I'll hold you and bloody Spinduo responsible when they take that bloody woman away!'

In the kitchen Mrs McKenna cowered in one corner and stared at her gleaming Spinduo Combined-Twin-Tub-and-Spin-Dryer in the other.

'What on earth's the matter, Mrs McKenna?' asked Jeffers, shocked at the state of her – and not a little fearful of the angry bulk of Teddy crowding in behind him.

'You'll get nothin' outa her,' bawled Teddy. 'Look at

her, skin an' bone, nails ate to the elbow – an' eight weeks ago she cudda flung a full milk bottle twenty-five yards . . . Till that bloody thing came into the house!'

'But what exactly's wrong?' asked Jeffers, crossing to the machine.

Mrs McKenna shrieked and fled from the kitchen. Her feet pounded on the stairs and a door slammed overhead.

'There y'are,' said Teddy accusingly. 'That's her for the day. You'd bloody better –'

'But if you'd only tell me what's the matter,' cried Jeffers, his own nerves beginning to jig in sympathy.

'Tell you!' Teddy jabbed a fag-pickled finger at the machine. 'No need to tell you anything. Just you pull that bloody switch there an' you'll see what's the bloody matter!'

Jeffers did, and within seconds realised with horror, and some awe, that for the first time in ten years he had drawn that one in ten thousand: a rogue; a 'Dr Who'.

He had often read about the phenomenon in trade magazines and had heard many tall tales of the havoc wrought on all who came in contact with it, never dreaming that one day he'd be called upon to cope. And it had to be today, of all days, and in this bloody place, he thought angrily, watching the machine waltz gracefully across the lino towards him.

'What did I tell ye! . . . What did I tell ye!' screamed Teddy, skipping into the hall and half-closing the door. 'An' wait'll you hear it. Wait'll it warms up.'

When it reached the extremity of its lead the machine paused. Clothes and suds swirled in the window of the main tub (after its last performance the McKennas hadn't dared remove the load). Then suddenly it gave vent to the first in a series of huge guttery farts, the red and green lights on its master panel began to flash on and off, and it started to skitter back and forth, swinging on the end of its lead, pirouetting and, eeriest of all, singing. 'Listen to it,' moaned Teddy from the hallway. '*Faith of Our Fathers* . . . an' there's worse.' Jeffers himself thought it more like a slow version of *The Battle of Garvagh*, but said nothing.

As though cued by Teddy's voice the machine had begun to gyrate faster, fart louder and sing shriller. Jeffers, fascinated despite himself, noted the curious fact that for all its wild shimmying it never touched anything; it skimmed cupboards, circled the table, birled down the length of the lead and up again, always missing by a hairbreadth as though it had evolved in itself some sort of radar screen. Then, just as music, lights and movement seemed to be mounting to a fused crescendo, everything stopped. ('This is it! Wait'll you hear it!' howled Teddy.) After a short pause – when, Jeffers was to swear later, the rogue breathed heavily – came the first part of 'it': the most ear-shattering fart yet. This was followed quickly by a deep but distinct groan 'Ah-h-fu-gg-h . . .' for all the world like an expression of sincere relief by a costive docker, as the 'Dr Who' voided its load of suds onto the lino. The lights went out.

'Did you hear that! Did you hear that!' screeched Teddy, outraged, bounding in to launch a kick at the satiated machine. 'Sure wouldn't that wreck the nerves of any dacent married woman. Now either you tame that baste or get it away to hell outa my sight!'

Jeffers had read and heard enough to know that there was no way of taming it. Indeed, as he now told Teddy, they were all very lucky that it had not yet reached the homicidal stage inevitable in such mutations. He quoted instances of householders, crisped to a turn, being flung through windows, crushed against walls . . . of toy poodles fragmented in the spin-dryer. 'The only thing for it,' he declared finally, 'is destruction.'

'I don't give one damn what you do with it,' said Teddy, 'as long as you get it outa here.'

'Well then, if you'd just lend me a hand to hump it down to the van . . .'

'Fuck you and it!'

The last thing he heard of Teddy was his mutton dummies on the stairs as he went to join the missus above.

Luckily all that chassying around had kept 'Dr Who's' castors in good order and Jeffers managed to get it into the van without rupture. Elated, he headed for the Cut without bothering about the other call in Kilbraddock's. No need now; he doubted if Sanders would even enquire about anything else once he learned about the captive rogue; triple-time was assured by the thousand-word article that would blazon the name of Sanders across the middle fold of the trade magazine. The only reason Jeffers decided to do the remaining calls in the 'safe' part of Ballyturdeen was to put in time before returning to Belfast, where the daily bomb-scare traffic chaos would be at its worst.

As the Reservist had said, it was a private estate, neat rows of semi-detached chalet 'Dun Roamins' with no sign of man, woman, child, dog or chimney smoke to denote human habitation.

At his first call the incontinent car in the driveway had a drip-pan underneath to save it soiling the virgin concrete. By a tiny artificial pool among the rose bushes a gnome (one of six) sat fishing, holding his rod, Jeffers noted with delight, at a most suggestive angle. It would be nice to think, he mused while awaiting an answer to his second thunderous knock, that whoever had purchased and placed that obscene dwarf had done so knowingly. But no, never, he decided, reading the varnished-crosscut-of-wood nameplace above the door . . . 'Bali Hai'.

What first drew his gaze upward, Jeffers was to recall later, was the preliminary snick of the catch on the chalet-bedroom window – like a cocked rifle-bolt in the stillness. Then the window wings flew outward, crashing against the brickwork on either side. The upper half of a woman fell out, waving its arms and making a noise like a small ship in a fog. 'Whoooooo . . . Whooooooo . . .'

It had a ball-freezing effect on Jeffers similar to that caused by the staircase scene in Hitchcock's *Psycho*. He gaped up at the mad cuckoo in quilted pink and curlers, paralysed.

'Whoooooooo . . . Whooooooooo . . . Bomber . . .'

All around dogs began to bark, doors slammed, men's voices rumbled . . .

'Whooooooooo . . . bomber . . . Whooooooooo . . .'

All around chalet windows opened and other female throats joined in . . .

'Whoooooooooooooo . . . bomber . . .'

But it was a man's voice, close at hand, that brought Jeffers out of his terrified trance. Whirling round he saw a big man in simmit and dangling braces running down the driveway of the house opposite. The big man shouted again – 'Git him, boys!' – and two dogs, one an Alsatian furred at the neck like a lion, the other a Doberman pinscher, hurdled the hedge and came for Jeffers. Jeffers, his back to Bali Hai's front door, looked wildly round as other doors opened to disgorge other men in police tunics, khaki tunics, combat coats; one brandishing a shot-gun, another ramming a magazine in a Sterling . . . 'Whoooooooooooooooo.'

Jeffers ran. The dogs caught him half-way across the lawn, the Alsatian by the forearm, the Doberman by the ankle, spreadeagling him and beginning a grisly, snarling tug-o'-war over his body. He heard himself screaming, 'Spinduo! Spinduo!' over and over as the dogs wheeled him round and round on the close-shaven grass. And all around a blur of dark-green legs, khaki legs, camouflaged legs as the men tried to get the dogs off him. Eventually they did – but only by dint of clubbing the Alsatian senseless with a pistol butt and rapping the Pinscher on his fulsome testicles.

The men hauled Jeffers to his feet and held him propped between gun muzzles as he babbled, 'Spinduo . . . Spinduo service . . .' The women and children had descended now and were crowding in all around, waving hammers, hatchets and kitchen cleavers, all howling, 'Bomber, bomber, give him to us! Killin's too good for him!' But presently the dog-owner, whom Jeffers recognised by his simmit and braces, spotted the firm's name on his overalls and shouted. 'Here, wait'll I have a dekko at that van.' And all the while Jeffers was being poked and pushed, one berserk lady managing to stretch over the phalanx of menfolk and grab a handful of hair, tugging tenaciously.

The dog-owner swam back into vision, shouting and gesticulating – 'Leave him be, Cynthia. He's only a washing machine man' – and the tension on Jeffers' scalp eased. The crush of bodies around him loosened and he sank down on the grass, the whooping faltered – but then . . . a lone, chilling soprano aria, 'He is, he is, he is,' and, looking up, Jeffers saw Cynthia coming at him over the heads of the men, lips white with spittle, a brass toasting-fork in her fist. Just as the fork seemed inches from Jeffers' eyes the dog-owner plucked Cynthia out of the air and subdued her with a neat right cross to the jaw. But the new screech rose in volume in all sides. 'He is, he is, he is!'

He came to briefly in a speeding, wailing ambulance and saw, in the stretcher opposite, a simmit and dangling braces.

During the following convalescent days the dog-owner (a police constable from whose skull they were removing pieces of a Kenwood mixer) told Jeffers of the terrible scenes after he had passed out on the lawn. The men had formed a square over his body and for half-an-hour had withstood a lynch-mob of their kith-and-kin. Visibly shaken by the memory, this veteran of Bogside battles described the fury with which ladies and offspring had flung themselves against the wall of breadwinners. He'd seen one man, a long service red-cap, being dragged out and garrotted with a garden hose by his wife and married daughter while his fifteen year old son had trampolined on his ulcerated gut; he was now in the intensive care unit. Another casualty had had his nose severed by a pair of hedge shears he himself had sharpened that morning. 'I'm tellin' ye,' said the dog-owner, 'if that patrol hadn't arrived with the CS gas we'd all have had it. That's one thing the bitches can't stand, the gas – it straightens their hair, y'see.'

Sanders came to visit with a bottle of Vichy Water and a copy of *Fortnight*.

'A monstrous fracas, Jeffers,' he said sternly. 'But I managed to keep the company name out of the gutter press.'

'I thought maybe you'd bring me my pay,' complained Jeffers. 'They don't hand out fags on the National Health, y'know. I could do with some of that triple-time.'

'Triple-time!' Sanders laughed. 'For what, Jeffers? Provoking a riot? Oh, I'm not saying it was all your fault; but in cases like this there's always a contributing factor on both sides.'

'And what about the 'Dr Who' in the van? Eh? Isn't that –'

'– A 'Dr Who!' Come, come, Jeffers, you're not yourself yet, I collected the van from the police barracks this morning, and I assure you that there was no 'Dr Who' or anything else in it. Pull yourself together, man.'

'Thievin', fuckin' Peelers!' exclaimed Jeffers. 'I hope it ates them!'

O'Fuzz

'A Turrible Booty is Borneo' I parodied to myself, after
O'Casey, surveying the splendour of it all: wall-to-wall
vinyl tiling; pneumatic armchairs with matching small
table – for coffee or feet – laden with confiscated
stock, *Playboy*, *Knave*, *Armpit*; discreet musak which
at that moment was relaying, appropriately, Eric
Weissburg's banjo-picking from *Bonny and Clyde*.
Approaching the inquiry aperture (really more a
proscenium arch, with subtle concealed lighting) I
admired the open-plan, nothing-up-our-sleeves design
which allowed one, indeed pleaded with one, to view the
back wall of the building through a progression of glass
partitions. In the middle distance a face that could belong
only to a remanded mass-murderer pressed itself against
the glass, glowering, then turned away, swept a match on
the glass and began to light a pipe. It would demand all
the ingenuity of a dedicated sadist, I thought, to so much
as tramp on the toe of a suspect in this environment –
forby the fact that one really heartfelt scream would
mean everyone up to his knees in shattered glass.

I pressed the inquiry button and was at once confronted with as near Miss Ireland as I've ever seen in the
flesh: auburn curls, peaches and cream – with freck-
les – a starched blouse bursting with goodies. 'Can I
help you, Sir?' she asked, genuinely concerned.

Anywhere else, even the Labour Exchange, I'd have
told her candidly just what help she could render me.
But I knew that Policewoman R69 (as God's my judge!)
would be just as likely to bound across the counter and

try out on my soft parts all the nasty things she'd been taught at training depot, so I told her, straight.

A small advert in the previous evening's paper had offered parts for a 1961 Morris van. The address given was a townland in the Ards (the name escapes me now, but it was long and glottal, half-roads between a Gaelic battle-cry and a Planter's curse). In which direction did it lie? I wanted to know, it being in the area served by this station.

R69 rolled the strange name on her lovely tongue for a moment. 'No, I can't say I've ever heard . . . Wait, we'll try this.' She produced a book from under the counter and began to run a rose-coloured fingertip through it. It was a postal codes directory, but suddenly the phrase 'Day Book' loomed to my mind and I remembered the last time I had cause to visit a police barracks – the day we lost Jimmy Gurney's corpse.

'No, I'm afraid it's not here,' sighed R69, pouting deliciously.

'Well, look, it's OK,' I said, 'I'll have a tootle around and ask –'

'– No, no,' she almost shrieked, brown eyes wide with pleading. 'That's what we're here for. These new code books can't be trusted, anyway; the Post Office seems to be making up their own names as they go along. So if you'll just take a seat for a minute I'll get on the R.T. and ask some of the mobiles if they know.'

It would have taken a heart of stone to refuse her. If I'd told her I had THE MAD BOMBER dead and stuffed in the back of the van she couldn't have been more delighted. She scuttled into the room at the back of the counter and began shouting things like 'Roger', 'Charlie' and 'Bravo' into a radio handset.

I went over to the porn-laden coffee table and sat down. There was a girl on the cover of *Armpit* who seemed about to do something quite extraordinary with a Kojak lollipop and I was reaching out for it, intending to see if the experiment was continued within, when I became conscious of the fact that I was being watched.

Looking up, I met the unwavering stare of the pipe-smoking, remanded mass-murderer. He had moved much closer, only two partitions of glass now separating us. Armoured glass, I assured myself; but there was something in that censorious gaze that made a browse in *Armpit* unthinkable, so instead I thought of Jimmy Gurney's lost corpse while I waited . .

One wet Tuesday in 1923 Jimmy had come in on a farm cart from Drumaness, bound for America. Late that same night Mrs Lizzie Tumath had found him sitting on her garden wall, drunk and drenched, all adventure spent. Lizzie, a war widow, had given him a bed, had gone with him the very next morning to sign him on the dole and, that same day, had guided his X on a proposal form for a shilling policy naming her as beneficiary (she was sure he'd never get over the drenching). Which was where I came in, forty years later, as an insurance agent collecting that weekly shilling.

Lizzie, on that second day when Jimmy was booting on death's door, had made the mistake of trying to grease the latch for him with a bumper of hot red biddy. One gulp kindled the coal in Jimmy, and there and then he decided to stay – though on a day-to-day basis, depending on the availability of the elixir. When I first met him he was sixty-eight years of age, his face was Prussian blue and he smelt like the Outpatients in the Royal Victoria hospital, inflation having long ago driven him to the meths – and worse. It was a bad tin of Kiwi dubbin, melted in hot water with sugar added, that finished him off in July, 1965.

I was on holiday when it happened, and I returned to find Lizzie Tumath camping on my doorstep with the shilling policy in her claw.

'Poor Jimmy's gone,' she keened, eyes streaming.

'Where?' I asked, knowing bloody well where. 'Back to Drumaness? They'll never have him after all this time.'

'Now none of yer smart Aleck stuff wi' me,' screeched Lizzie, suddenly businesslike. 'I've had dealings with youse graveyard bookies before. Yer not gonta flannel me outa my money this time.'

'Where's the death certificate?'

'I dunno. The Peelers came an' took him away an' that's the last I heard or seen of him. But he was as dead as mutton.'

Jimmy had been dead in his room for three days before Lizzie smelt him. And when Lizzie had gone screaming into the street in the traditional way, a police patrol car had just happened to be passing. They had radioed for an ambulance, collected Jimmy's bits and pieces of personal things, and that's the last Lizzie saw of them or Jimmy.

So it was up to me to find out what had happened to Jimmy's corpse and who had certified death. (If death, in fact, had occurred; the petro-chemical vintages have been known to cause a condition called 'Temporary Death', a classic case being that of a Brasso victim in the Short Strand who sat bolt upright in his coffin and snatched a bottle of stout from the lips of a waking relative.) Having ascertained the barracks to which the police patrol belonged, I called in to inquire with some trepidation, knowing how they felt about intruders.

At that time the duty room in every urban police barracks had a billiard-hall atmosphere, consisting mainly of plug tobacco and male B.O. plus a nuance of Sloan's Liniment; a place where heavyweight boxers, shot-putters and javelin hurlers put in time between training sessions. There was always one man with his tunic on, the duty-man who dealt with the odd inquirer at the minute hatchway – though he, I suppose, could have been trouserless. The rest lounged about in various stages of undress, from shirt-sleeves through simmit and braces to the occasional dressing gown. They sprawled in armchairs, sat on tables or held up walls, all exuding an aura of dozy well-being. The general impression, I'd often thought, was that of a crew of shipwrecked stokers taking their ease in the fo'c'sle of the rescue vessel – except, that is, for the row of .45 elephant guns hanging by their trigger guards from a rack on the wall.

The duty man on that day was a young fellow, not long out of the depot by the look of him; but he had learnt a trick or two already. For instance, when I rapped the hatch – causing a sudden silence within – and he stuck his head out, he didn't say, 'Can I help you, Sir' or even 'Yes?' He said 'Well?' in a manner which left no doubt that the next, unspoken phrase was, 'what have you been up to?' The motley of athletes in the background glowered at me and flexed their biceps.

I explained my problem. His response was another question. 'What business is that of yours?' The biceps stirred approvingly. I told him, whereupon he grinned, glanced over his shoulder and said, 'Well, you'll hardly find your man here!' The biceps shuddered with mirth.

'Yes, I realise that,' I said evenly. 'But perhaps you could tell me to which hospital or morgue he was taken. Your men must have kept a record, mustn't they?'

I could see that nobody liked my tone of voice. Obviously the depot had not prepared the lad for such repartee, for he flushed up, recoiled a step back from the hatch, and then looked towards the biceps appealingly. From these there erupted a rumble of growls out of which I discerned the phrase 'Day Book'. The lad ducked down behind the hatch and came up with a grubby double-entry ledger which I could see was ruled five days to a page.

'When was it, you said?' he asked.

'Last Wednesday afternoon about three o'clock.'

It took three minutes of thumb licking and page turning to find last Wednesday. A triumphant cry issued from the lad as he stabbed a blank space with his forefinger. 'There y'are – nothing.'

'Nothing at all happened last Wednesday?' I asked incredulously.

'See for yourself,' he said contemptuously, swirling the book round. I saw that not only had nothing happened on Wednesday but also that Monday, Tuesday, Thursday and Friday had been equally unfull of events.

'Try back ...' This, accompanied by a gust of Old

Crowbar, made both of us jump. Unnoticed by us a large grey man fully clothed in withered tweed had sidled up to the lad's elbow. His presence, I could see, unnerved the lad. 'Yessir,' he said, and his hand trembled slightly as he began to leaf through the book. 'Sir' leaned over his shoulder, now and then trapping a turning page with the stem of his pipe to read an entry. And each time, I noticed, a small puddle of brown spittle trickled from the mouthpiece onto the page. It was just as well there weren't many entries in that book; one hour's good drying and it would have been as solid as a brick.

'Here!' cried the lad suddenly, pointing. They both perused the entry, 'Sir's' pipe voiding its most extensive deposit yet. Then the lad looked up and said to me, 'Here's two oul' maids gassed themselves in Botanic Avenue Wednesday three weeks ago?'

That question mark is no slip of the pen. He was asking.

'Sir' straightened up, replaced his pipe between his teeth, and they both stared at me, awaiting my reply. I knew I had been check-mated. Certainly I could turn on my heel and walk away; but any reply I made now would trigger the inevitable denouement. Half in admiration of their cunning, I decided to go the whole hog.

'You mean,' I said quietly, 'that I can have the two old maids *instead* of Jimmy Gurney?'

You could see the tension go out of them. The lad gave something like a sigh and 'Sir' grunted contentedly, applying a match to his dead pipe. They looked at one another for a moment, and then 'Sir' nodded and turned away as if to say, 'It's your case, son.'

The lad was on sure ground now. He closed the Day Book with a resounding splash; he reached up and took the edge of the hatchway shutter in both hands; he fixed me with an icy stare. 'None of yer oul' lip now,' he said in a voice loaded with practised menace and a good octave deeper than his normal key. He then banged the hatch closed. As I walked away, beaten, but with an odd feeling of satisfaction, I heard an outburst of applause from inside the duty room.

114

Eventually I found the still glowing remains of Jimmy Gurney in the City Hospital morgue and gave him such a slap-up funeral that there was very little of the claims money left over for Lizzie Tumath.

Meanwhile, back in the New Look '70s, the remanded mass-murderer had submerged behind the glazing again. I reached for *Armpit*.

'Hello . . . Sir . . . I say, Sir . . .'

It was R69 at the counter, beckoning. I rose and obeyed – at the same time, a completely unconscious action, folding and stuffing *Armpit* into my hip pocket.

'I'm sorry to keep you,' she said breathlessly, 'but I'm waiting for a reply to your query from one of our mobiles. He's asking someone down the peninsula.'

'It's really not worth the bother,' I protested.

A crackle of verbal static arose from the radio room. 'That'll be him now,' cried R69, already in flight.

In her path between counter and radio room there was a door, a narrowish door leading onto a corridor, and once through it she had to negotiate a sharp left-hand turn. She was in the process of doing this, at top speed in Charlie Chaplin fashion, with one foot in the air while performing a sort of hopping skid on the other, when something extraordinary occurred. From nowhere, out of the floor it seemed, a hand and arm appeared. It swept up and under R69's short skirt from behind, catching her at the very apex of her manoeuvre, causing her to shriek and topple away out of my view. But almost at once she was back, framed in the doorway, little fists clenched on hips, stamping her foot, blushing madly and fairly spluttering with rage – all directed at some presence in the corridor hidden from me. 'Sergeant, you're . . . oh you're an awful . . .'

Then he was in the doorway, filling it, my remanded mass-murderer! Tired tweed with oxter bulge, brown boots. Old Crowbar . . . Oh God!

'Who's this?' he growled, meaning me, paying no heed

at all to R69's anguished bleating. He lumbered over to the counter, looking as if poised to vault it if I broke and ran. I caught a whiff of that sweaty-sheep smell that arises only from Long Johns at that stage of fission just before they have to be amputated. He took the pipe from his mouth and flicked it, projecting a jagged trail of spittle onto the dove-coloured floor.

'He's only looking for directions,' said R69 protectively, making a face behind his back. 'He wants to get to . . .' she spoke the name of the townland.

'Is that all he wants! Sure that's easy,' said the sergeant. Then he addressed me. 'And who would you be wanting up that way, Billy?'

'My name isn't Billy,' I replied, moving my first pawn in a game, I knew, doomed to end the one way possible.

'Oh, isn't it . . . Well, anyway, I'll tell you the best way to get to that particular quarter. Just you drive about two mile out on the north road, stop at the first unmarked crossroads, get out of the car, shout "Up The Rebels!" and before you know it that place you're looking for will come looking for you!' He laughed and waves of Old Crowbar lapped over me. R69 smiled obsequiously. 'What d'you think of that for a joke, Paddy? I'm thinking of sending it to the papers.'

'My name isn't Paddy,' I stated recklessly.

'Ah sure we'll get to know your name soon enough; that's part of the joke, y'see,' he said jovially. 'Is that oul van outside yours? The one with no tax disc, baldy tyres all round, one headlamp gone and the handbrake cable trailing on the road?'

I nodded philosophically.

'You'll be sorry to hear that it's been towed to the pound for further investigation. I wouldn't be surprised if they found bits of old people sticking in that front grille.' He turned to R69 and beamed. 'So there you are. Problem solved: he's not going anywhere so he doesn't need to know the direction of where he intended to go.'

R69 looked sheepish and avoided my eye. At that moment I had the chance to go, silently, and perhaps retain her sympathy. But, as before, I couldn't . . .

'Thank you, sergeant,' I said. 'I realize that it's all for my own good and that of the general public at large. And I know that you are only doing your duty in the finest tradition of the Irish Constabulary.'

He grinned and removed his pipe. Her eyes, suddenly wintry, met mine. And they came in together on the cue like Jeanette McDonald and Nelson Eddy in *Rose Marie*.

'None of yer oul lip now!'

Cromwell's Day (The 1st of April)

Father Coyle stood in the bay window of the chapel house and gazed down over a bank of fuchsia ablaze in the morning sun, to the white cluster of the village below, to the calm amethyst sea and the shadowy islands lurking in the morning mist. He raised his eyes up beyond the islands to the wastes that spread unhindered to that farther shore and crossed himself, murmuring an aspiration. In Boston it would be nearly midday; his sister Patsy, the children at school, would be at her job in the local hypermarket; his brother Sean would be touring in his patrol car; and brother-in-law Frank, a Christian Brother, grappling with a cage of fourteen-year-olds. Father Coyle always liked to think they remembered this hour and responded to his blessing . . . But he doubted it.

The door behind him opened and the widow O'Malley, his housekeeper, came in bearing a creel of turf for the fire.

'Isn't that the fine morning, Mrs O'Malley,' said the Father, stretching himself in the window. 'Sure if you were to die now and wake up on a morning like this in a place like this, you wouldn't give a damn if God turned out to be a Protestant after all.'

The widow groaned to her knees beside the grate and said: 'God forgive you, Father.' Mr O'Malley, a ganger with Wimpey's, had smothered to death in a trench near Scunthorpe five years ago, whereupon Mrs O'Malley, at thirty-eight years of age, had fallen into the role of Priest's housekeeper as though groomed by the best coaches in Hollywood. 'I think maybe you're after forgettin' what day it is, you're so fond of it,' she said.

'The second into the fourth week of Lent, thank God,' sighed Father Coyle, casting a longing glance at the padlocked brandy cupboard.

'It's Cromwell's day.' Saying this, Mrs O'Malley settled back on her haunches and watched the back of his neck in anticipation. She wasn't disappointed. He spun round, just managing to grab the cigarette as it fell from his slackened lips, all tranquillity gone; from cold grey asceticism to the purple sweats in one second flat.

'It's never that!' he cried, dashing for the calendar.

'It is,' said the widow coolly. 'Didn't I see with me own eyes Abu Ben gittin' out the number one Mercedes this mornin', an' himself all done up in his Ballsbridge best, off to Westport to meet the eleven o'clock.'

Father Coyle groaned and punched the calendar. There it was, marked with a red skull-and-crossbones in his own hand: "Cromwell". He must be getting old. 'How long will it take them from Westport, d'you think?' he asked.

'No more than four bottles of stout, with Abu Ben in his number one yoke,' replied the widow.

Anthony Joseph O'Malley, alias Abu Ben, was an eighth cousin of the widow and the nearest the Barony had to a jet set. A self-made man, from a standing start as a navvy with McAlpine's Own he had created 'Western Manpower Services', otherwise known as 'Muckshifters Unlimited', supplying labour to the English construction business. In his home place he had been called 'Abu Ben' ever since his fourth cousin, the schoolmaster O'Malley, had given a public lecture elucidating the Arab role in the African slave trade. He owned three Mercedes and the best hotel in the county.

Father Coyle gazed out the window again, trying to recapture that earlier mood. But now the blue helmets of the Twelve Pins of Connemara seemed to threaten across the bay, like a besieging army. A light wind had risen to set the fuchsia quivering nervously and carry up from the shore a cloying stench from the rotting carcasses of last season's sharks. Of the village that had sparkled, all he could see now was a cluster of television aerials and the entire resident male population, four spavined ex-navvies and the postman, making their unhurried way to O'Malley's bar. It must be pension day again . . . and near ten o'clock . . . an hour and a half to Cromwell . . .

Then he spotted Mary O'Malley herself coming down the main road. She looked up at the chapel house, as she always did, and waved, raven strands of waist-length hair streaming out in the wind. The priest smiled and waved back, his old heart warmed by the sight.

'There's Mary now,' he said; and murmured to himself: 'Grainne . . .'

'How many has she?' asked the widow, now recharging the oil lamps that were the hamlet's only source of light, electricity having been held up three miles east in a bog and bankruptcy this ten years.

'Two,' replied Father Coyle. 'Oh, and she's just dropped into the post office so that'll make five.'

'Includin' her own, that's only six. Five to go for Cromwell,' said the widow ominously.

Father Coyle frowned, watching as Mary emerged from the post office and continued up the road with the five young ones scampering round her, all done up in their party best . . . The Pride of the county, he mused; a runner-up in the 'Rose of Tralee' beauty stakes; a singing hostess in Bunratty Castle; and at the heels of the hunt, one single solitary child! . . . Oh he'd warned her often enough, from the first he'd heard of it to the very day of the wedding, against having anything to do with a Currane O'Malley. He remembered telling her, his head bowed with embarrassment, about the scandal of the wild goats and their exile to the desolate wastes of Currane over a century ago. And when he had raised his head she had been smiling that transcendental smile of hers, revealing the full glory of the most flawless set of teeth in the four provinces. 'I've often wondered what driv' the poor craturs wild,' she had murmured softly.

Oh, she was a charmer, all right, the same Mary O'Malley.

'It's a bit like Al Capone, when you think of it,' said the widow, giving the Blessed Martin a buff with the grate polish.

'What?' snapped Father Coyle testily. The widow had a way of lurking quietly, as though tapping his thoughts.

'The goat O'Malley gittin' caught like that, after all the hot water he's been in.'

It irritated Father Coyle to hear her use the expression. There had been a time, not so long ago, when a virgin girl or a woman with child would have run a mile across the bog sooner than pass a 'Goat' O'Malley on the road. Unspeakable as it was, their original crime was as nothing to the near-Satanic myths that had gathered around them since. No fisherman would crew a boat with a 'Goat' O'Malley; no one buy or take milk from a beast that had been owned by the black tribe . . . Yet, despite all, the Currane O'Malley, like the Hebrew of old, had thriven in adversity. Where others had stayed, they had gone out in the wide world and made their mark as builders, politicians, policemen, shop-stewards, always on the top rung of the ladder. Mary's 'Goat' was no exception.

'Hot water, is it,' said Father Coyle: 'Boilin' oil more like. You'd think with this Cromwell thing going on he'd have the decency to lie low for a bit. But no, not the boul O'Malley. Sure wasn't it only yesterday I heard him mentioned on the English news, up to his dirty neck in some strike or other. 'Wildcat' O'Malley, they're callin' him now – the Bolshevik heathen! If it was anybody else but Mary I'd let them throw the key away on him.'

'There she is now, the darlin',' groaned the widow, now beside him at the window. 'And with a full house at her heels.'

Father Coyle counted the distant heads and sighed 'Ten it is – and the eldest scrapin' fourteen – a well-balanced litter if ever I saw one.'

Priest and housekeeper watched the procession disappear up the road in the direction of Mary's cottage. Then the widow, glancing at the clock, said: 'Better make a move yerself, Father, for if Abu Ben's in a good way of goin' yis'll have Cromwell roun' yer necks before you can spit.'

'I suppose I'd better. What'll I wear, d'you think?'

'The full regimentals, if I was you,' the widow advised. 'He's probably some class of Christian Scientist, an' there's nothin' like a bit of the oul purple an' gold when yer dealin' with that sort.'

But when Father Coyle made his way down the hill fifteen minutes later he was soberly clad in decent broadcloth – though he had retained his biretta in deference to the Widow's theory.

Mary's cottage was a brave step from the village, up the road that followed the lip of the cliff above the cauldron of seething water known as The Ganch's Mouth, a wild fulcrum of currents that had claimed more local lives than the Great Hunger itself. And then, as he paused at the half-way mark up the steep incline, there arose before the old Priest a sight that never failed to lift his heart, looming like a great jagged tooth on the far foreland, evanescent through a scrim of seaspume: Grainne's Keep, the ruined fortress of the ancient sea-witch, Grace O'Malley. At times like this he could picture her standing on the high battlements, raven hair wind-blown, fine white teeth bared in defiance of her sea-borne ravishers, Albion's pirates . . .

But fancy thrives on lack of oxygen, and, as always, when his breath returned the vision vanished. Looking back down the road he saw his housekeeper on her way up, cowled in her Grandmother's black shawl. In discussing the matter, the widow had wanted to go the whole hog and wear the traditional red petticoat and pampooties; but he had decided that that might be carrying it all a bit too far.

Mary herself met him at the garden gate. From inside the cottage came a terrible hullabaloo of squealing children and crashing delft. 'God, Father, they're a wild lot!'

she gasped. Though obviously under a strain she looked, as ever, a patriot's dream of Celtic maidenhood – and dressed at the height of Cleveland, Ohio, fashion, her sister in that city being very free with the parcels.

Father Coyle saw at once that it would never do for Cromwell, and told her so. It being in its way a compliment, she agreed, saying that she had just the thing in mind. But in doing so she treated him to one of her shy, dazzling smiles, and with a sinking heart he saw the impossibility of it all: in a beggar's rags she'd still be a Queen.

Just then a piercing whistle drew their attention down the road to where the widow stood, pointing dramatically across the bay. They looked and saw, on the road beyond the village where it squeezes through the great cleft in the mountain called 'The Westport Gap', a flash of sunlight reflected on the chromium maw of Abu Ben's number one Mercedes.

'Sacred Heart! It's them!' cried Mary, and ran indoors.

Father Coyle stood his ground by the garden gate. The cloud of dust that was Abu Ben had almost reached the village when the cowled widow panted up beside him. 'The rate that idjit's coming there'll not be a hen layin' between here an' Westport for a week,' she said.

'I trust Mr Cromwell has a strong stomach,' said the Priest.

But obviously Mr Cromwell had not . . . When the car screeched to a halt he was the first out. A small grey man in a brass-buttoned blazer, he stood still for a moment, his eyes closed as though in prayer. Then the driver's door opened and Abu Ben all but fell out. Father Coyle saw that the cocktail cabinet situated beneath the dashboard in front of the wheel – a unique extra – was open and in use.

'God blesh all here!' cried Abu Ben. 'Father Coyle, let me introduce Mister Nigel Cromwell of her gracious Majesty's Inland Revenue.'

Cromwell came round the car unsteadily, clutching a

123

briefcase to his chest as if it were a lifebelt. The emblem on the briefcase, Father Coyle noted with disgust, was the crown of England. You'd think they'd have the wit to make him cart his bits and pieces under plain cover. But sure, what could you expect, sending somebody called Cromwell in the first place.

'Good morning, Padre,' said Cromwell, smiling wanly and extending his hand, oblivious to the sudden flush of fury to the 'Padre's' face. It was all Father Coyle could do to touch the proffered hand briefly. The widow crushed in almost between them, scanning the visitor's face intently, looking for the wart.

Cromwell went on: 'I'm sorry my first visit to your beautiful country has to be on such an unsavoury errand; but as you've been informed, the matter of Dermot O'Malley's returns is one of three test cases to do with a very serious case of mass fraud, and your government has given permission –'

'Say no more,' commanded Father Coyle. 'Sure the last visit by one of your tribe was every bit as unsavoury, but we overed it. The woman of the house is inside, if you'll follow us.'

Cromwell did, though looking slightly mystified. Going in out of the bright sunlight, it took a moment for their eyes to adjust. The children were lined round the walls, silent and motionless now. Mary herself was a shadow at the end of the room.

'Well, Mister Cromwell, here's what you've come all this way to see,' said Father Coyle, indicating the children: 'eleven little O'Malley's. And this is Mrs O'Malley herself.'

Mary came forward into the half-light of the window. The Priest looked – and couldn't believe his eyes. Behind him he heard the widow gasp. Could it really be Mary, this hatchet-faced creature swaddled in dirty Aran? She didn't speak, her mouth puckered and her cheeks clapped in as though sucking through a straw. God! she could be fifty if a day. Then he remembered Bunratty Castle and Mary astride the small harp . . .

Make-up! That was it! – the actor's art; an illusion created by colour and light.

Cromwell was saying: 'I hope you'll pardon the intrusion, Mrs O'Malley; a mere legal formality.'

A mere five minutes later, shaking hands with Father Coyle at the gate, Mr Cromwell said: 'That husband of hers must be Peter Pan. He looks half her age.'

'Dermot's a Currane O'Malley,' said Father Coyle darkly, 'and they age only when they've a mind to.'

Mr Cromwell looked uncomfortable. 'Well, that's the matter cleared up satisfactorily, Padre. I'll be off.'

The Father watched Abu Ben's number one well down the road before re-entering the cottage, again a bedlam of shrieking children. The widow and Mary were standing giggling by the window where he'd left them. They appeared to be looking at something in Mary's hand, and what with the noise of the children they didn't notice until the Priest was upon them . . . 'Mary, you were tremendous!' he cried. 'How in heaven –'

He stopped dead, his question answered by the object in Mary's hand, which she tried unsuccessfully to conceal; a glass of water out of the depths of which the glory of Grainne smiled eerily up at him . . . Mary clapped a hand over her mouth and ran to the kitchen. The widow looked at Father Coyle's face and burst into peals of laughter. Dazed, he turned to the cottage window in time to see a cloud of dust disappear over the Westport Gap.

'Curse you, Cromwell,' groaned Father Coyle.

Chinese Knackers

On the second morning of my stay with the Bard in his seaside fastness I stayed safe in my 1943 issue kapok sheath (stencilled 'Pte. 1st class S. Kowalski. 2nd Tennessee's Own') and read *Porterhouse Blue* by Mr Tom Sharpe, In the next room a guitarist from the Holy Land screamed intermittently – a bad case of hot curry and cold porter (sic.). Outside, the perennial gale carried sods of turf from Donegal ten miles across the bay and hurled them against embattled window shutters. Around the foot of the house the Atlantic clamoured like a lynch mob and in the living-room below the Rolling Stones played hell (in person – it had been some party). And above all, suddenly, a piercing shriek as, I learnt later, the woman next door discovered what the guitarist had done nocturnally all over her Georgian doorstep . . . As the Bard said later, in mitigation, while picking two dead tits out of the mess: 'At least your milk will be safe from them in future.'

My own quiet death seemed imminent. It must be the strong air, I decided; all that iodine being forced into and up every bodily orifice, ridding the bloodstream of a life time's homoeopathic resistance. A scathing experience indeed for lungs that not so long ago had fluttered in distress when taken outside a quarter-mile radius of the Belfast gas-works . . . A door banged nearby and I prayed that it wasn't the cook; one whiff of bacon essence would finish me off for sure. Thankfully, it was the guitarist; he fell downstairs, screaming; I heard him hit every fret all the way to the ground floor.

In the middle of chapter nine I had to let *Porterhouse Blue* fall. I had tried harnessing each painful guffaw, eking it out through clenched teeth, but it had merely spread the agony. (Unclenching, I discovered that the clenching itself had been an illusion; my tongue, a strip of flayed, nerveless rubber, had been between my teeth all along.) I assumed the foetal position, belongings in hand, and for a time was distracted by a display put on by multi-coloured liver spots on the insides of my eyelids. But presently this took a menacing turn, the whirling atoms tending to explode suddenly and painfully. So instead I lay on my back and stared at the ceiling, thinking of Tom Sharpe, Bishop McNamara and Aggie Smiley's Arseless Wonder.

He was yellow – the Wonder, not the Bishop – a good head taller than Aggie, and had, as Uncle remarked, little or no rear end. Of course the uniform of the US navy does tend to give its wearers that kipper-hipped look, but Aggie's captor sticks in my mind as being inordinately deprived – perhaps because he was a sturdy banty in other ways. I particularly remember the whiteness of his teeth clamped on a big black cigar as Aggie and he rounded the corner of River Street, Aggie hanging on his arm like a skin bucket.

'Poor wee bugger,' sighed Uncle as they disappeared into Aggie's house. 'She'll blow him out in bubbles. She'll kill him stone dead.'

At the time I didn't understand what Uncle meant. The year was 1943. I was fourteen, school-leaving age, and was being allowed to get my shoulder moulded to the corner in preparation for manhood. I knew that the other Aggie, the one in Gas Works Lane who read tea-cups, poisoned people regularly; but this Aggie had always seemed benign enough. An orphan, she lived alone in the middle one of seven terrace houses in River Street, a short cul-de-sac bounded by the river Lagan. People, especially other women, called her 'poor' Aggie, and I once heard my eldest sister say that she was an 'unclaimed treasure', though she couldn't have been much over thirty at the time.

But that was before Pearl Harbour; by 1943 very few baubles, no matter how antique, went unclaimed for long in the Plaza ballroom. The Wonder, a cook off a cruiser in for a three-day repair job, wasn't Aggie's first claimant, nor was he her last, but he was certainly the most memorable. It was well into the third day before he emerged from Aggie's house, alone, and wiggled past the corner and out of our lives forever, oblivious to the furore he had caused in the interim.

Ten years were to pass before I learnt the full story, and only then because of a bad batch of elderberry wine. The harrowing economics of the first six months of married life had made me a home-brew addict, so when a workmate offered the season's crop of elderberries from his allotment behind Windsor Park football ground I jumped at the chance to experiment. Which is why, six weeks later, Uncle and I spent an entire Saturday afternoon flushing ten gallons of blood-red, undrinkable vinegar down our lavatory, pint by slow pint.

I had recently moved into one of the seven terraces in River Street, in fact the one next door to Aggie's (though she was long gone, having married a hero home from Burma in 1946 and produced a child a year since). I had known all about the damp walls, the bugs, the aggressive mice; what I was now discovering, pint by slow pint, was the terrible inadequacy of our sewage system.

The houses had been built by a local mill owner before the invention of the water closet – you could still see the marks of old cesspit walls in the backyards. When it became legally necessary for him to install the new machine the mill owner, true to form, had improvised everything bar the article itself. A shoulder-high, doorless, brick and corrugated-iron kennel enclosed the throne ('Six fut high!' I can hear him scream. 'Yis'll bankrupt me! Sure they'll be sittin' down ...'). If it rained you had to wear a cap. And when it came to laying a main disposal pipe along the seven houses to the river the old gentleman really had cut his corners.

'Two-inch guttering must have been on offer that

year,' said Uncle gloomily, dribbling elderberry into the bowl. 'Or maybe he thought the serfs wouldn't ate so much if they kept getting it back up every time they pulled the chain.'

The next morning, Sunday, the wife went off to Kirk and left me in bed with a hangover and *The News of the World*. On the pavement outside she was accosted by Old Sarah, who lived in the end house next to the river bank. The bedroom window was open an inch or two and I heard every word . . .

Old Sarah: 'Here . . . is yer man all right?'
Wife: 'Oh aye. The usual stocious headache, that's all. What makes you ask?'
Old Sarah: 'Well, niver come over this, mind . . . but there's somebody along this row knockin' on death's door.'
Wife: 'Who? . . . I can't think of anybody that's that bad.'
Old Sarah: 'I dunno. But since last night every time I pull my chain their lifesblood comes bubblin' up the bowl at me.'

The wife, who had helped in the latter stages of elderberry disposal, made some sort of incoherent reply and clattered off up the street.

Old Sarah, said to be well over ninety, lived alone. She had left Tyrone as a girl to work in the city house of the family that owned the local mill – but Tyrone had never left her. She looked like a character in the foreground of one of those brown photographs in a book about life on the Blasket islands – navy-blue collarless blouse, long aproned skirt and men's boots – and she always kept a pig or two fattening in the backyard and along the sloping river bank. For generations the children of the district, whom Sarah hated without fear or favour, had been reared in the belief that if caught trespassing on that part of the bank which Old Sarah considered hers they would end up in a sow's belly.

'Poor oul Sarah,' said Uncle when I told him about the

129

'lifesblood'; 'she never knows what's gonna happen when she pulls that chain – especially when the river's high an' nothing's gettin' away. Like that time Aggie Smiley's Yankee Chinaman killed the Countess.' It was then, prompting him, that I heard the full story of the ruction ten years before.

Aggie and her navy cook had been closeted for two full days (Uncle and the other cornerboys being greatly entertained by the range and variety of Aggie's vocal ecstasy trumpeting from the front bedroom). It was well into the morning of the third day when Old Sarah came running up the street, screeching: 'The Countess is dead! . . . They've kilt the Countess, the cruel wee buggers! . . . They knew she'd ate them.'

Uncle and the others hurried down to her house and found that The Countess (Markievicz), a prize sow, was indeed dead, lying trotters up in the two inches of river water and assorted sewage that covered the yard.

'As soon as I pulled the chain up they came . . . hunnerds of them . . . all the colours of the rainbow,' sobbed Sarah.

Uncle counted seven of the lethal objects still floating in the scum – baby-blue, yellow, tangerine . . .

'Wouldn't you wonder where the wee ghetts would get that many balloons in wartime,' keened Sarah.

Uncle and company left quickly without a word and poor Old Sarah went to her grave convinced that the Countess had been the victim of a devilish plot by the children of the neighbourhood. The next morning our local butcher bought the cadaver and in the course of his dissection found eleven more foreign bodies lodged in the gullet.

For me the revelation brought to mind the scene at the corner of River Street when Aggie Smiley's arseless cook had minced past on that third day, a big black cigar between his grinning teeth. I had never understood why the entire complement of the corner, on Uncle's cue, had removed their caps and stood to attention as he passed by . . . 'There's seven hunnerd million of them wee

130

huers,' I remember Uncle saying as the jaunty figure disappeared from view, '– an' now yis know who done most of the work.'

Thirty years later, under the Bard's quaking roof, the memory was painful – worse than Tom Sharpe, for it made me suddenly aware of my bladder. Struggling out of the tube I opened the bedroom door . . . and there on the landing, in strength, was the bacon . . . the smoked bacon.

The next fifteen minutes in the bog opposite were very debilitating. But on returning to the bedroom I discovered with careful joy that the storm had packed it in. I could hear the chug-chug of the first tourist buses idling in the street outside. Through a crack in the shutters I saw a double-decker with a banner along its side which said: 'Cullybackey Co-operative Guild', and I knew that the Bard was up and doing his daily nude calisthenics on the second-floor front balcony. (His critics and rivals allege that he has a financial arrangement with the local Tourist Board.)

An hour later I met him on the stairs and we ran past the kitchen, holding our noses, into the street. We visited an ice-cream parlour where I watched him devour a double Knickerbocker Glory, his normal summer breakfast. Afterwards we followed a clear trail of blood, porter and curry which led to the beach area. Behind a line of bathing boxes the guitarist from the Holy Land had an elderly deckchair attendant by the throat, lecturing him on the merits of the Gibson D 18. We wiped the man down and delivered the guitarist to a nearby nursing home where the Bard gets stomach-pump facilities at cost.

I craved antibiotics, any sort, so our next stop was a chemist's shop. On the counter, to one side, stood a dispenser of 'Multi-hued Ticklers'. Above it, incorporated in the display, was a blown-up photograph of a well-known fundamentalist clergyman who urged: 'Plan – the Protestant Way!'. His words were trapped in a lip bubble, cartoon fashion. The shape of the bubble was a stroke of genius, very much in keeping with message and product.

Behind the counter sat a cool-looking girl, buffing her nails with a rough lolly stick.

'And a very good morning to you,' boomed the Bard. He gave the 'Tickler' dispenser a hearty thump and asked, 'How's stocks?'

Without looking up from her nails or missing a stroke the assistant replied: 'Medium, Large and Outsized only. Try Woolworth's down the street.'

Sects

As always, the journey into the city centre wound him up to High Doh – despite his having breakfasted on three Valiums, a dosage usually reserved for Speech Days, Sports Days, Interviews with Parents and 'Chinwags' with the Head. Bad enough the half-hour wait at the bus-stop in that degree of windblown rain called 'spittin''. Infinitely worse, the hour-long tour of the city's hellish inner circle which included a thirty-five minute dawdle behind the paramilitary cortege of some martyred racketeer, all to a leit-motif of aggressive obscenity and Wunnerful Radio One from an entire stream of Intermediate truants in the back seats. But mind-blowing, at the heels of the hunt, to be told by a semi-literate bitch in the music library that she'd 'niver heard tell of' the great Festy O'Spoon, last of the singing thatchers of West Tyrone!

For one fuming moment, facing her across the counter, he wanted nothing more than to emulate that highly-strung local poet who, faced with like bovinity over a book, had leapt up on the counter and viciously sandalled his tormentor in the throat . . . But he didn't; instead he delivered a short impassioned lecture on what he thought of so-called librarians who professed ignorance of a man whose divine ornamentation was the talk of the folksong world. In the middle of it he observed her pressing a bell behind the counter and thought she had been moved to seek a higher opinion on the matter. It wasn't until later that he connected this action with the thick-set, uniformed person who appeared at his elbow, grasped it in a most excruciating way and began to propel him towards the door.

'Come on, Shakespeare, that's enough dirty verse outa you for one day,' growled the veteran squaddie, depositing him in the corridor, completely ignoring his protests. Two other uniformed men were passing at the time and he heard one say: 'Another bloody poet,' and the other reply: 'That's the third this week. They're getting to be worse than the winos.'

It was then he lost his temper. He tried to get back in, but the brute had locked the door and now stood inside making shooing motions as he, outside, pummelled the plate-glass panelling. The cow at the counter stuck out her tongue. Dazed with wrath, noticing that the pane of glass level with his mouth had become slightly misted, he wrote '!TIHS' with his fingertips. (Later, contemplating the mindless dexterity of the act, purely reflex, he marvelled again at the durability of small skills learnt in childhood. The postman, he remembered, had been particularly vulnerable to that sort of window graffiti on cold mornings. Then, of course, there had been an E in the composition and no exclamation mark, American literary influence having eradicated the former and Grammar School and University supplying the latter.)

The cow gaped; the bemedalled bouncer shook his fist and started towards the door; he turned away, intending to get offside quickly, and found himself to be the focal point of a small gallery of spectators. And there in the front row lolled the sixth-formers Davis and Kyle, hanging on to one another, faces red with bottled guffaw . . . At that moment he was as near suicide as he would ever be.

Minutes later, in a cafe opposite the library, he gulped stewed tea and tried to calm himself. What he really craved was a large Bushmills, but all the nearby pubs were in ruins and to stray too far from the centre meant breaching some ghetto where one whisky, or merely asking for the wrong brand, could be your death.

It was a total disaster, he knew. Davis and Kyle would

have a highly coloured version going the rounds of the school in the morning and the Head and his terrible wife would be discussing it over dinner in the evening. It would mean, at the very least, another 'chinwag'; and coming so soon after the one about the concert it would not look well on his file . . . 'Considering the present – ah-volatile situation, Mr Chambers, and considering also the-ah-religious and political background of our establishment, your choice of song might seem to some to have been somewhat-ah-perverse . . .' While not relishing the prospect of another session with that silver-haired pomposity, it was the one which would surely follow he dreaded most . . .

'Fourteen verses in Gaelic!' his wife had shrieked after the concert. 'Fourteen verses about Fenian sheep drowning in some Kulchie bog! You must be out of your bloody mind! Do you realise you were standing up there for a full half-hour with your hand cupped round your lug!'

It had been the worst yet. His quiet protestations regarding the content of *Ana Cuen* had merely brought her to the brink of physical attack. As she towered over him he had kept calm by telling himself that somewhere inside that muscular bulk in the bottle-green uniform still lived the shy tourist in the National Folk Culture who had played her way into his heart on the mountain dulcimer. That had been in their early days, before another aspect of the National Culture had caused her ancestral farm in Fermanagh to burn down. The very next day she had joined the full-time Police Reserve and had purchased – illegally – the .22 automatic which she carried, the holster attached to an old suspender belt, inside her regulation knickers (where his weapon, incidentally, had not been allowed in many a day).

And now this . . . At the height of her fury that last time it had crossed his mind that, if provoked much further, she might shoot him. There was plenty of precedent for private mayhem on the male side, he mused, from that heroic UDR man, off-duty and rutting on the side of the Cave Hill, who had winged three peeping-Toms without dismounting, to the scores of would-be music hall artistes who had tried to shoot cigarettes from the mouths of their dear ones. Should he phone anonymously and tell them about the gun in her knickers before she learnt of the library fiasco?

At this point in his forebodings an altercation outside the cafe attracted his attention. A security gate bisected the pavement just abreast of the window at which he sat. A large foul-mouthed lady appeared to have been touched up the wrong way by one of the 'civilian' searchers. The searchers, of course, disdained to rise to her abuse. They stood around in various attitudes of martial unease, the men twirling the waxed moustachios that were all the rage with the uniformed population, blinkered by cap peaks that rested on the bridge of each nose, Guards fashion (some one of them, some day, he knew, would discover the monocle), the women balancing their air-hostess kepis on top of elaborate *Come Dancing* hairdos. Two loitering soldiers approached and persuaded the affronted lady to be on her way. Beside the searchers they looked like a pair of undernourished Displaced Persons.

Then he saw her coming through the gate, being patted by one of the Amazons (the precarious hair and, in the case of the men, those cap peaks, rendered impossible anything more than a brief benediction). Despite the years and the change in fashion he would have recognised her anywhere. Clogs, frayed jeans and tee-shirt – especially the tee-shirt, which bore, he learnt later, the statement: 'They're all Mine!' And so they were, if he remembered rightly.

He rapped the window sharply with a ten pence piece. She turned, looked, removed her sunglasses, squinted, waved, and came running into the cafe.

'Carson Chambers!'

'Deirdre!'

She flung her arms around him and fastened her luscious mouth on his. And at that moment he wished, oh how he wished, that those bastards Davis and Kyle were among the rubberneckers in the cafe . . . 'It's a good fish supper that one needs,' girned a shawlie at the next table. And Deirdre, with that quiet panache he remembered so well, released him, put on her sunglasses, turned them on the crone, and said: 'Fuck off.' The crone pretended not to hear and disinterested conversation broke out all around.

They held hands across the table and told each other how glad they were. She produced French cigarettes and after four years of Walnut Plug he inhaled luxuriously, by the way catching a disturbing nuance of her deodorant.

'P.P.P.!' she exclaimed, laughing. 'Piss, Pernod and Periods. I remember how you used to say that after your first drag of a Gauloise.'

'Ah yes, the Metro . . .' And they talked about that time in Paris (a CND rally), that time in Dublin (the 50th commemoration), that time in Dungannon (the first Civil Rights march) and, in particular, that time in Clones (the big Fleadh Ceoil) which had culminated for them in a drunken, sweaty tussle in a pup tent.

' "The Night of the Brewer's Droop" ', she reminded him coyly.

'And you expressed the wish that I had taken up the flute instead of the guitar. Cruel bitch . . .'

She talked about herself. She had finished at Queen's three years ago (Arts), had gone to Essex for two years (Psychology) and was now in her second year at N.U.U. (Social Science). She was firmly unattached and intended, if possible, to make the grant system dovetail into her Old Age Pension . . . 'And I'm busting for a jar,' she said. 'Let's go round to the Prince.'

He had to tell her that their old sanctuary had been heap of rubble for nearly two years now. Which led them to talk of Liam in Long Kesh, Francie (dead), Sinéad (exiled in Donegal) . . . 'And your mate,' she asked, snapping her fingers, '. . . Billy. The one with the great voice. What about him?'

He told her that if she should ever see Billy, at any

time of day or night, she must take to her heels in the other direction.

'Billy! A Prod gangster!' she gasped. 'My God, he's the last person you'd have thought that of.'

'Well, I suppose he thinks of himself as some sort of patriot,' he said. Then, a bit nettled at the look of bland incomprehension on her face, as though she had never heard the word before, he went on: 'You know, like Liam and Francie; the last refuge of knaves and the feeble-minded.'

There was a hiatus while she polished and readjusted her sunglasses. Then she said: 'Thinking back, doesn't it make you weep, all this sectarianism?'

Had the question been posed at any other time he would have replied by demanding a definition of sectarianism. Was the schism to be condemned merely the Big One, or was the condemnation to include those between Republicans (six or seven sets of initials at the last count), Prods (from five known to infinity), and the 57 varieties of Trotskyite, all potentially as bloody as the Big One? But he sensed that this was not the time to pursue a line of aggressive moderation – if, as he had begun to hope, things were to progress between them.

'What else can you expect from the 17th century mentality?' he began, and went on to talk about the 'Tribal Mentality' and the 'Cornerboy Mythology' and to suggest that it all stemmed from a dearth of O levels. It was a line that always went down well with even the most ultra-left or -right academic, Mick or Prod – and particularly well with those from lowly backgrounds. She responded warmly as if to a Catechism, revealing a weakness for *Belfast Telegraph* first leaders and, worse, a browser's acquaintance with the front pages of *Fortnight*. Hard to stick. But with 'They're all Mine!' thrusting eagerly across the table ('They' having nudged her cup and saucer a good three inches towards him, he observed lewdly) he would gladly have listened to excerpts from *Hibernia* all afternoon.

But presently her thirst began to act up again and she

suggested that they adjourn to the Europa Hotel for a scoop or two, it being in the general direction of the flat which she shared when in Belfast.

Ten minutes later he followed her through a scree of broken glass around the hotel (yesterday, for the umpteenth time, a car-bomb had brought the windows cascading into the street like crumbling teeth in a *Tom & Jerry* cartoon). He barely noticed, however, being at that moment taken up with the hypnotising motion and counter motion of her dungareed buttocks. All a matter, he knew, of rigid bone and wayward gristle; but there was always that split second at the end of each rotation, before the skeleton asserted its stricture, when all order seemed lost; a quiver in the mass, like a heart flutter, that had always seemed to him to be the very root of jazz. Much as he loved the traditional dance music of the Celtic people he realised that it was, and should be kept, a wholly male preserve, at its best when that feline quiver was simulated by the backlash of a kilt. To watch a well developed girl forcing her body to conform to the animated puppetry of, say, an Irish jig, was to understand the traditional expression of dedicated agony . . .

'That'll be two pounds seventy pence, sir.'

Stating this, the barman grinned maliciously. The effect of the first round on a new customer always made his day. And this one made no attempt at a stiff-upper-lip: 'In the name of Christ!' screamed Carson. 'Are you making me pay for all the bloody windows?'

It made the barman laugh for the first time in weeks, and he cashed Carson's cheque for a tenner without the usual reference from a Minister, J.P. or Commissioner of Oaths.

Deirdre sipped her brandy-n'-port – the sure tipple of a 'sixties folk-groupie – and apologised for the price. 'But it's the only really safe place, I suppose. They blow out the windows now and then for the benefit of the Press, but at least you're not liable to get ten pounds of gelly through onto your lap.'

He could see what she meant: familiar television faces

all around, though not now in their 'Serious Commentator' mould. A quartet from Lord Toronto's *In Depth* team crooned *Adeline* in the next booth. On a high stool at the bar a brilliant and beautiful expert on the life-style of the Urban Guerilla talked meaningfully into the sullen moustaches of, while squeezing the knee of, his latest anarchist.

'A haven of hacks,' said Carson.

'A scribble of scribes,' giggled Deirdre.

'A piss-up of Pommies.'

'Racialist!'

'I'd choke my sister first.'

'You didn't used to be like that. What changed your tune?'

'Birmingham.'

'The bombs? ... God, wasn't it awful ... All them people just –'

'– Nine died in the Prince and it didn't make the front page in any of the Nationals.'

'Perfidious shits!' hissed Deirdre.

They traded atrocity stories through a second two pound seventy pee's worth (one more round, he computed, and they'd have swallowed the price of O'Spoon's latest LP). Deirdre detailed a couple of hair-raisers and he realised that she was one of those people for whom the bullet is not enough, even though it had been for murderer and murderee. For her the drama was incomplete without the knife, in most cases applied to the male organs with a view to re-arranging them elsewhere about the cadaver. Horny old wives tales, he knew; generally, urban murderers have little time to indulge in Mau-Mau refinements, much as they'd probably like to. But he said nothing to this effect, considering it no bad thing that her thoughts should be on male organs, detached or otherwise. What worried him was the effect another round of draught stout would have on his should the opportunity arise (would it?). A repetition of the Clones debacle would be just too much for his ego in its present parlous state. Fortunately, for both pocket and prick, Deirdre drained her second brandy-'n-port and said: 'Come up to the pad and I'll make you a coffee.'

The suddenness of it took him by surprise. Helping her gather her bits and pieces he got another whiff of her perfume, this time with the added ingredient of that which it was supposed to suppress, causing a joyful surge inside his Y-fronts which necessitated a furtive frame of pocket billiards as they crossed the lounge to the door.

They emerged into the sunlit bustle of the late afternoon. She took his arm and they wandered chattering through the homegoing crowds, oblivious to the continual lament of police sirens in the distance and the fact that the foot patrols of skulking, scurrying troops were wearing helmets, a sure sign of some major security crisis.

The flat was in a terrace near the University, not far from the one in which he had spent his student days. Climbing the stairs behind her he inhaled an essence of old curry, nicotine and damp rot and became giddy with erotic nostalgia. Only eight years ago and it seemed a lifetime away: breakfasting on stout and chocolate digestives; rutting in an unmade bed in the afternoon; piss in the sink, used condoms under the carpet and Lenin on the wall; lovely squalorous days when all ambition ended in a herringbone Martin, a beard like Barney McKenna's and a hardner that would materialise, like Pavlov's dog, at the snap of a suspender.

Deirdre opened the door of the flat and went in quickly, glancing left and right in the way of the communal flat-dweller, to ascertain that nothing really obscene was going on or had been left in view. 'You'll have to excuse the state,' she said; 'I hadn't even time to make the – whoops! . . .'

The literary exclamation was caused by his hands coming up from behind her, the right to cover 'They're', the left 'Mine!' as he heeled the door shut. His teeth closed gently on her left ear lobe. Wriggling backwards, she said: 'Oh ho . . . you did take up the flute after all.'

'My client,' he chewed, 'demands a re-match.'

'Challenge accepted,' she groaned. 'Now if you'll just let go a minute while I clear the ring . . .'

When they called quits three hours later – round three – it was dark outside. His wife, he knew, would have the Special Patrol Group scouring the city for him; and he didn't give one tinker's fart. Clearing the cobwebs of her hair from his face he lit a Gauloise, sighed contentedly and inquired: 'You wouldn't have such a thing as a guitar about the place?'

' 'fraid not,' she replied sleepily, 'and I doubt if you'll get much of a tune out of your flute for a while.' So saying, she demonstrated what she meant, which led to a further bout in which he demonstrated the efficacy of creative improvisation.

At rest again, Gauloise re-lit, he ruminated dozily on the possibility of future generations evolving bottom teeth with bevelled edges – or none at all. Still, it was great to feel even the ache of old callouses. Who was it said something like: 'The English have only two ideas about sex – both horizontal?' If that were so, he mused, his wife at least had no identity problem . . . Deirdre now . . . say what you like, speak as you find, but if you can manage to get the Pope's foot prised off it they're the best –

He shook himself awake, shocked at this unconscious lapse into schoolboy sectarianism. Deirdre's head stirred on his midriff and she giggled softly. Wondering if he had unwittingly uttered the abomination he asked: 'What's so funny?'

'Do you realise,' she said, picking playfully at his naval, 'that we have been performing an old folk rhyme of the country?'

'What one's that?'

'Your Orange balls
Beat 'Derry's Walls'
Agin my Fenian arse.'

The Gandhi Gong

Shadows jigged on the curtained bay-window, though the music within was discreet enough for us to make out voices and laughter; soft rock from Edinburgh . . . just what the doctor ordered.

'He's not a doctor. He's some sort of lecturer,' said The Poet, lurching off the short path that led to the front door and decimating what looked in the gloom to be a border of geraniums. He held his ear against the window. 'I discern the gulder and guffaw of people I hate,' he said with relish. I leant on the doorbell, though with some mounting trepidation. Even on gin he smoulders gently, but on whisky he tends to go out-of-control-and-spreading.

We waited what seemed an age, me with our token bottle of Hungarian Red at the ready, he sucking pre-emptively at our personal half-bottle of Bushmills.

'I know he's not a doctor,' I said. 'His thing is Social Science or some such. A sound man.'

'A limey yo-yo. And she's worse,' snarled The Poet.

'What I said was that this used to be our doctor's house. McGregor, a Scotsman. His surgery was in the front room there. D'you know, I was once carried down these steps straight to six weeks quarantine in Purdysburn Fever. Diptheria. I had it twice, though they say –'

'– For God's sake, will you for one night spare us reminiscence of your alleged deprived childhood. Say another bloody word and I'll tell everybody you boarded in Campbell College and your Da was secretary of the Unionist party. Hit that door a dunder.'

That wasn't necessary. Our host flung it wide and cried: 'Welcome!' The Poet ducked in under his arm.

He looked like the Captain of the 1st Eleven dressed up to play the lead in *Private Lives* – cravat, pipe, horn-rims – but his accent was Black Country, the sort that makes even far-left clichés sound just right. A nice man called Bert. Up the hallway, his not-so-nice wife, a hennaed Ardboe anarchist, class of '69, off-duty in split-to-the navel, see-through chiffon, confronted the Poet. 'Who the hell let you in?' I heard her say – and saw him lean close to make what I knew would be a carefully studied riposte.

Oh God.

'I was just remarking,' I said to Bert as we moved partywards, in an attempt to divert his attention from the impending slaughter in our path, 'that this was our doctor's house in the old days. McGregor, a Scotsman. D'you know, I was once carried . . .'

The food and drink were in the back room, which had been McGregor's waiting room. I recalled the rising-damp marks on the flowered wallpaper that had taken on odd shapes during my pre-Purdysburn delirium; and the guttering gas-fire from which, now and then, red-hot fragments had fallen onto the oil-cloth, causing wheezing consternation among the regulars; and the pile of old *Picture Posts* and *John Bulls*, pages tacky with strange emissions; and the yellowing poster above the mantle-piece that told the square of speechless worriers, clutching their pre-NHS half-crowns, that 'Careless Talk Costs Lives'. Impossible to believe it was the same place. The walls, where not hidden by posters depicting handsome, bearded terrorists and andro-gynous musicians, were painted glaring white. Plants overflowed from baskets hanging from the ceiling, ten-drils almost touching the heads of the people gathered around the food and drink table. I imagined the air full of small, green, crawley things parachuting into the quiche and decided to leave it alone. Blowing cannily into two tumblers, I poured a drink for myself and Bert, who was saying: 'I think it's absolutely marvellous how chaps like you emerge *sui generis*, as it were . . .'

'I'm just a dandelion on a dunghill,' I said flippantly, embarrassed by Saxon forthrightness. 'As long as I stay put, I might even be mistaken for a yellow rose in a bad light.'

'Grandma Moses,' sneered the Poet in passing. He grabbed a handful of quiche and proceeded towards the main area of battle in the front room. Glancing back into the hall I saw one of his ex-mistresses comforting the Ardboe woman, whose face wore an expression I knew of old, as if some small flaw she had hitherto considered an ornamental slub in her personal fabric had recently been sliced open to reveal a mummified earwig; a 'beauty spot' diagnosed as a malignant mole. The ex-mistress was applying the sutures with practised skill. At least one other would be in the front room, I feared, waiting to bind up the wounds he was sure to inflict there. Thus everywhere they hovered in his bloody wake, comforting the fallen with tales of worse carnage – and, by the way, hoping to damp a fond glow kindling, perhaps, in the shattered breast of some sister masochist.

'He's changed a lot since those days,' said Bert (which was the very mildest observation I'd heard made on the Poet's condition in many a day).

He said it whilst drawing me through eye-level shrubbery towards the far end of the room and indicating what has become known in cynical circles as The Shrine. This consisted largely of a display of framed photographs, posters and newspaper cuttings relating to the early days of Civil Rights. It covered the upper part of the end wall of the room, tastefully arranged around a photograph (not larger than, but with a slightly heavier frame than the rest) of the Ardboe woman, in the drab fatigues and haystack hair-do of those squalorous times, receiving what has been called the 'Gandhi Gong' from the hands of the Mahatma's daughter.

The thing itself stood on a table directly under the display. Anyone with half a jaundiced eye could see at

once the *double entendre* in the nickname. A nine inch
high figurine of Gandhi himself, complete with walking
stave, stood in front of, and faced away from, another,
twelve inches high, of a man in shirt sleeves and big
boots who carried a sledgehammer, two-handed, across
his left shoulder. A 'Worker-of-the-World', of course;
but people of the same early vintage as myself had
detected a resemblance to Bombardier Billy Wells, an
ex-boxing champion who used to strike a huge gong as a
prelude to some old British films. Viewed from a certain
angle, some said, the Mahatma appeared to be cowering
away from the threatening hammer.

The ensemble was reputed to be nearly solid gold. The
sizable cheque that had come with it was nowhere to be
seen.

'There he is,' said Bert, pointing to a photograph in the
display.

And there indeed was the Poet, posed on the steps of a
bus whose windows bristled with golliwog heads, all
bound for the first big confrontation in Derry. Even then,
aged twenty, gaunt from living on cold tinned beans,
chocolate digestives and whiskey, he had set himself
apart: his was the only crew-cut in sight, and instead
of the uniform denim he wore a traditional Republican
trench-coat (with grenade cleeks on the belt). That coat
had been frowned on at the time; now it could be seen as
an early demonstration of the sometimes brutal honesty
which the Ardboe woman had just sampled in the hallway. As always on these reunion occasions, tonight he
was sporting, or rather, flaunting its soiled and tattered
remnant, slung cape-wise around his shoulders.

'Did you know,' I said, 'that the nearest he got to Derry
that day was Lavery's bar – two hundred yards down
the road?'

Bert looked around to see who was within earshot.
Not having been there himself, as much in love with the
myth-making industry of which the Ardboe woman was
managing director as he was with the woman herself, to
him it must have sounded close to rank heresy – as

though saying that Saul of Tarsus had made up a yarn as an alibi for getting drunk and disorderly instead of getting on with his business in Damascus. The Poet, since his eminence, had been co-opted into the myth whether he liked it or not.

'Yes . . . well . . . I have heard gossip to that effect,' said Bert nervously.

'It's the God's truth. I was in Lavery's waiting for him with the drink ordered. We saw the first blood on the six o'clock news.'

There was a photo of that too. It was the original of the famous press shot, syndicated world wide, of Arnie Fowles being led away to captivity by two baton-wielding Peelers. Arnie is slumped backwards; his handsome face, streaked with blood from a damaged scalp, has on it an expression of beatific satisfaction similar to that displayed by clapped-out marathon runners.

I asked Bert if Arnie was here, and a well known voice from behind answered: 'Try an' bate him away. He's holding a Durbar in the front room and breaking-in a new pipe.'

'Conor, you bitch,' I said, turning to face the wild, toothy grin of Dr O'Trew, out of which hung a huge and shining Peterson hooky. 'I see that you too have taken to the hallmark of the charlatan.'

'But, y'see, mine's empty,' he said, removing the pipe to demonstrate. 'I brought it to annoy Big Head and yourself, you opiniated old fart . . . This, by the way, is Ms Dymphna Doyle.' A pretty, dark-haired teenager in a too formal, too scintillating shift dress blushed and bobbed her head. His latest probationer . . . 'Dymphna's from Hackballscross, a terrible handicap for someone wanting to be theatre nurse . . .' Dymphna protested that she was from Forkhill, but Conor ignored her and went on: 'And this, Dymphna, is our host Bert Barraclough, and Johnnie Windrim, the well-known writer of remaindered fiction. There you are, m'girl –

your first Englishman and your first Protestant in one go.'

Dymphna fluttered purple eye-lids frantically and pleaded that we were not her first. Bert, equally embarrassed by attention being drawn to something that he himself succeeded in forgetting for long periods at a time, like a hunchback his hump, told her to pay no heed to Conor and drew her towards the shrine. It never crossed his nice English mind that her blushes were for the Protestant, not the Englishman.

To me, lowering his voice, Conor said: 'I saw your poetic mate in the front room, gargling a half-bottle, playing snakes and mongooses with Bernie Cope and Big Head. Could be a joyous evening. Anything I can do to hinder?'

'Oh look, Conor!' cried Dymphna. 'There's you. A hippy! With a headband an' all!'

Dapper Doctor O'Trew looked at his young self, one of a row sitting on wet tarmac at the back of the City Hall, and grimaced. 'Only in appearance, dear. The previous night I'd lost what remained of my grant in a poker school. Even then money, or the lack of it, was never far from my mind.'

'Don't believe a word of it, Dymphna,' I said. 'I remember him as a very serious young man. What about the night you arranged the 'packing' of that meeting in St Mary's hall, Conor? You can't tell –'

'Sure I knew no better,' said Conor dismissively. 'But times since have taught me, in more ways than one . . . Here, Dymphna, do you see that fella there? –' He pointed to a face in the row behind him at the sit-in. '– Remind me to show you a bit of his pelvic bone tomorrow. I use it all the time for lectures. They gave me three pieces of him, and if I'd had even a bit of the fourth I might have done something. He was one of my first lessons.'

'I read your article on bomb blast in *The Lancet*. Excellent,' said Bert reverently, aware that the mood had changed and, like a good host – or a good chairman

148

(for an academic, the same thing) – wanting to draw a line with a brisk summing-up.

'Easy,' said Conor, grinning again. 'Ample scope for trial and error. If Burke and Hare had lived around here these past ten years they'd have starved to death ... One thing I have learnt is that that there' – he pointed to the photo of Arnie's martyrdom – 'makes medical nonsense. People suffering from baton rash naturally tend to the foetal position. Only the Blessed Arnie folds backwards. Could it be due to an evolutionary development in the metabolism of Great Men, d'you think? An involuntary tic activated by photographer's flash bulbs?'

Bert gave a dry cough/laugh and said: 'Shall we join the others in the front room? It gets a bit sticky in here if too many linger.'

It was on the tip of my tongue to suggest that if he threw half the foliage into the yard there might be enough oxygen left for us few lingerers – and to point out that things could not be anything but stickier in the front room. But without comment I followed him and O'Trew and Dymphna out past the obligatory crumple of journalist-retainers guarding the drinks table and into the hallway.

The Ardboe woman and the Poet's ex- now sat on the stairs, holding hands. Bert paused and spoke soothingly: 'You shouldn't take on so ... He doesn't mean half what he says ... You should know that ...' So, in spite of my covering action he had been aware of the Poet's assault. Also, something in his tone of voice led me to believe that he was aware of much more. It didn't surprise me. They belonged to the truth-telling generation, for whom the surreptitious joys of adultery came a poor second to the operatic havoc of the subsequent confession. For someone like the Ardboe woman it can also be seen as a marital application of the political theory of 'continuous revolution' – always providing, of course, that your confessor is someone like Bert, a nice man, and not someone likely to try and cleave you to the bare navel with the domestic hatchet – such as, say, the Blessed Arnie Fowles.

In the front room his current mistress, as yet unmarked, sat unheeded at his feet. He sprawled on the sofa, having an intense conversation with Bernie Cope. As we entered he removed the hooky from his mouth and traced an aerial benediction in our direction while Bernie, leaning over the sofa back, still whispered in his ear. It was a tableau symbolic of their association from the early days, when Bernie had played Dr Goebbel's to Arnie's Hitler, to the hatchet incident involving wife number one in which Bernie, it was rumoured, had acted the part of Iago. In recent times their relationship had developed and ripened profitably in their chosen professions, Arnie being a barrister-at-law and Bernie a solicitor, both specialising in the Special Powers legislation relating to terrorism.

'You know everybody here, I'm sure,' said Bert.

Indeed. The room swam with faces which, for a brief period ten years ago, had figured daily in the media and in Special Branch 'action' files. And the swimming sensation, I suddenly realised, had quite a lot, but not all, to do with the amount of plonk I had downed in the fraught minutes since arrival – and that on top of whiskey. The walls and ceiling were painted black (bar the ornamental rose in the ceiling, which was white), the walls liberally hung with paintings, antique gilt mirrors and psuedo adverts for long defunct brands of Irish whiskey. The vestigial lighting came from a square chromium rack suspended from the central rose, each side of the square bearing four directional units, silver cylinders throwing pencils of light meant, presumably, to illuminate some artistic gem on the walls. Some did, but most, whether by accident or festive design, fell haphazardly on the company beneath, giving a chiaroscuro effect to the scene that tended to compound the effect of the drink.

A woman greeted me from behind, and I turned to find only a disembodied decollage spotlighted from above,

150

the rest of her in darkness. But I recognised the voice as that of Ms Mathilda Brown, once a suety student of scholastic philosophy, now a BBC presenter – radio, not television; she hadn't matured all that well.

'Better watch out for your friend, the ageing Byron,' she said. 'He's heading for another dose of his kind of trouble.' A pudgy hand joined her boobs in the spotlight and indicated, the wrist curved to make a snake's head, the forefinger its fang.

The Poet was sitting on a low settee. Because of this most of him was visible, the area of light being wider at that depth, wide enough to include most of his prey. She was pressing – or being pressed – back against the cushions, clutching a glass of coke to her breast with both hands like a shield. It could have had dark rum in it, but I didn't think so. The Poet was leaning towards her, talking rapidly, and I could guess the gist of what he was saying by the size of her eyes, like saucers, a Disney faun at bay.

'She's the niece of the house,' supplied Fat Mattie. 'Up from Drumquin on her way to the college of the Big Nuns. There'll be hell to pay if he tries to nobble her.'

That didn't concern me just then. What did was the bottle of whiskey, our bottle of whisky, which the Poet was just then raising to his lips. When lowered again there was barely an inch left in it. Another time, in another place and in a less altered state I'd have been only too glad to rescue the virgin and, by the way, per-haps postpone the Poet's inevitable coronary a few hours. But here, now, in my thirsty rage he became part of the old crowd, as old and smug and selfish in their thirties, as if in adverse reaction to the extraordinary theatre of their youth, as most old craps in their fifties (like me). The near empty bottle was a symbol of it all – or so it seemed to me just then. Advancing as swiftly as the murk allowed I snatched it from him.

'Gannet!' I snarled.

'You're no gentleman,' he slurred, the fourth son of a hill farmer in County Tyrone. He attempted to rise but had to slump back again, a ploy that brought him even closer to the shrinking virgin. He waved an imperious dismissal. 'Anyway, with you whiskey is mere affectation. Frog's piss or soap-suds are good enough for upwardly mobile cornerboys: whiskey is for poets.'

'Bollocks,' I said succinctly and put the bottle to my head.

It was not a wise thing to do. Besides everything else it had the affect of sustaining my wrath, so that when the Blessed Arnie summoned I went to him like a bull out of a gate, hunting for trouble. (Included in 'everything else' was compression of time and a facility for auto-censorship. I have been told since of various dramatic events in which I became involved and of which I have no recollection whatever – one being an obscene tongue-lashing of Fat Mattie, causing her to crack up and flee the room. But I recall my corrida with Arnie word for word, perhaps because of its bearing on what happened later.)

'I mentioned this to our poet friend earlier, but he wasn't too receptive,' he began, puffing at the hooky and glancing uneasily down his long nose into the bowl in the way of the recently reconstructed cigarette smoker. The sleek black head of his floored mistress, level with his knee, gleamed like that of a water spaniel. On his right shoulder sat the head of Bernie Cope, or so it appeared in the confused perspective of drink and lighting.

'Whatever it is, I can imagine his very words,' I said. 'Him and you never exactly licked thumbs to the elbows, as they say in Lurgan.' (A reminder to him of his rural roots in County Armagh.)

Despite numerous rebuffs over the years – verbal and, once, physical – to hear it said seemed to shock him deeply. Bernie's face made a despairing moue.

Arnie showed immaculate teeth clamped on the black stem and conceded: 'Comrade-in-arms, then. I admit we haven't always seen eye to eye.'

'Arms?' I queried belligerently. 'Surely they were always for other people? – your clients.'

'Every man to his calling, for better or worse. And there are degrees of success in soldiering as there are amongst lawyers and scribblers. Your friend and I, now, would have made very bad soldiers, whereas we have turned out reasonably good in our own fields. I just had the thought that we might do something for the bad soldiers Bernie and I deal with – the ones who get caught. I'm told there's some very promising but uncultivated literary talent emerging up in chokey. I thought a series of readings and lectures by established writers might be an acceptable contribution. I could arrange it.'

'I'm sure you could. But if I was in their position I think I'd prefer you to arrange for a bag of vodka-spiked oranges instead, or a dozen French Letters stuffed with plastic ... What had your 'comrade-in-arms' to say about the idea?'

Arnie removed the hooky and, again suddenly the mischievous student I'd known before his apotheosis, giggled, hooking a thumb at Bernie hovering behind. 'He said he'd do it for the same hourly rate that Bernie gets for a 'consultation' visit. What is it now, Bernie? A hundred and fifty quid?'

It is said that their conversation consisted almost entirely of quibbles about fees. Bernie muttered something nasty and moved back out of his spotlight.

I was about to get stuck in, determined not to let drink or the emergence of the attractive joker in Arnie put me off, to possibly say a thing or two about 'guilt' and 'conscience', when I was grabbed suddenly from behind and literally dragged towards the door – though I couldn't tell on the moment in which direction I was going. On the moment too, I thought it might be the Poet, in delayed reaction to our words over the whisky; he had a reputation as a furtive kidney puncher. But no blow came, and the voice in my ear, when it came, was that of his ex-mistress, last seen comforting the Ardboe woman. 'For Christ's sake come out here quick,' she said unnecessarily: 'there's trouble.'

My first thought was that the Poet had somehow managed an Olympian quickie with the nun-bound niece. But even as I was tugged through the door into the hallway I glanced back through the gloom and saw him still on his mark on the sofa – at about the 'Age Concern' chapter of his presentation, I judged, to be followed by the penultimate 'Vicarious Happiness' section. What, then, was the trouble?

I posed the question to our hostess, who awaited us in the hallway, black-eyed (because, I registered later, of being abnormally white-faced) and eating the varnish off her fingernails. She shushed me with a lip-crossed finger, glancing fearfully towards the back, Gandhi Gong, room. The ex- put a hand over my mouth from behind and both pushed me down the hall towards the street door. There they began a litany of incomprehensible responses . . .

'You're the only one from around here . . .'
'So you might know them . . .'
'God, the heart's crosswise in me . . .'
'I darn't tell Bert. He'd think I'm an eejit . . .'
'A Brit accent would be a red rag to a bull . . .'
'It's my own bloody fault . . .'
'But how were you to know . . .'

I could see that both were in a state of genuine fright. A sobering observation when those observed were two of the hardest nuts imaginable. The Ardboe woman's teeth all but chattered and she held her arms wrapped about her, as if longing for a shawl – and, by the way, drawing my attention to the fact that since my last viewing she had drawn her decollage together by means of a small safety pin near the throat. The ex-, a dark, nicotined whippet of a girl, kept dropping her cigarette on the floor.

Piece by piece, like in some crazy guessing-game being played by hysterical deaf-mutes in a telephone box, I discovered the nature of their 'trouble' . . . It was now 12.30 am (where had it gone!). At approximately

11.45 pm the Ardboe woman had answered the front door bell. On the step were two men, strangers, one of whom placed himself between the door and jamb and pleaded to be let in, saying that they were being pursued by the police. Whether he had recognised her famous face on the moment, or knew beforehand what sort of gathering it was, is immaterial; it was the right thing to say. Responding to her rural nationalist upbringing in the ever-open-door-for-felons tradition, the Ardboe woman, half-pissed anyway, let them in.

There is a probably apocryphal tale told about a family of dog-loving English tourists in Mexico who befriend, and then fall in love with, a small terrier which comes out of the blue to share their carpark picnic. Only after defying international quarantine laws and smuggling the beast home in their luggage do they discover, by way of a visit to the vet, that their pet is a species of desert rodent which has adapted to civilisation by taking up residence in urban tip-heads . . . Similarly, the Ardboe woman, for whom the phrase 'on the run' evokes an image of young men 'on their keeping' in some misty glen (preferably in Donegal, her week-end home), had caught to her bosom a pair of urban poison dwarfs.

Though nothing specific was said, I gathered that her bosom (hence the safety pin?) or some other portion of her, had come in for attention.

'Any sign of weapons?' I asked.

'No,' she snapped; 'they're not like that. More like . . . burglars . . . or worse.'

Had they come with guns hot from a killing she'd have secreted the weapons in her cleavage, risking the tit burns that terrorist courier girls are said to treasure like duelling scars; or with the stink of marzipan about them, from planting a surprise on a packed commuter train, she'd have sat with them at the television while they awaited casualty figures like actors the reviews of a first night. But burglars!

'What are they doing now?'

'Lowering all the drink they can get their hands on,'

155

she said. 'They were both rightly when they got here, so Christ knows what state they're in now.'

'Who's in there with them? What about the newspaper men?'

'There were only two left, and they bolted when they laid eyes on that pair. They're on their own now.'

That was ominous: it was a rare wild animal that could chase a hack from his waterhole.

'Who were they? The reporters, I mean . . .'

The Ardboe woman tugged her hennaed dreadlocks despairingly and whimpered: 'They're awful. They shouldn't be in my home.'

The ex-wife snarled at me: 'Why all the fucking questions? What the hell does it matter who's who?'

'Because,' I said firmly, 'I want to have at least a fair idea of what's in there before I go near it. Unless you want me to call the Peelers, that is.'

'Oh God no!' screamed the Ardboe woman in *sotto voce*, eyes wide with shock. 'Not them. They'd have a press release out in the morning . . . Wait . . . Yes, one of the press fellas was that lig from the *Morning Mick* . . . Shay something . . .'

Shay Doran: mouthpiece of paramilitaries, chronicler of hard man, organiser of backstreet press conferences. If they frightened Shay they must be beyond the blackmail of Public Relations, mustn't care about their 'media image'. That was bad . . . Werewolves at the waterhole . . .

The ex-mistress hissed: 'For Christ's sake do something . . . before somebody else barges in and says the wrong thing.'

I knew who she meant. The thought was enough to push me to a decision.

'I'll go,' I said, 'on the understanding that if I don't know them and can't talk to them, I'm straight out and we call the Peelers.'

The ex- nodded agreement and the Ardboe woman murmured, shiftily: 'Alright, we'll see. But for God's sake go on.'

156

Sober, I'd have gone out through the front door and left them to it. Still half-cut despite the sobering turn of events, I told myself that I bore a certain responsibility, being the senior citizen in the house – not for the shits, of course, but for my friends present, in which grouping I included the ex-mistress as I remembered her in her pre-Poet days. It was she who now gave me the strong push from behind that carried me almost to the closed door of the front room. I heard Arnie's guffaw above the music and wondered briefly if I should gather a posse. That, I knew, would make a punch-up certain. Deciding against – anyway, none of them had ever shown much aptitude in the lists, except for martyrdom – I passed on under my own steam and entered the Gandhi Gong room.

The sight of the little blue hat started my blood running backwards. Snap-brimmed with a white band, a hard plastic imitation of the headgear worn by gangsters in 'fifties movies, it perched on the back of a head bent over the drinks table just inside the door. The head turned towards me and said: 'Have a bevvy, squire. Where'd all the weemin go?'

The sharp, droop-lidded face looked young until you were close enough to see the tiny silver scars above the eyebrows and realise that the droop had nothing to do with the drink: an ageless bantamweight. The clink of a bottle neck on the rim of a glass located his mate, out of sight behind the food table and foliage, near the Shrine. The bantam's head turned towards the drink again, humming happily to itself. He seemed to forget me, still standing just inside the doorway, giving time for quick thought.

The little blue hat placed the bantam in a nearby ghetto of dealing-men, previously horse-copers and cattle drovers, now into everything from rags to other people's riches; a raffish bohemia of sporting and gambling men with a reputation for style . . . When ordered onto the streets at the height of confrontation eight years ago, they, seeing no immediate profit, had responded reluctantly but with characteristic flourish. Casting around for a badge, a distinguishing symbol, they lit on a job-lot of little blue gangster's hats that one of their number had acquired at an auction in a bombed cinema, part of an old promotion campaign for the film *Guys and Dolls*.

I remembered seeing them on their first outing. It was the time of 'No-go' areas and they had placed a barricade across the main road into the ghetto. Similar obstacles, meant to hinder the entry of army and police, were to be seen all over the city. But here, instead of the defenders taking up positions *behind* the pile of wrecked cars and assorted junk, as in other places, the little blue hat brigade had lined up *in front* of theirs, standing shoulder to shoulder, four square, in the great shiny brown boots that are an enduring relic of their horsey roots. Style, you see . . . It was a British soldier, peering up the road at the barricade, who coined their nickname: 'Fuck me . . . It's the Mick Mafia!'

The police had loved the little blue hats. When the army finally smashed through the barricades and internment began, all they had to do was find a little blue hat and whoever was wearing it, in possession of it, or standing near it, was in the bag.

I had rejoiced at the round-up, I recalled, for the good reason that the little-blue-hats had made the ghetto 'No-go' – or rather 'Get-out' – for more than the army and police during that time of sectarian sundering. Nowadays, a little-blue-hat was the mark of a veteran – but of internment only, that one barricade having been their sole service, and not very active at that. Perhaps that's why the wearers have gained a reputation for aggressiveness; I've heard it said that those martial standard bearers in the British Legion are mostly pensioners of such non-combative units as the Pay Corps.

'Jasis, would you look who's here . . . Oul home week,' exclaimed the Commando behind the foliage, from where he could see me but not I him. Not needing to, not wanting to, I thought that Shay Doran's reaction had been the right one after all and craved nothing more than to emulate him. A werewolf indeed . . .

'Dunty!' I cried, walking quickly round to where he sat against the wall beside The Shrine, 'Long time no see.'

He had been a middleweight in the '50s, when famous local boxers were called 'Rinty' and 'Bunty'. His sobriquet had arisen from a habit of hitting opponents with his head, for which he had been banned from the ring for life, blocking forever his only legitimate route out of the gutter. His subsequent career as a street fighter and small-time protection racketeer had earned him some charisma amongst those who set the seeds of urban myth – journalists and sociologists – and some short prison terms. No little-blue-hat ho; during that period he was already on-the-run, having gatecrashed a jailbreak by some activists and become part of 'The Struggle'. Re-captured in the act of armed hold-up, he served what some thought a surprisingly light sentence, and I have heard him referred to as a 'grass'. This accusation is not borne out, however, by his continuing existence. My own opinion is that 'The Struggle' had given him up.

He was super-heavyweight class now, most of the addition sitting on his lap as he sat overflowing one of our host's cushioned milking-stools. Yet surprisingly, like a pregnant teenager, his features had not changed all that much since I'd last seen him, long before the little-blue-hats. (He and I had been reared neighbours in the ecumenical enclave they had destroyed.) The tiny eyes above the spread of boneless nose still had that calculating squint, even in booze, that saw everything in terms of mass and movement in relation to the huge scarred fists now resting on top of his paunch. I was glad to see they were filled, a glass of our host's whiskey in one and an open half-bottle of wine in the other. I was not glad to see that the wine was of a vintage unknown and a provenance abhorred in this household: cheap, sweet, South African: 'Red Biddy', 'Blow-e-up', 'Climb-the-walls' . . .

159

He took a swig from either fist and made a wide-armed gesture encompassing the room. 'McGregor's house,' he said. 'Eh? The oul bastard'd birl in his grave if he saw us now . . . Used to go out of here with our heads shaved, like sheep from the dip. D'you mind, Johnnie? The donkey-fringe gang?'

Johnnie did mind. He minded very much being reminded of something that surfaced now only in the occasional nightmare. Diptheria might be OK for a bit of nostalgic bravura with those of the Welfare State generation; but not the nit and ringworm parade.

Dunty had hit his mark, and he knew it. 'An' here we are, mixin' with the nobs,' he said. Then, nodding in the direction of The Shrine, he asked: 'That's her there, isn't it? . . . in the middle photo . . . the one with the big jugs that let us in?'

I nodded. 'It's her house, y'see, and she's a bit worried about you having the police after –'

'Peelers!' laughed Dunty. 'Sure that was only a geg. We've nothin' to fear from the Peelers these days. 'Least I haven't. I don't know about Kevvie here.'

Following his gesture with the whiskey fist I saw that the little-blue-hat had moved to join us. He favoured me with a long, dour stare and then, with a muscle-loosening shrug of shoulders unnaturally wide in relation to his pinched, colourless face, he asked: 'Who the fuck's this?'

'Johnnie Windrim: an oul residenter . . . An' this here is young Kevvie Roche. Sure you knew his Da.'

I did – and decided that I liked the son even less.

'Kevvie's eldest sister – you mind Mary, the dancin' one – she's just moved into your Ma's oul house in Abbot Street,' Dunty informed me gratuitously, grinning, and I knew then for certain that he wasn't after drink or women; he craved trouble.

'What has you here, Dunty?' I asked, trying to keep one eye on the full fists (reminding myself not to watch the glass or the bottle, either of which, or both, could be let drop as a dummy, taking my gaze with them to the floor whilst the empty fists made for my jaw) and the other on Kevvie Roche to my flank.

'Just knockin' about, like. Kevvie saw two oul friends of ours comin' in earlier on. Bernie Cope an' Mister Fowles –'

'The fuckers,' groaned Kevvie passionately.

'They once made a crafty deal for Kevvie that went wrong, y'see. Nearly cost him both knees. Anyway, them pair of boys have made a fair bit of cash out of us in their time, so we thought we'd get some of it back in kind.'

He hoisted the whiskey in a toast and drank deeply. But I knew he hadn't necessarily meant that kind of 'kind'. And by the sounds of him, Kevvie certainly didn't.

They weren't about to shift in response to anything I might say or do; of that I was sure. My only possible recourse, therefore – bar the Peelers – was to get Mister Fowles to face his fans. I made the decision without any vindictive motive or anticipatory relish. Arnie, I knew from experience, had a way with rankers totally at variance with his egalitarian philosophy. Waiters, whom he treated like panes of glass or suppliant beggars, grovelled before him. Even in his student days I had seen him reduce a tailor to tears over the cut of a bespoke combat-coat. So the result of a confrontation with Dunty would be no foregone conclusion – and, I conceded to myself, could be intriguing from a neutral observer's point of view.

'Cope and Arnie are in the other room. I'll get them for you,' I said casually and, turning, took two steps towards the door into the hallway. That's as far as I got before the door opened to admit . . . chaos.

The Poet, caped in his trench-coat and clutching a bottle of wine by the neck, posed in the doorway and glared malevolently at me. 'Ingrate!' he cried. From behind him came a soft scream and I saw the Ardboe woman's frantic face briefly over his shoulder.

I stood still and said nothing. Behind me, I sensed that Dunty had risen to his feet. The Poet's gaze slid past me,

161

theatrical wrath tempering to bold curiosity. He advanced into the room and came to a halt in front of me, giving Dunty and Kevvie his famous curled lip, head-to-toe treatment. He too could act the Orderly Officer when the situation required it. He also had an unerring talent for 'saying the wrong thing', which he now did.

'Christ, they're emptying the bins early this weather.'

It took a second or two to sink in. In that time I saw Arnie's face (with pipe) appear in the doorway, and Conor O'Trew's, and behind them the posse-gathering Ardboe woman and the ex-mistress.

'I'm no fuckin' bin man, ya fruitmerchant ye!'

So shouting, Kevvie launched himself at the Poet – who did an effective Toreador swirl with the trench-cape before going down under the charge. Behind me I heard whiskey glass and Biddy bottle hit the floor as Dunty freed his lethal paws. Then I was in mid-air, hurdling the tangle of Kevvie and Poet, managing to avoid a screaming inrush of the Ardboe woman, the ex-, Arnie, Bernie et al, and ending up sprawled in a neutral corner, from whence I viewed the first round . . . Kevvie was on his feet again, making a fighting retreat to The Shrine before an onslaught of drunken pacifists, still being reinforced by the dregs from the other room. Fat Mattie had returned and was in the thick of it, apparently having some sort of ecstatic seizure, leading the women in that terrible ululating war-cry of the feminist left (appropriated, appropriately, from Arab women who keen thus whilst happily snipping testicles in the aftermath of battle). I saw Dunty towering at bay in front of The Shrine . . . and then, traumatically, the Gandhi Gong hoisted above his head. For a frozen moment I saw Arnie's uplifted face, blood-streaked again, and the Ardboe woman's, screaming, both with hands upstretched like frenzied Corybants pleading for a rub of the relic. But Dunty was not in a giving mood. The floor shook as the Gandhi Gong hit it – and the lights went out. (No mystical significance: Fat Mattie had pulled the Cona coffee ensemble bodily out of its wall fixture and fused the circuit.)

Total confusion reigned. A renewed pitch of screaming – some of it from Dunty, I thought – sent me scuttling on all fours along the wall towards the door. The heel of my left hand ground painfully on something round and hard. People were careering about the hallway, but there was light there and I headed, upright now, for the street door.

The caped Poet stood against a street lamp smoking a cigarette. Around his feet were clustered five or six full bottles – one at least, I saw, of whiskey.

'What in the name of Christ kept you?' he demanded as I stumbled down the path to the pavement. 'Grab a hold of these bottles ... Here, what's that you've got?'

An enquiring left hand came out from under the trench-cape and I, half-dazed still, extended mine and opened it. The heel was bleeding and the blood had smeared the severed head of the Mahatma, which must have skited the length of the room and on which my hand had closed involuntarily. He smiled up at us forgivingly.

The Poet took it from me and held it up to the light, squinting. 'Hollow and gold-plated. Not worth the full of your arse of roasted snow,' he judged, tossing it into the Ardboe woman's geraniums. 'Grab them bottles and we're off. The night is yet a pup.'

There were six bottles in the cache. Tired, bleeding, in the tightening grip of what I can only describe as a crash hangover, I revolted. Lifting three, I said: 'The rest's yours.'

Grinning his sly-little-boy grin he said: 'I have other things in hand.' And like the same little boy showing off his new pet hamster, he lifted the right-hand wing of the trench-cape to reveal ... Bambi: the Drumquin niece tucked in under his oxter, her loving arms wrapped around his waist!

'That woman'll have a contract out on you tomorrow,' was all I could say.

'But then again,' he replied, gently re-parcelling his prize, 'if things go well, I may not survive the night. Let's walk.'

'Let's run,' I said, somehow managing the other three bottles.

Dublin Indemnity

The deputy warder swung open the solid door to the cell block and the palpable stench of morning buckets flushed through the Minister's tender sinuses like drain cleaner.

'Sacred heart of Jesus!' he hissed, pausing inside the door as it slammed closed behind them, gripping the bridge of his nose between finger and thumb and shaking it violently. 'What the hell do you be feeding them? That can't be natural.'

'Sure we're well used to it,' said the Warden as they followed the warder the few yards to an inner, barred, gate. 'Though it does be worse on a Saturday – after the wholefood dinner on Friday night, y'see. Far better than spiking the tea with Epsom salts, like in the old days.'

When they had passed through the barred gate the Warden asked the warder to hand over his keys, saying that they could find their own way from here in. The warder, obviously disgruntled, insisted that the Warden sign for the keys before he would comply. The Warden did so meekly and they proceeded down a long echoey corridor.

The Minister had taken advantage of the pause to light a short, dark cigar and now moved in a protective screen of blue smoke. This had not prevented him from observing the tense little scene between Warden and warder with scarcely concealed impatience. 'I sometimes wonder about your methods, Hooley,' he said, 'I'd have shoved that notebook up his arse and kicked him from here to the front gate . . . And feeding wholefood to

165

these carnivores, no matter what the shite return, is asking for trouble in the long run. Too much of that trendy nonsense and they'll start atein' each other.'

Hooley mumbled something about trade unions and the price of meat, but abstractedly, his mind plotting ahead through the labyrinth of passages in an attempt to avoid contact with any grouping of inmates at morning association, dreading their reaction to the sight of the Minister, who had come straight from the golf course. He wore a baby-blue zippered jacket, plus-fours and white shoes with huge serrated flaps. But most potentially remarkable of all was the effect of his cap, tartan with a green pom-pom, crowning a russet and purple face that suggested a lifelong diet of Chateaubriand (rare) and Remy Martin. The Warden himself, tall, thin and prematurely grey all over, had been converted to vegetarianism by his wife, who was artistic and a niece of the Minister.

'I still can't think what can be urgent enough to drag me off the links at this hour,' puffed the Minister. 'Sure there's a whole wing in Grangegorman full of eejits like this one. Isn't it the time of year for it.'

The Warden's hard heels clacked in the corridor leading to 'the farm', as the warders called it: a cul-de-sac of six cells reserved for violent and unmanageable cases. The Minister's shoes squeaked and flapped. The noise of their passing brought a pair of large, wild eyes to a small grille high on a blank door; the eyes, seeing, closed as if in doomed acceptance.

'And isn't that where I was for sending him,' said the Warden in *sotto voce*: 'the 'Gorman. But aren't they packed to the gills with that crowd from Milwaukee University. I was down and had a look. Eating the walls they are, and still with braces on their teeth, some of them. Brandy and port mixed, on top of God knows what else. Himself says it's corroding the rubber in the stomach pump. That Joyce, for all his undoubted greatness, has a sin to answer for.'

'Greatness! A Godless gather-up this country was well rid of,' the Minister almost shouted, causing the

166

Warden to wince nervously. 'Why the hell don't they go
to the kips in Paris and Trieste where he spent his time,
instead of fouling up our pavements every June . . .
What makes this one so special anyway? And all this
bloody play-acting . . . Sure he's bound to know my face.
It's in the papers often enough, thank God.'

'It's the things he does be saying, Minister,' said the
Warden, a mite testily, sorting through the warder's keys
as they approached the main door to 'the farm'. Someone
inside was singing, a sound like a bee in a biscuit tin.
Perhaps in mitigation for his previous shortness the
Warden went on: 'I'm a good party man, as you well know,
Minister, and what with the elections coming up –'

'Point taken, Hooley, say no more. I'm just wondering
what a looney Yank student would know about me or
mine that's worth a round of golf.'

'I'd sooner you heard it from himself. He'd talk the leg
off a stool. I declare to God he hasn't shut his trap since
they pulled him out from under that bush in the park this
day last week. I got them to put him down here, well out
of the way.'

'Full of brandy and port, I suppose?'

'Not a trace. Malnutrition, exposure and nervous
exhaustion, the doctor says . . . Just through here now . . .'

The solid door to 'the farm' swung open, revealing a
short corridor with six cells rowed along one side, on the
other a blank wall. The released singing voice, soft and
unhurried, was distinct now.

Tim Finnegan lived in Walkin Street,
A gentleman Irish mighty odd,
He had a brogue both rich and sweet,
To rise in the world he carried a hod.
But Tim had a touch of the tippler's way.
With a love of licker he was born,
And went upon his way each day
With a drop of the cratur every morn.
Whack for the dal, dance to yer partner,
Welt the fluer –

'Shut up!' shouted the Warden with uncharacteristic heat. The singer did.

'Who's that?' asked the Minister as they walked along the line of cells, the Warden again fiddling with the keys.

'Some class of a scribbler from Belfast. Drunk and disorderly. He's in the cell next to his nibs – and that's what worries me: just how much them lugs of his have been picking up . . . Here we are now – and remember: you're the DA.'

'God help us!' groaned the Minister as the cell door opened.

The Warden entered first, switching on the cell light and saying: 'Good morning, Hank. I've a visitor for you.'

The cell furniture consisted of a minute wash basin, a bucket, a chair and a bed. Sneakered feet on the ends of long, thin denimed legs swung to the floor, but their owner didn't rise any further. The Minister, coming in behind the Warden, had a first impression of large, square, rimless spectacles and the sort of listless fair hair that looked oddly out of place, as if it were a temporary covering for a head meant by nature to ripen into early baldness.

'This is the person you've been waiting to see,' said the Warden, stepping aside. The inmate on the bed had removed his spectacles and was polishing them on a loose shirt-tail. He looked up, squinting, his top lip reefed up to reveal a full house of perfect American teeth. Out of a mid-Western batch, the Minister judged . . . polished Okie . . . matt-finished, aerodynamically stable (vestigial nose and ears). Spectacles readjusted, his eyes bloomed, traversing the Minister from head to toe.

'This is the District Attorney?'

The sentence was finely balanced between question and exclamation, the delivery recognisable as being of the human-word-processor type perfected by American television commentators of the 'singing chipmunk' school.

Aware suddenly of a silence, the Minister saw the

Warden looking at him significantly and realised that he was 'on'.

'Well . . . yes,' he began, wondering again how a lovely child like Sinéad could grow up into the sort of affected bitch who would give house-room to a lig like Hooley. Still, looking after your own was one of the perks of the game, no matter what. 'Y'see, we have a different name for it here,' he went on: 'we call ourselves "Deputies". But it's the same thing.'

The inmate, he could see, was not convinced. So could Hooley. 'Now Hank,' he said, in a petulant, "tether's end" tone of voice, 'I've gone to a lot of trouble, and if you don't –'

'OK, OK,' said Hank, holding up both hands not so much to placate as to shield himself from Hooley's alien uncoolness. 'All I want is to make a statement to someone in authority who looks like he might have an IQ over fifty. If you say this guy's the goods, OK. I guess I'll have to adjust to the crazy get-up.'

Hooley, knowing the Minister's short fuse and sensing its initial splutters, admonished: 'I've told you before, Hank, a civil tongue at all times or you'll get nowhere.'

'I was on the links,' the Minister explained, quietly and reasonably, the cigar a pulp between his teeth.

'I guess that's Gaelic for golf course, right?' said Hank, head nodding sagely. And again he made the shielding gesture with outspread hands, this time in anticipation of their boisterous pleasure as he conceded: 'OK. I've been in this Goddam country long enough to get used to cops who look like traffic wardens and traffic wardens who act like cops, I guess I'll have to accept a DA in a Buster Keaton cap and purple trousers.'

'Oh you will, will ye, y' cheeky skitter! Well let me tell you that if you don't bridle your impudence I'll be back on the ninth green in ten minutes and you'll be on your way to the Joyce-nutter's cage in the 'gorman'.

By the end of the first sentence the Minister's suffused face had moved to within a foot of Hank's, pickles of flung cigar leaf stippling his spectacles. Hank lay down on the bed, closed his eyes and covered his ears with his hands. 'I'm an American citizen and I demand to see my Ambassador.'

'He's been on a health farm in Florida this two months and it's whelps like you has him there,' shouted the Minister, enjoying the acoustics, forestalling an intervention by Hooley with a raised, clenched fist. 'If it was up to your Ambassador, poor man, he'd have the Sandycover Tower converted to a gas chamber. So less of your lip and just state who you are and what you want or I'm off and you're for the rubber walls.'

At this point Warden Hooley sat down on the edge of the bed, placed a hand on Hank's right knee, and said, gently: 'He's not foolin', Hank.'

The words and action had a dual affect on the Minister: of acting like an ice-pack on his blood temperature, and of raising an old question that had never been answered to his satisfaction. The words had been spoken in a superb reproduction of Hank's own mid-Western accent. This in itself did not surprise the Minister, he having had previous experience of Hooley's unconscious mimicry, an unfortunate trait that had led to his removal from the Department of Trade and Industry, the Minister's first placement for him, to virtual incarceration in the prison service. Indeed, the repercussions from his final virtuoso performance, at a trade fair which had attracted representatives from all nations, were still being felt in the department. The Japanese delegation in particular had taken grave affront, Hooley in their case having excelled himself not only vocally but also with much histrionic use of eyes and teeth.

The action, now, was more to the point of that unanswered question, a question that had first loomed in the Minister's mind at his first meeting with the young Hooley. The occasion had been a backstage party after an amateur production by the Castlebar Thespians of 'The Importance of being Earnest', in which he, Hooley, had given a highly acclaimed performance as Lady

Bracknell. Throughout the party, which had gone on into the small hours, he had remained in costume and in character, a sight and sound that the Minister had never quite been able to erase from his memory, even on the day he had walked up the aisle with Sinéad – who, he also wanted to forget, had played a creditable Algernon in the same production . . . It takes all sorts of relatives, he told himself resignedly as the sullen Yank heaved himself upright and again placed his sneakers on the floor. Hooley gave his shoulder an encouraging squeeze.

'Right. OK,' said Hank, addressing the floor. 'Who am I? My name is Henry Taft Scropenhauer. I am twenty-five years old and I'm a research student in Anglo-Irish literature at the University of Athens, Idaho.'

'And tell me now, Mr Scropenhauer,' asked the Minister in a manner gauged to suggest that anything he was about to be told was a downright lie. (He himself had once practised at the other facet of showbiz, the Bar), 'tell me just what you were researching under that bush in Phoenix Park? Or maybe you were waiting for the holy mushroom to sprout? Was he tested, Warden?'

'Grass, coke and mushroom – not a trace,' replied Defending Counsel Hooley.

'I'm not a junkie,' protested Hank. 'My mental and physical condition at the time was due to the intensity of my research and to the traumatic effect my findings were having upon me. It is my intention to reveal those findings to you now, as a preliminary to pre-Christmas publication which I am confident will get me tenure for life in the University of Athens, Idaho. Also, four days ago I was robbed by a woman.'

The Minister whooped triumphantly: 'Oh ho . . . I knew there'd be one of them in it somewhere. Didn't I tell you, Hooley? – drop any copy of *Ulysses* and it'll fall open at the Night-town chapter.'

'I deeply resent the suggestion implicit in that remark,' said Hank huffily, though without any change in his vocal delivery. The Minister thought of brown toothpaste oozing evenly out of a tube. 'It happened in broad daylight on the canal bridge in Baggot Street. She had a gun and she said she was from Prisoner's Aid.'

It was the Minister's turn to be resentful. 'Where do you think you are? Belfast? That sort of thing doesn't happen here. You might as well admit you were mugged in the kips by the Great-Grandaughter of Fresh Nelly. Sure isn't that what the Grand Joyce Tour is all about?'

'I am not with any tour. I tell you again, I'm a research student. I came here to follow a specific line of inquiry – related to Joyce, sure, but in a peripheral way.'

'And what is it this time? Not laundry lists again! Pawn tickets, may be, plenty of scope there. Or IOUs?'

'No. My brief is the legend of Tim Finnegan as related in the famous ballad and used by Joyce as one of the main structural themes in his novel *Finnegans Wake*. You know the legend, right?'

Hank still talked to the floor, so the Minister's reaction to his last words and the ensuing passage of facial mime between Minister and Warden were lost to him. The Minister registered in quick succession alarm, rage and furtive query. Hooley answered with a classic mask of 'I told you so' smugness.

'Ah ... yes, I know the story, Mr Scropenhauer, none better,' replied the Minister, wanting nothing more than to stub the cigar butt on Hooley's long, thin nose. 'Now perhaps you'll tell us just what aspect of it you were investigating.'

'I requested your presence here, as an officer of the courts, to do just that. For what I have to tell is of such serious portent that to publish without first bringing it to the notice of legal authority would be unethical. I guess now's the time to ...'

This last ellipsis he addressed to the Warden who, to the Minister's amazement, immediately dived head and shoulders under the bed. He emerged grasping a Japanese cassette player. Placing it on the bed, he turned to the Minister, bright-eyed, explaining eagerly: 'This is something Hank and me worked out as a way to illustrate his story. Maybe if you'd take a seat – er-Deputy.'

The Minister sat down heavily on the chair, gazing at Hooley with a stunned, slightly fearful, expression. 'Will it get me out of here any quicker?' he asked, now watching Hank, who had extracted a slip of paper from the pocket of his jeans and, referring to it, was twiddling about with the tape in the player.

Hooley prefaced his reply with an unbelievably high, nervous giggle. 'Well, we can only hope that it will seem quicker. You see, what we've done –'

'Right. Here we go,' said Hank, and pressed the 'play' button . . . Someone cleared his throat earsplittingly, sending Hank's hand darting to 'Volume Control' . . .

One morning Tim was very full,
His head felt heavy which made him shake.
He fell off the ladder and broke his skull.
They carried him home his corpse to wake.
Wrapped him up in a nice clean sheet,
Laid him out upon the bed
With a bucket of whisky at his feet
And a barrel of porter at his head.

Hank, having pressed the 'Stop' button, began to speak: 'Now that, Deputy, is by way of being an introduction to –'

'Hold your tongue just a minute,' commanded the Minister. Throughout the singing he had watched the rapt expressions on the faces of his two cellmates, the dangerous ringing in his ears mounting until it had all but drowned the final stanzas. Turning to Hooley he asked: 'Is this what I was dragged the whole cut from Killiney on a Saturday morning for? To hear some bowsie of a scribbler yowling on a tape? It was him we heard outside, wasn't it?'

'Yes, it was,' snapped Hooley irritably. The Minister could scarcely believe the venomous glare that accompanied this outrageous hubris. Worse was to follow . . . 'I'm sick telling you that *this is something you should hear*,' Hooley went on, leaning forward, eyes hard and unblinking, stressing the words with a nodding motion of his head, like an unvocational schoolmaster traducing a thick pupil. 'Surely another twenty minutes away from playing with your wee ball is a small price to pay. You can leave now if you wish, of course – but if you do you'll regret it, I promise you.'

The Minister's aural bells had now reached the intermittent 'bleep' stage, reminiscent of the bedside monitor during his last stay in Intensive Care. Nevertheless, his response was calm and dignified: 'We'll speak about this later, Warden Hooley. Now, Mr Scropenhauer, perhaps you'd continue what you were saying.'

Hank looked from one to the other, then resumed his perusal of the floor, head shaking back and forth, and sighed 'Jeez, you guys,' before continuing briskly.

'OK, I was saying that the song on the tape was an introduction to our problem as stated in the ballad of *Finnegans Wake*. I should tell you first of all that my Alma Mater, the University of Athens, Idaho, is sponsored almost entirely by the Life Assurance Corporation of North America. It was during a visit by the President of the Corporation to the campus last fall that the legend of Tim Finnegan came up, the Corporation having recently granted a further bursary from Anglo-Irish studies, with a bias towards the folklore aspect. The prime relevant interest for the Corporation was, of course, the resurrection angle – Finnegan apparently dead, presumedly certified so, therefore the death claim, if there was one, must have been registered. So what happened to the claim when he suddenly came back to life? I say relevant because the Corporation has been having this long term hassle in the Supreme Court over some dead heroes in Vietnam who turned up hale and hearty, via Canada, long after the war ended. Then there was a secondary interest: the ladder from which Finnegan fell to his putative death. I don't know how much you know about insurance men, Deputy, but I can assure you that they are haunted by ladders, especially painted ladders. One of the main tenets of life assurance since time began is that no ladder should ever be painted, the reason being that though the paint may protect to some extent, it also covers up any potentially dangerous wear-and-tear in the structure. So if somebody falls off a ladder and there's a claim, if that ladder's painted, then the claimant has no mission. Anyhow, the President thought that here was an area of research appropriate for the University of Athens, Idaho. Are you with me this far, Deputy?'

The turning of the Hooley worm was uppermost in the Minister's mind. He had watched the Warden's lips moving with only a split second's lag behind Hank's narrative and had pondered on the phrase 'stir crazy'. But surely that was only prisoners?

'Deputy?' prompted Hank.

'Oh yes . . . carry on, carry on.'

'The first thing, of course, was to establish that there was a factual base for the legend. This I quickly did. Tim Finnegan, a builder's hodsman, had lived in Walkin Street around the turn of the century. He was, as the first verse of the ballad adumbrates, a notorious drinker. He was also what is known as a 'hard case', and I have good reason to believe that he made a subsidiary living as a pimp –'

'– What did you say!'

The Minister had heard well enough. He was making a threat, not asking a question.

'He said pimp,' replied Hooley with a contemptuous toss of the head that the Minister recognised as one of the bits of business he had brought to his Lady Bracknell. 'And if you think that's bad, wait'll you hear the rest of it. Carry on, Hank.'

'I was just going to complete this part of my introduction,' said Hank, 'by suggesting that that might account for the enigmatic line in the first verse which calls him a "gentleman Irish mighty odd".'

The Minister cleared his throat noisily, seeming to be having difficulty with his breathing. 'I wonder, Mr Scropenhauer,' he said, 'if you happened to come across a counter . . . legend, as you call it, about a decent, hard-working man, strong in his faith, who served his country in her hour of need, who –'

Hank interrupted with what can only be described as a 'hollow laugh' (an imitation of a laugh, that is, a facsimile of a sound he had heard issuing from other folk from time to time). 'I sure did! All that stuff about rising from the dead after a vision of the Virgin Mary – a sort of Matt Talbot without the chains! Pious eyewash. All my evidence points to the fact of Finnegan being a totally bad character. And I'm not just talking hearsay. Through my connection with the Life Assurance Corporation of North America I gained access to the records of companies that were active in the Dublin area at the time. And boy, did I ever strike uranium! There was this half-assed outfit called 'The Gaelic Hibernian Friendly Society' that was on its last legs about then. The local office was down to a manager and one agent. And by the purest of coincidences the office itself was directly across the street from the building Finnegan was working on the morning he fell off the ladder! The manager was this great character called Cassidy, who later put the whole thing down on paper. He begins by telling how he and agent Feeney were in the office that morning, and how Feeney, looking out of the window, saw everything.'

Here Hank stopped and looked sideways at Hooley. And Hooley, as if on cue, took over (he was, the Minister observed bitterly to himself, on eggs – like a big Girl Guide before the annual display) . . . 'To encapsulate matters, as it were, I suggested to Hank that we dramatise the situation as a sketch for voices. Hank then wrote a script – to which I contributed something from my knowledge of local dialect and such. I also directed the production. Now . . . Deputy, if you're agreeable we have only to start the tape.'

To the Minister it seemed eons since he had walked in a haze of sunlight and cigar smoke in the company of sane men (a Bishop, a Supreme Jurist, the leader of the opposition). Worse for one whose success in life was partly due to being one step ahead, able to anticipate the next move, was to find himself in the strange position of not knowing what would come next, of being on the edge of a void. There was too a vague feeling of captivity, perhaps only because of the environment . . . but it had something to do with the new, aggressive Hooley. He could not shake off the ridiculous notion that if he got up to go, Hooley would somehow stop him. He nodded agreement and Hank pressed the 'play' button.

What followed first was a chorus of *Finnegans Wake* sung by the same voice as before.

'Whack for the dal, dance to yer partner,
Welt the fleur with yer trotter's shake,
Isn't it the truth I tell you,
Lots of fun at Finnegans Wake.'

Then a speaking (male) voice exclaimed: 'Holy Mother of God!', and another (also male) said wearily: 'Feeney, would you ever come away from that winda and quit lustin' after every ankle that passes. There's work to be done.'

Feeney (excited): 'I've seen it, Mr Cassidy! I've seen it!'

Cassidy: 'Get a grip on yerself, man. You couldn't have.' (Here Hooley sniggered and glanced slyly sideways at the Minister. The latter, behind a screen of fresh cigar smoke, had recognised Hooley – for all the overdone Narth Wall adenoids – as Cassidy, and had decided there and then that an annulment was not out of the question. A telephone tapper he knew, formerly an investigative journalist in the North, did a thriving sideline in salacious scenarios for the eyes and cameras of Private Inquiry Agents. He wouldn't even have to bother the Bishop; a well known society monk, also of his acquaintance, had a hot line for the well-heeled to St Peters itself.)

Feeney: Come over here quick, Mr Cassidy. I'm only after seein' a donkey's death!

Cassidy: Never. You'd be the first in the history of Ireland. The folklore people would never allow it.

Feeney: But look, look here. D'you mind tellin' me that for an insurance man to witness a claim happening is as rare as seein' a donkey die? Well, I'm after seein' one of our Lives Assured bouncin' on the cobbles off the top of a ladder!

Cassidy: Holy God! Are you sure? Who is it? I can't see for that crowd of gapers round him.

Feeney: It's Finnegan the hodsman. Y'know . . . the hard case from Walkin Street. Oul wreck-the-house.

Cassidy: Him! He's never one of ours. Who in his right mind would take on a bowsie like that – and a hodsman to boot!

Feeney (snivelling): Ah, Mr Cassidy. You'll ate me.

Cassidy (aghast): You! You never did! When?

Feeney: Three weeks ago. When you were down in Skerries. It was a terrible bad week for business, Mr Cassidy.

Cassidy: A bad week, he says! My God, Feeney, do you realise that that Finnegan's coffin could be the last nail in ours! . . . Is he dead? Can you see if he's dead?

Feeney: I think so. They've pulled a bag over his head.

Cassidy: How much, Feeney? Tell me how much before I forget myself and put you through that winda after him.

Feeney: Tuppence a week.

Cassidy: Not the premium, man – the pay-out. How much? Quick now.

Feeney: Ten pounds. Oh Mr Cassidy, I'm heart sorry –

Cassidy: Ten quid! Feeney, you've sunk the Gaelic Hibernian with all hands. What'll I tell the board in Jurys' Hotel the night? Ruined!

Feeney: Wait, Mr Cassidy. Something just struck me.

Cassidy: Not yet, Feeney, but I'm lookin' around.

Feeney: The ladder! I'm after seein' somebody draggin' it into the yard there. Just when they took Finnegan away in that cart.

Cassidy: God! Yes! the bloody ladder! Why didn't I think

of that? Feeney, you're a genius. Let's have a look.

Feeney: It's outa sight now. But I saw this fella draggin'
it in with a rope.

Cassidy: And it slabbered in paint from head to toe!
Isn't that what you saw, Feeney me lad? Isn't it?
Tim Finnegan, y'low rip ye, you're for a pauper's
grave after all!

Feeney: I'm afeard not, Mr Cassidy. Spankin' new by
the look of it – and not a drop of paint.

Cassidy: Feeney, I'll lave marks on ye –

Feeney: But wait . . . look, there's a paint shop up the
street. Ten minutes would do it if there was nobody
about. A pint of chape paint and an oul brush – a
tanner at the most.

Cassidy: A sprat to save a mackeral! Good man, Feeney.
The Gaelic Hibernian will not forget you for this.
Take it from the petty cash and away ye go this
minute. And mind – I know nothing about it . . .

At this point there was the sound of a door slamming,
and then a whirring silence. Hooley broke it. 'Here,' he
said to the Minister, 'you have to imagine a passage of
time, say twenty minutes. The machine hasn't the capa-
bility to do proper fade-outs and fade-in, like on radio.'

The Minister responded slowly, as if waking from a
doze. He removed the cigar from his face and managed
to say, 'Who –' before the door slammed again and
Hooley silenced him with a kissed finger.

On the tape the sound of heavy breathing was followed by:

Cassidy: Feeney. What happened? You came outa that
yard like a scalded cat.

Feeney: Ah God, Mr Cassidy, I was near a goner. Paddy
McGee was there, workin' at the ladder.

Cassidy: McGee the tinker? Finnegan's butty?

Feeney: The very one . . . Came at me like a wild animal.
I took to me heels.

Cassidy: And the paint and brush? Where the hell's the
paint and brush?

Feeney: I dropped them in the yard. Oh, if you'd seen him . . .

Cassidy: Go back there and get them. Wait your chance, but get them. He'll not be there all day. We'll have plenty of time to do the job.

Feeney: But he's took the ladder away, Mr Cassidy. He had it across a handcart . . . Look, there he goes now.

Cassidy: Scuppered. Ten quid on a wino that spent his days goin' up and down unpainted ladders! I'll be the laughin' stock of Jurys'! All it needed was a dollop of paint – but no, you couldn't even manage that, could ye. Well let me tell you, me fine fella-me-lad, you'll be a tanner short in your last pay packet from the Gaelic Hibernian. You'd think with your entire livelihood at stake you'd have stood yer ground, McGee or no McGee. And what the hell's bells was he doin' there anyway, futherin' about with the ladder?

Feeney: Takin' the rope off it.

Cassidy: What rope? What was a rope doin' on the ladder?

Feeney: Sure I told you about seein' somebody draggin' the ladder into the yard by a rope.

Cassidy: It must have been McGee then. But surely he wouldn't tie a rope on the ladder just to do that – the brute could carry two like it in one hand. So the rope must have been tied to the ladder all along . . . Now think, Feeney . . . did Finnegan fall off the top of the ladder, or did the ladder fall and he with it? Think, man!

Feeney: The ladder couped. Sure I saw it with me own eyes.

Cassidy: Feeney, me brain's boilin'! We could be saved yet. A brand-new-lookin' ladder – you said so yerself – a brand-new-lookin' ladder coups from a wall for no reason. But there's a rope . . . A long rope, would you say, Feeney?

Feeney: Well, I suppose –

180

Cassidy: – a long rope tied to the ladder. And what if
the other end of this long rope leads back into the
yard, and Mr Paddy McGee is in the yard, and the
same Mr Paddy McGee just happens to give this
long rope a good tug? Eh, Feeney? He came at you
like a wild animal, didn't he? And you said he was
workin' at the ladder. Doin' what? I'll tell you,
Feeney: untyin' the rope; removin' the evidence!
It's murder, Feeney! Glorious, premeditated murder! And if you know your fine print like I do you'll
know that the Gaelic Hibernian pays out only on
deaths natural and accidental. In Holy Ireland,
Feeney, murder is a beaten docket!

Singer: Whack for the dal, dance to yor partner,
Welt the fleur with yer trotter's shake,
Isn't it the –

Click. End of tape.

Hank snapped open the holder and extracted the
cassette.

Hooley said: 'Pipped at the post. Still, there was only a
couple of lines left of the song and that ended the first
. . . 'act', I suppose you'd call it.'

'I'd call it the greatest load of balderdash I've heard in
all my born days,' said the Minister very loudly, rising
from the chair and flinging the butt of his cigar to the
floor, there grinding it messily into the well-scrubbed
tiles with the sole of his shoe. His face throbbed with
anger. Indicating Hank, who was intent on his manipula-
tions with the cassette, he said: 'He can't help being a
Yankee pill-head, I suppose – but you, Warden Hooley,
a supposedly responsible civil servant, giving credence
to this slanderous rubbish by acting the eejit on tapes
when you should be about your bounden duty. I sensed a
slackness in discipline as soon as I put foot in here this
morning, and now I know the reason why. What the hell
must your staff think of such goings-on!'

Hooley rose from the bed, drew himself up until his
chin was level with the Minister's pom-pom, and

squared his shoulders. 'Outside,' he ordered, hooking his thumb towards the cell door.

Twice before in his life that word had been said to the Minister in just that manner and accompanied by that same unequivocal gesture: once in a public house and once in the Dail; the first invitation he had accepted and been badly beaten up in the car park, the second he had declined. Though it was inconceivable that even this new, strange Hooley would lay hands on him, something caused him to hang back as the grim-faced Warden opened the cell door and stood aside expectantly. 'Come along,' said Hooley, stretching out his arm, a one-man Guard of Honour which the Minister eventually passed, without a glance, into the corridor. 'Back in a sec, Hank,' said Hooley, and followed.

Outside, the Minister turned, quivering finger raised – and was immediately struck dumb by the sight of Hooley's quivering lower lip. The Warden was slumped with his back against the closed cell door, his long face a caricature of 'hurt feelings' . . . 'How could you speak to me like that in front of a prisoner,' he whispered. 'Forby anything else, I think your attitude is making him suspicious about your identity, and it's been hard enough egging him on this far.'

'Egging him on!' blared the Minister – and was shushed by Hooley's finger. He continued in a hoarse whisper: 'Is that what you call it? I'd call it aiding and abetting.'

'With all due respect, Minister, you obviously know nothing at all about the handling of a nut-case like that in there,' he said forthrightly, but with all the old deference. The Minister, having difficulty in relating this Hooley to the one in the cell, did begin to have some doubts about his own attitude. Hooley went on: 'Sure you can see that the books have him half round the twist. The only thing fellas like that respond to is a bit of buttering-up. Anything else and they crawl back into their shells.'

'But you surely don't believe that that stuff on the tape

is anything but a literary nutter's fantasy, do you?'

'I believe it,' said Hooley firmly, 'because I've seen chapter and verse in his research papers. And you can't tell me, Minister, that certain facts about Tim Finnegan's early character revealed so far on the tapes weren't known already by those, let's say, directly concerned with the legend.'

The Minister said nothing in the eloquent way he had developed through dealing with ill disposed television inquisitors: he stared blankly, with a faintly quizzical furrowing of the brows, as if he hadn't heard what had been said or as if what had been said was so stupid as to be beyond belief.

'Anyway, that is not why I got you down here,' said Hooley, content with the response. 'The bit that matters comes on the other side of the tape, and when you hear it you'll realise why I had to get everything out of this fella before he started shouting it abroad around election time.'

'What is it, for God's sake?'

'You'll hear in a minute. If we linger too long out here he's liable to start losing his marbles again. But when we do go in, Minister, would you please try and not rock the boat . . . Oh, and I should tell you that Sinéad plays a part on this side, as Mrs Finnegan. The part of Feeney, by the way, is played by a discreet friend of hers in the church dramatic society. So you see,' said Hooley, with just a trace of hauteur, 'the tape wasn't made within the walls.'

As he spoke he was turning to open the cell door; and by his tone of voice, and in the facial reconstruction that went with it, the Minister could already discern the re-emergence of the other Hooley. Determinedly suppressing his growing dislike of both manifestations – for the time being – he followed the Warden into the cell.

Hank was sitting on the edge of the bed, elbows on knees, head in hands. He didn't look up as they entered.

'Well, Hank,' said Hooley breezily, taking his place beside him, 'I've explained some aspects of your project and our presentation to the Deputy and I think we're now ready to proceed with the flip side of the tape.'

'Before we proceed, Warden,' said the Minister, ignoring the expected 'I thought we'd agreed' glare from the Warden, 'I'd like to get an aspect or two straight with Mr Scropenhauer, if he doesn't mind.'

Hank removed his hands from his head, which began at once to nod at the floor, and sighed: 'OK, man. I ain't going anywhere.'

'It's just that with all this talk about murder, Mr Scropenhauer, I'd like to make sure that we're talking about the same Timothy Finnegan. The one I have in mind, God rest him, died a natural death at the age of 85 and was buried in Glasnevin with full military honours.'

Hank shirt-tailed his glasses, reefed his lip and squinted up at the Minister. 'I do not dispute that', he said: 'quite a lot of my time has been spent researching his exceedingly well documented life: in the garrison of Boland's Mill with De Valera in Easter week; active with the Wicklow Column in the Black and Tan war; chairman of Fianna Hotels Limited and President of the South Eastern Vintners Association, etcetera, etcetera. All will be documented in my book.'

'Another thing, Mr Scropenhauer: about this alleged attempted murder. Isn't it odd that Mr James Joyce made no mention of it? You'd think he'd have made certain of all the facts before making it a "main structural theme", as you yourself called it. Makes a bit of a pils of his book, wouldn't you think?'

'Writers like Joyce are rarely concerned with facts; the myth suffices for their purpose,' said Hank, communicating his long sufferance by exaggerating the monotonal delivery of a bored lecturer. 'It's from the private papers of men like Cassidy that the historian unearths the realities beneath legends. In later life Cassidy became very religious and was tortured with remorse over his part in the actual happenings at the wake, which occurred on the night following the day of the ladder incident. Maybe to salve his conscience he wrote it all down in detail and gave the sealed manuscript into the keeping of his old company, the Gaelic Hibernian. It disappeared in a flurry of takeovers and mergers in the early fifties, but his papers survived intact and unread by anyone until I came along.'

'And they just handed you these private papers when you asked for them?' queried the Minister, eyebrows raised.

Hank grinned – or rather bared his incredible phalanx of teeth, shark-like. 'To a Yankee pill-head, you mean? . . . Well, I guess it makes a difference if the pill-head asking has a letter of introduction from the President of the North American Corporation that owns two-thirds of their action.'

Hooley laughed, rocking sideways and placing his arm around Hank's shoulders. 'You're the boy, right enough, Hank! Never lost for an answer.'

The Minister gave something between a growl and a moan and sat down on the chair, tearing off the end of a cigar with his teeth and spitting it accurately into the bucket. 'I think perhaps it's time we heard the rest of your story,' he said.

'Cassidy's story,' corrected Hank. 'You said something about "all that talk about murder", but all you've heard this far is about an *attempted* murder, for we're all agreed on the subsequent career of Tim Finnegan. What I brought you here for is to inform you of an act of *actual* mayhem, up till now concealed from all but a very few. That I shall now do . . . If you remember, Cassidy was jubilant when he deduced that Finnegan had been murdered by Paddy McGee – a deduction which turned out to be correct in all but effectiveness, as you'll hear. But in order to save the ten pound claim, murder would have to be proved in a court of law; and that, Cassidy realised, would be extremely difficult. Motive was no problem. By means of agent Feeney's contacts in the district he learnt that not only were Finnegan and McGee rivals in their part-time pimping interests, but also that McGee was having a clandestine affair with

185

Finnegan's wife. Furthermore, it was she who had taken out the policy on Finnegan's life with the express wish that he should know nothing about it. An abundance of motive, but no proof. Cassidy and –'

'A moment, please,' said the Minister in someone else's voice. The normally blotchy areas of his face had turned a uniform battleship grey, his lips blue. 'I want to get this straight. You're saying that Tim Finnegan's wife, who I happened to have known in her saintly old age, was an adulteress who plotted with her paramour to murder her husband for ten pounds insurance money? Is that what you're saying?'

Hooley intervened, both vocally and bodily, managing, under cover of a large explanatory gesture with hands and arms, to sway his long trunk forward and to the side until it came between Hank and the Minister's whitened knuckles. At this angle, with the back of his head towards Hank, he also managed to transmit a conniving wink as he said: 'Hank's merely reporting the gist of his findings, Deputy. The allegations are all in Cassidy's papers.'

The Minister, pleased that his stock display of barely governable rage still convinced at close quarters, blustered: 'No matter who. It's hard to sit and listen to such slanderous aspersions on the character of a great and good lady – on top of everything else.'

'I think,' said Hooley, resuming an upright position, 'we should reserve judgement until we've heard the whole story . . . Hank?'

Hank sighed. 'OK. According to Cassidy then . . . He and Feeney canvassed the area for one other eye witness, but without success. The only one to see Finnegan actually fall was agent Feeney, and even he couldn't swear to seeing the rope being pulled by McGee. And so,' he said, swivelling his head round and reaching out to the cassette player, 'Cassidy and Feeney had no option but to attend Tim Finnegan's wake, the traditional time for settlement of all transactions to do with the deceased . . .' He pressed the 'Play' button . . .

Singer: His friends assembled at the wake
And Mrs Finnegan called for lunch.
First they brought in tay and cake,
Then pipes, tobacco and brandy punch.
Mrs Biddy O'Brien began to cry:
'Such a nice clean corpse did you ever see.
Ah Tim avogue why did you die'
'Ah, houl yer gub,' says Paddy McGee.

Cassidy: Terrible to see a woman making an exhibition of herself like that. I don't hold with hitting them too often, but I'd say she deserved that welt McGee just gave her. Here, maybe it's his conscience . . . D'you think, Feeney, is he breaking up with the strain? A dramatic, last minute confession over the coffin would save our bacon.

Feeney: Not a chance. He was only assertin' his rights as her new boss. Biddy was in Finnegan's stable, y'see. None of them liked Tim much – but they hate McGee.

Cassidy: Ah well, all we can do now is try and recoup as much as we can in kind, for there's hard days coming . . . Away and grab that tobacco bowl before it disappears.

Feeney: And a pipe, Mr Cassidy?

Cassidy: Not at all. I've brought me own. Take a look at that brute: one of Peterson's special Wake pipes. I can pack a quarter pound into that. Between it and the poacher's pockets I'll get enough the night to do me the winter . . . Houl yer tongue, here comes the grievin' widda . . . Ah, Mrs Finnegan dear . . . what poor words of mine could console you at this terrible time.

Mrs Finnegan: Ah sure, Mr Cassidy, it's a grief we all come to bear. Have you brought the money?

Cassidy: Indeed I have. And let me assure you that the Gaelic Hibernian is only too pleased to be of assistance in your hour of need. Here you are now: ten of the best. So if you'll just put your X on the form there for Mr Feeney. I'm sure the good man, God rest him, wouldn't mind us using his last roof as a desk for such a worthy purpose . . . No, Feeney . . . on the brass plate . . . you'll scratch the varnish. That's it, Mrs Finnegan, asy done. Ah sure, doesn't he look just fine lying there on the bed – as robust in death as he was in life.

Mrs Finnegan: He'd a drap taken. I suppose the good of it's still with him.

Cassidy: Sure the worms'll think it's Christmas, Mrs Finnegan.

Mrs Finnegan: His only thought in life was the pleasure of others.

Cassidy: A public benefactor. A friend to the lonely and unloved.

(Here there was an outbreak of shouting and screaming and the sound of glass breaking)

Mrs Finnegan: Holy God! Has them bitches no respect at all at all. Let me out amongst them . . .

Singer: Then Biddy O'Connor took up the job,
    'Biddy,' says she, 'you're wrong, I'm sure'.
    But Biddy fetched her a belt in the gub
    And left her sprawlin' on the floor.
    Civil war did then engage,
    Woman to woman and man to man,
    Shillelagh law was all the rage
    And a row and a ruction soon began.

Cassidy: Shut that door, Feeney.

(Door slam)

Cassidy: Gaugers and gather-ups. It's well the corpse himself is in here or they'd be breakin' him up for clubs.

Feeney: I'm glad you're here too, Mr Cassidy. For all me experience I'm never at ease in the same room as the Dear Departed.

Cassidy: For this job, Feeney, you need the mind of a politician and the nerves of a morgue attendant. Maybe it's just as well you're on your last legs . . .

(Sound of door opening. Thin tumult of male and female shrieks – and another breaking glass.)

Cassidy (angry): McGee . . . y'great yahoo! That bottle near cleft the scalp of me! Is one murder a week not enough for ye, y'trollop drover ye! And look at the bed, would ye . . . not content with killin' the poor man you drown him in whiskey.

Feeney: Jesus, Mary and Joseph! . . . Mr Cassidy . . . Finnegan . . . he's movin' . . .

(Chorus of gasps and screams. Door slams.)

Singer: Then Mickey Cassidy ducked his head
When a bottle of whiskey flew at him.
It missed and fallin' on the bed
The whiskey scatters over Tim.
Bedad, he revives now, see how he rises,
Finnegan rising from the dead,
Sayin': 'Whiddle yer whiskey round like blazes,
Thunderin' Jasus did yis think I was dead!

Mrs Finnegan: Tim! Tim darlin' . . . yer alive!

Finnegan (Hooley again, this time with a barely decipherable, deeply adenoidal, Liberties snarl): Shut up, woman will ye. Me head's splittin'. Hand us that bottle, Mr Feeney, till I get me bearings . . . that's better. Me tongue tastes like carbolic.

Feeney: It's a Holy miracle, Mr Finnegan. You've been dead and shriven. Can you remember anything? What was it like?

Finnegan: Dull and dry . . . But I mind one thing very clearly, Mr Feeney, since you ask. I was a burd, flappin' me arms like they were wings . . . hoverin' . . .

Feeney: A Holy Angel!

Finnegan: Ah no, Mr Feeney; just a hodsman takin' a helluva long time to hit the ground. It's like they say when you're drownin' your whole life passes in front of you – when you're fallin' it's as if you're driftin' gently down, with all the time in the world to look around ye and see all sorts of strange goin's on. Things like a rope tied to the bottom of a ladder and me oul butty Paddy McGee draggin' on it like he was anchor man in a tug-o-war team . . . Eh,

Paddy? And you needn't try to hide behind her
skirts, y' durty low cur ye, for I'm gonta corpse you
with this bottle!

(Furniture falls over. Mrs Finnegan screams. A third
glass breaks.)

Mrs Finnegan: He's kilt him!

Feeney: Is he dead, Mr Cassidy?

Cassidy: As mutton, Mr·Feeney.

Feeney: And Finnegan too?

Cassidy: Notatall – sleeping like a baby. Here, give us a
hand to get him back up on the bed. There y'are
now . . .

Mrs Finnegan (keening): Ah Paddy me darlin'! Paddy,
where are you!

Cassidy: Now cut that out, Mrs Finnegan. The first
thing is that you get your affections sorted out once
and for all. Feeney, put your back agin that door
and we'll keep this between ourselves for the time
being . . . Now, Mrs Finnegan, what do we do? Get
the Peelers and send Tim for the eight o'clock walk
and yourself to the Bridewell for conspiracy to
murder?

Mrs Finnegan: Conspiracy is it! Sure I couldn't have
stopped him any more than you.

Cassidy: Oh, you're the cute one . . . But never fear,
your mark on the policy on Tim's life and our evidence about the rope, could put you away for a long
time. Eh? Now, would you like to hear my alternative plan?

Mrs Finnegan: Pure bloody slander. I'd deny every
word of it. But talk away all you like – bad breath
costs nothin'.

Cassidy: Right. First of all – give us back the tenner.

Mrs Finnegan: What! It's mine, legally signed for when
he was certified dead.

Cassidy: Then you'd better spend it quick, Mrs
Finnegan. Feeney, open the door and run for the
Peelers. It doesn't matter to us if they hang him or
not – we've paid the claim.

Mrs Finnegan: Wait ... wait now ... Here y'are, you
　　bloody twister.
Cassidy: One, two, three ... all present and correct.
　　Right, Feeney, Give us a lift with McGee here.
Feeney: Onto the bed?
Cassidy: Into the coffin, man. We've had a wake, it's
　　only right we should have a funeral. A very private
　　funeral. Mrs Finnegan, open that back window. As
　　soon as we get the coffin through and away, throw
　　a bucket of coul water over your husband and get
　　him out to meet his public. Right, Feeney, lift and
　　put yer back into it. You and me'll see our pensions
　　from the Gaelic Hibernian yet.

A hiss of silence was terminated by Hank's finger on the
'Stop' button.

'So there you have it, Mr Deputy,' he said, pressing
'Rewind': 'the murder – or manslaughter – of Paddy
McGee, and the cover-up.'

The Minister made no response. Now it was he who
gazed at the floor, head on hands, elbows on knees.
Hank looked at him and then, quizzically, at Hooley –
who with closed eyes, pursed mouth and shaking head
signalled him to pay no heed. So, with a shrug of the
shoulders and a spread of defensive palms, he continued:
'Cassidy and Feeney spirited the body out the back way
and disposed of it secretly. Finnegan appeared before
the multitude in triumph – the first draft of the ballad
was penned that night – and in the confusion McGee
was never missed. Even later his absence was never
remarked, which isn't as odd as it seems when you realise
that the entire neighbourhood must have known all
along that McGee had murdered Finnegan. So when Tim
arose, it seemed natural to them that McGee should
make himself scarce ... Finnegan, of course, never
looked back – as you obviously knew, Mr Deputy. As
Ireland's own Lazarus he found at once that he could
make more money charming warts and ringworm than
carrying a hod or pimping. This led to some success as a

political ward-heeler in pre-revolutionary days, and so on to Boland's Mill, the Tan war and the first Dail. The hotel chain is in the family to this day. One of his Grandsons is a Bishop; two or three others are involved in politics ... And that, Mr Deputy, concludes the true story of Tim Finnegan, which I intend to publish when I get back to the University of Athens, Idaho.'

Warden Hooley jumped to his feet and clapped his hands, a standing ovation. 'Bravo, Hank. Very nicely done. And I'm sure the Deputy appreciates your bringing this matter to his attention. Deputy?...'

The Minister responded on the question mark, rising to his feet in one sudden movement, ivory coloured stumps bared in a smile, hand out-thrust.

'Thank you very much, Mr Scropenhauer, for a most informative morning,' he said heartily as Hank, after some hesitation, touched the tips of his fingers. 'I'm sure you have quite a lot of work still to do on your project, so I'll arrange for your transfer to a more salubrious situation while I ponder the implications of your discoveries – and until, of course, your Ambassador returns from Florida. He will have to consider your case and arrange for your repatriation to Athens, Idaho.' Whilst talking, he had been moving steadily towards the cell door and was already in the corridor when he said: 'Thanks again, Mr Scropenhauer, and goodbye,' and shouted: 'Come on, Hooley.'

The Warden, inside the cell, made a face that was an astonishingly accurate caricature of the Minister in anger and said: 'See you later, Hank.' Outside the cell, outside the main door of 'the farm' and proceeding side by side towards the main gate, he asked: 'Well, what did you think of all that? Wasn't I right?'

'Inishdoom,' the Minister pronounced: 'that's where he's going. By the first available helicopter.'

'Where's that?'

'It's a sharp rock four miles off the Clare coast, inhabited by a dozen or so demented monks who live on kelp and seagull droppings. It's in the brother's Diocese, so there'll be no bother ... Sure won't yer man's book be all the better for a long period of contemplation in solitude.'

'Ah but how long? Won't his Ambassador have something to say about it?'

'As long as it takes to sell the hotel's to those bloody niggling Germans and/or the result of the election – which I've a notion will be my swan song in politics. The Ambassador, poor man, will go along with anything we say. Things like this happen all the time. At the moment we have three or four of their political embarrassments locked away in drying-out clinics all over the place. And they've kept an unwanted poet of ours orbiting the Irish-American reading circuit in a drunken stupor for nearly two years. It's a case of scratching backs ... But what about you, Hooley?'

Scratching backs; quid pro quo; an end-play in the game that Hooley had anticipated ... 'I'd very much like permission, and some funding – nothing great, mind you – to set up a theatre group in the prison. I saw this crowd from San Quentin on tour –'

'I read about them,' said the Minister gruffly. 'Heavy, anti-establishment stuff. I can see nothing but trouble with that sort of thing.'

'No, no,' protested Hooley, skipping along half-turned towards the Minister, gesticulating, 'nothing like that. Something more in the entertainment line: comedy, a good farce, pantomime –'

'*The Importance of being Earnest*?' asked the Minister, stopping abruptly to turn and glare accusingly at him, his thoughts again on the machinations of annulment.

Hooley was delighted. 'You remembered that! A marvellous piece ... Yes, definitely ... And then there's –'

'Well, if that's the case I see no reason why not,' lied the Minister, walking on. 'I'll have a word with Patcheen on Monday; he owes me one or two ... Oh, and Hooley ...'

'Yes, Minister?'

'That singer fella, the Belfastman,' he said with the

warm smile that had struck terror in the hearts of opponents down the years: 'make sure there's a seat for him in the helicopter. I wouldn't want things to be too cosy for anybody on Inishdoom.'

The Visitation

Harry did not want to go. It was too far to travel on a day when the buses would be packed with last minute shoppers. And besides, he said, he had made arrangements to see some friends early in the afternoon.

'You'll have to go – and bugger the Buffaloes,' said Minnie, his wife, emerging from the scullery and indicating with a wet, steaming hand the single card propped on the mantelpiece. 'That's the one and only card we've had from any of your tribe in twenty-five years. He must be bad. And he *is* your brother.'

A thin voice issuing from a dug-out of cushions and shawls on the end of the sofa next to the fire sobbed: 'He was the best of yis all . . . His Mammy's pet . . . I mind the time he won a medal in the Boys Brigade . . . An' him with his lovely home an' all . . .' The voice faded into a snore.

'You wouldn't reign long in his "lovely home", I can tell you that,' said Harry sourly, though knowing that his mother, even if awake, had long since stopped listening to voices other than her own. 'Thon one of his,' he said, 'would have you off to the knacker's yard in a week.'

'That's another thing,' said Minnie: 'it's too late to send a card, and I don't want her to have one up on me. So stick one in a box of chocolates and take it with you.'

'I'll be all day getting there an' back. That place of his is a fair step from the head of the lines, y'know.'

'Where?' Minnie screeched from the scullery. 'The head of the lines? Sure they tore the lines up years ago, y'eejit ye. You can get a bus right up till his doorstep . . .

Look,' she said, coming into the kitchen again, hands red to the wrists with turkey innards, 'if you like I'll get yer man to come out on his bike for you when he gets back.'

'Ah well, I suppose I'll have to,' groaned Harry, hurling his butt into the grate and starting to hunt under the sofa for his shoes. 'What a lovely way to spend your Christmas Eve, ah? Visiting a death bed an' getting a lift back with bloody Evil Knieval. Wait'll our Tommy catches sight of him – that'll finish him off an' no mistake!'

'Look you, get it into your head: Tommy's not dying. It wasn't even the full coronary. Ida that works with me says it was just a warning, like – but bad enough.'

'A trailer for the Big Picture – "Coming next Week",' said Harry, lifting his mother's dangling feet and extracting his shoes from beneath. Before pulling them on he turned each upside down and shook it thoroughly.

'And no cracks like that when you get out there,' warned Minnie. 'Bad enough for a lifelong teetotaller to see a boozy blaggard like you still on your feet, without you doing your Jimmy Durante act . . . Oh, and get some sweets or something for the kid on your way.'

'Whose? . . . oh, Tommy's lad. I near forgot about him. What age would he be now?'

'Twelve or therabouts. God help him, with that one for a Ma. Go on now, and I'll tell yer man to call into the Buffs on his way and let them know you'll be a bit late.'

'They'll never let him across the door,' said Harry, on his way down the hall, 'but he can shout through the letter-box.'

From the bus-stop on the main road he had to walk past forty-two identical doorsteps on forty-two identical chalet bungalows before he found Tommy's. It, at least, was different in that you could actually see the doorstep, the long front garden being entirely devoid of tree, bush or flowerbed, an immaculate bowling green which, it was rumoured, she vacuumed by torchlight in the small hours. And instead of a garage, a plastic-roofed car-port flanked the house, sheltering Tommy's three-year-old Escort. How had she let him away with that, Harry wondered.

He rang the front doorbell and was answered by a tap on the front window – from which signalled an identical Christmas tree. Through the double-glazing her cherry-tinted bubble-head mouthed instructions for him to come around the side of the house. She half-opened the side door for him, holding it with one hand, the other clutching her throat, and looked down, wide-eyed, at his feet.

'You found us,' she accused, holding the door until he had scraped his soles thoroughly on the iron scraper.

'Easy,' he replied, entering in the knowledge that there was still a fair packing of dog's dirt secreted in the deep ridges of his Commando soles. 'They told me yours was the only one in the row without a garage.'

If he'd been Tommy, she'd have hit him. Harry remembered the first time he met her with Tommy, at a Saturday night jig in the Plaza. He, Harry, drunk, had made a pass in the Moonlight Saunter and had suffered the full weight of her diamante stiletto in his instep. A fine-looking bird then; hard to believe that this starved clothes-horse with the collar of pearls and the Mickey Mouse hair-do was the same woman.

'Tommy was getting round to the garage when he finished the extension,' she explained. 'We have planning permission, but it'll have to wait for a while now . . . But not too long; the doctor say's he'll be up and doing in no time . . . Here's Harry to see you . . .'

Tommy looked no different from the last time he'd seen him, five years ago, on the day he'd collected his voluntary redundancy and hammered his last rivet. A bit thicker around the middle maybe – and a lot cleaner. 'A dry back and no sweat' was how he had anticipated his new job in security. But then, thought Harry, there were different sorts of sweat.

He was sitting in his new plaster-smelling extension,

cushioned in an easy chair, an arm's length from a portable television. At one end there was a kitchen bar,
behind it a miniature chip-shop of stainless steel
extractor vents.

'Harry Lad, it's great to see you!'

They shook hands in the arm-wrestling way, reminding
Harry of the day Tommy had beaten their Da across the
kitchen table. Then, he could have struck a match on the
palm of his right hand, the gun hand; even now it was lean
and hard, the tool of a handyman.

Harry dissolved the incipient lump in his throat with a
barrage of cracks: 'God, you must be well on the mend
when they have you parked in the scullery!' . . . 'And
what the hell's wrong with your telly? – she must be
washing it in the wrong powder or something' . . . 'Navy-
blue grapes are out of season, so I brought you a box of my
favourite sweeties – and some for the bucko, wherever
he is.'

Tommy grinned contentedly, knowing Harry. She
fussed about, plumping Tommy's cushions, smoothing his
sparse hair, like a nervous Matron at visiting time after a
catastrophic day, answering point by point. It wasn't just
a kitchen, it was a living area, she said, and anyway, they
were in the process of re-doing the lounge in which, if he
wanted to know, was a full colour, 23 inch set of immov-
able proportions. The doctor had said that Tommy wasn't
to eat sweets, but she was sure Gary would love them.

She went to fetch Gary from his room above where,
Tommy explained, he was doing homework. 'He's at the
Grammar now. The amount of homework's shocking,
even at Christmas time. Up there boring the eyes out of
himself.'

Harry prowled the extension, admiring, though not
uncritically, Tommy's handiwork. 'A lovely job – for a
shipyardman like. You'd have done better with a sheet of
half-inch plate . . . But here now' he said, in his only reference to Tommy's "trouble", 'after this touch you'll have
to take it easy for a bit. The bloody garage can wait.'

'All right for you, sitting down there at four-quid-a-week rent. A garage fairly jacks up the price if you're doing to sell.'

'You're not thinking of selling, are you?'

'No . . . but you never know, like.'

She came back with the young fellow at her heels, a bespectacled, acned beanpole in the family tradition. He seemed delighted with Harry's surprise present, a box of chocolate toffees. Watching him tearing off the wrapping and wiring in, Harry remarked on his facial likeness to their father. Tommy agreed, and they had a minute's silent loathing in memory of the old brute, while she went on like handbell about the moneysworth of worthwhile presents they had bought Gary: a pocket calculator, a chess set, a condensed encylopaedia . . .

'I forgot to ask about your fella,' said Tommy. 'He's the only one left now, isn't he?'

'Aye, the girls are away,' said Harry. 'Him . . . as thick as champ and as happy as Larry; a copper-bottomed lig if ever there was one. You'll see him in a wee while. He's coming up to collect me on the bike – but I won't mind at all if you shut your eyes.'

'A motor-bike?' asked Gary, eyes wide, chewing industriously.

When he did come, an hour later, they were in the middle of a cup of tea; and at least two pieces of her best china very nearly didn't get over the shock of his coming.

Front doors were not his scene. He came dipping through the side door, without knocking, as nonchalantly as if into a public house or lavatory. Had he kept his helmet on, Harry thought, a six-foot-four skeleton sheathed in worn black leather, epauletted and looped with gold chains, would have been shock enough: but bareheaded, the full glory of his Mohican plume, dyed emerald green with scarlet tips, the gold ring in his left earlobe . . .

'God save us!' gasped Tommy.

She made choking noises and tried, two-handed, to place her cup and saucer safely on a nearby table.

Gary's toffee-crammed mouth hung open in wonderment.

'This is the son, your namesake, Tommy,' said Harry. 'Only he answers best to "Sticks", being a bit of a drummer in a band and all.'

'What about ye, oul han',' said Sticks, lurching, creaking, clinking in the general direction of Tommy, who would have retreated if he could. 'I heard you were bad?'

Harry heard her moan quietly, cowering behind him, and decided to cut the introductions.

'Are you a Punk?' asked Gary.

Sticks turned to him, relief causing a spasm of exuberance, and took up a sparring stance. 'What's it to you, Specs,' he drawled in his gangster voice, tapping him on the cheek. Harry felt the blood rush to his face and didn't dare look at Tommy. But he needn't have worried: 'Specs' grinned delightedly and feinted back, gabbling . . . 'What's your bike? Is she fast?'

'A Suzuki 500, man,' sang Sticks with accompanying hip movements; 'sheet-lightning – King of the road. Fancy a burn, kid?'

'Can I, Dad?' pleaded Gary, dancing around Tommy's chair. 'Please, Dad.'

Tommy, nonplussed, looked quizzically at Harry.

'He wants to take Gary a ride on the pillion,' Harry translated. 'No sweat. He looks mad, but he's safe enough.'

'I dunno,' said Tommy, still mesmerised by the green and red plume. 'Ask your Mum.'

But there was no sign of Mum. 'Trust her! She must have went upstairs out of the road,' said Tommy irritably. And by way of revenge for her defection, he said 'OK. But only a short run, mind.'

Gary whooped and put his arm through that of Sticks as they headed for the door. Just before it closed behind them, Harry heard him ask: 'Is that ring right through your ear?'

Tommy sighed explosively. 'Well, I never seen anything like that in all my born days. I hope to God she stays above till they're back, or all the Librium in the world'll not keep her from doing the four-minute mile round them walls.'

They were back in ten minutes, Gary glowing from the fast burn, and she still had not appeared. Harry decided that now was as good a time as any to make an exit – before she made an entrance, heard of the burn, and threw one of her famous tantrums. Anyway, he could see that Tommy had had enough of Sticks for one day.

Tommy's last words at the moment of leaving, with Sticks and Gary already half-way down the drive to the bike, were: 'How's Ma doing?'

'Doting and thrawn,' replied Harry, and, making again what had always been a sore point between them, added: 'It can be tough on Minnie sometimes.'

A minute later, perched on the pillion of The King Of The Road, waving to Gary at the garden gate as Sticks revved the engine for a spectacular takeoff, Harry noticed something.

'That must have been some burn,' he shouted in Sticks ear: 'You've lost your earring.'

'Aye,' shrieked Sticks, 'so I have.'

At lunch time on the day after Boxing Day, Harry, who had wallowed with the Buffaloes into the small hours, shared the sofa with his mother and watched his wife beating their son over the head with one of his own drumsticks. Sticks was used to that treatment and seemed hardly to notice.

'What made you give it to a child like that, you big looney,' screamed Minnie. 'Have you no wit!'

Harry, head bursting, tried to soothe: 'Don't get yourself worked up over nothing, girl. Sure nobody's the worse for wear. Didn't your mate Ida say Tommy was all right and the wee fella –'

'– "the worse for wear",' shouted Minnie, turning to Harry. 'His mother's under permanent sedation, after coming across that wee fella with a carpenter's awl through his lug, bleeding all over the bedroom carpet, and you say nobody's the worse for wear! Are you right in the –'

'It'll do him good,' said Sticks.

'What!' gasped Minnie, too dumbfounded even to hit him.

'It'll do his peepers good. Granny told me that one time. Didn't you, Gran?'

The bundle at the end of the sofa stirred and the thin voice fluted:

'With a ring in yer ear
You'll see like a deer.
With a ring through yer snout
You're safe from the gout.'

That was all. In silence, Harry parted the shawls and saw that she was fast asleep again. 'Did you ever hear the like of that?' he said. 'Black Bottom Champion of the Ormeau Band Hall 1921, and she's startin' to give out like the oul' witch from the back of the mountain!'

'The world's oldest Punk poet,' said Sticks, blinking as the butt-end of a drumstick again shattered his Mohican plume.

THE END

Coming From Behind
Howard Jacobson

'A literary comedy which cuts through and beyond the
Portnoy school of self-absorbed Jewish fiction, the
English University Novel and the best of Tom Sharpe'
THE TIMES

Sefton Goldberg: mid-thirties, English teacher at
Wrottesley Poly in the West Midlands; small, sweaty,
lustful, defiantly unenamoured of beer, nature and
organised games; gnawingly aware of being an urban
Jew islanded in a sea of country-loving Anglo-Saxons.
Obsessed by failure — morbidly, in his own case,
gloatingly, in that of his contemporaries — so much so
that he plans to write a bestseller on the subject. In the
meantime he is uncomfortably aware of advancing years
and atrophying achievement: and no amount of lofty
rationalisation can disguise the triumph of friends and
colleagues, not only from Cambridge days but even
within the despised walls of the Poly itself, or sweeten
the bitter pill of another's success . . .

Coming From Behind is a shrewd, articulate and
consistently hilarious successor to *Lucky Jim* and *The
History Man*.

'Very funny, clever and engaging'
TIMES LITERARY SUPPLEMENT

'A sort of Jewish version of *Lucky Jim* updated for the
eighties, witty, observant, clever, a first-rate
entertainment and something more besides'
ROBERT NYE, THE GUARDIAN

0 552 99063 9   £3.95

─ **BLACK SWAN** ─

Catch-22
Joseph Heller

'Blessedly, monstrously, bloatedly, cynically funny, and fantastically unique. No one has ever written a book like this'
FINANCIAL TIMES

Catch-22 has become a byword in its own time. It is a novel of enormous richness and art. It is deeply serious, yet at the same time, brilliantly funny. It is without question one of the great novels of the century.

Catch-22 is, said Philip Toynbee in *The Observer*, 'The greatest satirical work in the English language since "Erewhon" ' — an hilarious, tragic novel in which an American airforce base on a small island off Italy becomes a microcosm of the modern world as it might look to someone dangerously sane.

'Remarkable, mind-spinning rave of a novel. Uniquely funny'
DAILY MAIL

'Wildly original, brutally gruesome, a dazzling performance that will outrage as many readers as it delights. Vulgarly, bitterly, savagely funny, it will not be forgotten by those who can take it'
NEW YORK TIMES

0 552 99195 3   £4.95

BLACK SWAN

God Knows
Joseph Heller

'Mr Heller is dancing at the top of his form again . . .
original, sad, widly funny and filled with roaring'
MORDECAI RICHLER, NEW YORK TIMES BOOK REVIEW

Joseph Heller's powerful, wonderfully funny, deeply
moving new novel is the story of David — yes, *that*
David; warrior king of Israel, husband of Bathsheba,
father of Solomon, slayer of Goliath, and psalmist
nonpareil . . . as well as the David we've never known
before now: David the cocky Jewish kid, David the
fabulous lover, David the plagiarised poet, David the
Jewish father, David the (one-time) crony of God . . .

At last, David is telling his own story, and he's holding
nothing back — equally unembarrassed by his faults,
his sins, his prowess, his incomparable glory . . .

God Knows is an ancient story, a modern story, a love
story. It is a novel about growing up and growing old,
about men and women, about fathers and sons, about
man and God. It is a novel of emotional force, imaginative
richness, and unbridled comic invention. It is
quintessential Heller.

'Joseph Heller is the outstanding clever ideas-man of
modern fiction . . . brilliantly inventive'
JONATHAN RABAN, SUNDAY TIMES

'The unforgiving genius still flares, and the book is
worth the price of admission for the first few pages
alone'
MARTIN AMIS, THE OBSERVER

0 552 99169 4   £3.95

BLACK SWAN

Peeping Tom
Howard Jacobson

'The funniest book about sex ever written'
VAL HENNESSY, TIME OUT

'I'd be prepared to say it was my own fault for tampering with the secret arts, except that it confers too much dignity on all parties. This isn't a Faustian story'.

So what kind of story is it that Barney Fugelman must overcome his own refined distaste for accuracy and candour in order to tell? Far from his native Finchley, why is such a confirmed antagonist of all things green and growing bound to the daily ritual of roaming the cliffs of his Cornish exile, his fur coat and snakeskin shoes an offence to the serious ramblers? Whence the burden of the cliffs, in whose shadow the hapless Barney seems compelled, in all his incarnations, to tread?

In this wickedly erotic, ferociously funny amalgam of the psychological thriller, the rural idyll and the literary novel of romance, Howard Jacobson displays all the exuberant wit and sharp intelligence that distinguished *Coming From Behind,* his first novel (also available in Black Swan).

'Brilliantly funny and inventive . . . an astonishing display of irreverent wit, marvellous situational set-pieces and biting one-liners'
ROBERT NYE, THE GUARDIAN

'Howard Jacobson comes from behind the "tropic swamps of the imagination" to drag admirers into them again, kicking and screaming and laughing our heads off'
GAY FIRTH, THE TIMES

'Brilliant and original'
PAUL BAILEY, THE STANDARD

'Peeping Tom' is a Jewish gambol through English literature as seen from the bedroom; it throws sex at the bookish and books at the sexish'
VICTORIA GLENDINNING, SUNDAY TIMES

0 552 99141 4   £3.95

BLACK SWAN

The Water-Method Man
John Irving

'John Irving, it is abundantly clear, is a true artist. He is not afraid to take on great themes'
LOS ANGELES TIMES

An hilarious novel about a man with a complaint more serious than Portnoy's, *The Water-Method Man* is a work of consummate artistry, bizarre imagery and sharp social and psychological observation, by an author whose original brilliance has already placed him in the front rank of contemporary American writers.

'Brutal reality and hallucination, comedy and pathos. A rich, unified tapestry . . . something of beauty'
TIME

John Irving is the author of six extraordinary novels, including his latest, *The Cider House Rules*.

0 552 99207 0   £3.95

BLACK SWAN

The World According to Garp
John Irving

'Absolutely extraordinary . . . a roller-coaster ride that
leaves one breathless, exhausted, elated and tearful'
LOS ANGELES TIMES

One of the most acclaimed novels published in the last
ten years, *The World According to Garp* is 'a social
tragi-comedy of such velocity and hilarity that it reads
rather like a domestic sequel to *Catch-22'* (The Observer).
In it, the reader can rampage through the hilarious and
chaotic world of Garp and his companions: kindly
whores, assassins, schoolteachers, wrestlers and earless
Newfoundlanders.

'A wonderful novel, full of energy and art, at once funny
and heartbreaking. You know it is true. It is also terrific'
WASHINGTON POST BOOK WORLD

John Irving is the author of six extraordinary novels,
including his latest, *The Cider House Rules.*

0 552 99205 4   £4.95

BLACK SWAN